The Fox From His Lair

Max Hennessy was the pen-name of John Harris. He had a wide variety of jobs from sailor to cartoonist and became a highly inventive, versatile writer. In addition to crime fiction, Hennessy was a master of the war novel and drew heavily on his experiences in both the navy and air force, serving in the Second World War. His novels reflect the reality of war mixed with a heavy dose of conflict and adventure.

Also by Max Hennessy

The RAF Trilogy

The Bright Blue Sky
The Challenging Heights
Once More the Hawks

The Captain Kelly Maguire Trilogy

The Lion at Sea
The Dangerous Years
Back to Battle

The WWII Naval Thrillers

The Sea Shall Not Have Them
Ride Out the Storm
Cotton's War
North Strike

The Flying Ace Thrillers

The Mustering of the Hawks
The Mercenaries
The Courtney Entry

The WWII Collection

Take or Destroy
Swordpoint
The Fox From His Lair
Army of Shadows

JOHN HARRIS WRITING AS
MAX HENNESSY
THE FOX FROM HIS LAIR

CANELO

First published in the United Kingdom in 1978 by Hutchinson & Co

This edition published in the United Kingdom in 2021 by

Canelo
31 Helen Road
Oxford OX2 0DF
United Kingdom

Copyright © John Harris

The moral right of John Harris writing as Max Hennessy to be identified as
the creator of this work has been asserted in accordance with the
Copyright, Designs and Patents Act, 1988.

A CIP catalogue record for this book is available from the British Library.

Print ISBN 978 1 80032 011 6
Ebook ISBN 978 1 78863 730 5

Look for more great books at www.canelo.co

Printed and bound in Great Britain by Clays Ltd, Elcograf S.p.A.

...For the sound of his horn brought me from my bed
And the cry of his hounds which he oft-times led,
For Peel's 'View Halloo' would awaken the dead
Or the fox from his lair in the morning.
Yes, I ken John Peel, and Ruby too,
Ranter and Ringwood, Bellman and True;
From a find to a check, from a check to a view,
From a view to a death in the morning...

John Peel, Old English hunting song

Author's Note

The Allied invasion of Europe on D-Day, 6 June, 1944, was plagued in the planning stages by a number of mishaps which came very close to causing its postponement. Papers were mislaid or misdirected; men, caught by excitement and enthusiasm, talked too much; even the crosswords in the *Daily Telegraph* put Security on the alert by using among their clues and answers code names which had been set aside and guarded with the closest secrecy.

The night action off Slapton at the western extremity of Lyme Bay at the end of April provided one of the biggest of all the scares. Ten officers, all of them well briefed as to the plans for the invasion and for the events of the following weeks, were found to be missing, and it was with the greatest alarm that the Allied chiefs viewed the possibility of their having been picked up by the Germans. This disaster was one of the most closely kept secrets of the war – little of it leaked out even to Torquay and the coastal villages round Lyme Bay – and few people know what it led to in the following weeks and its climax on the D-Day beaches.

Little has ever been written about the affair of the Fox and most of it recently came to light in the papers of the late Colonel Linus C. Iremonger, of Providence, Rhode Island, USA, on which this novel has been largely based.

Colonel Iremonger was the man most heavily involved in the affair but he never spoke about it. He had obviously intended at one time to write a book about it himself as his papers were detailed and frank in the extreme, even to his opinions on the people he worked with. These details have since been confirmed – and embellished – by his old friend, Colonel Cuthbert William Randall Pargeter, of Milton Abbas, Dorset, England, who as a young officer became Iremonger's deputy in the weeks preceding the invasion.

Colonel Iremonger remained a bachelor without as far as can be ascertained any close relatives. Because of his lifelong taciturnity, further details have had to be sought elsewhere. For information on the virtually unknown disaster in Lyme Bay I am indebted to Mr D. B. Nash, of the Imperial War Museum's Department of Printed Books; Samuel Eliot Morison's *The Invasion of France and Germany, 1944–5;* and General Omar Bradley's *A Soldier's Story.* The information on Ultra was obtained from *The Ultra Secret,* by F. W. Winterbotham. For obvious reasons certain names have been changed and the shadowy figure of Colonel Ebert Klaus Reinecke cannot be filled in completely. Inevitably, little was uncovered about him beyond what Colonel Iremonger's team dug up or reconstructed, and in the holocaust that descended on Germany in 1945 any German papers there might have been referring to him vanished completely.

Part One

From a Find to a Check

1

As the destroyer drove westwards across the waters of Lyme Bay, the two officers standing by the Carley float lashed to the side of the bridge huddled deeper into the high collars of their khaki coats against the wind that bit sharply at their flesh. As they searched the misty coastline, the ship bucked, taking the tip off a wave, and a slash of spray lifted across the deck, blurring their night glasses and the view of a landing ship packed with infantrymen just visible to starboard, pitching in the heaving sea.

Ashore, a cluster of cottages on a narrow strip of land marked the village of Slapton Sands. Obscured by darkness, it was silent and empty of villagers because the inhabitants had been moved away to enable the troops training for the great invasion of Europe, that everyone knew was coming before long, to practise on a beach as much as possible like the ones they were to attack in France. Nobody liked the added realism of live shells and bullets or their effect on property – least of all the villagers – but in a country which in April, 1944, was bulging at the seams with troops, it had been accepted that if the invasion on which the future of the world depended were to succeed, then sacrifices had to be made.

Indeed, the whole south coast of England had become one vast armed camp, packed with men, all speculating on the date and destination of the assault, and worrying whether, when it came, they would be killed. Perhaps the only things they didn't know at this late stage of their training were these very facts, and security was so strict that a few days before, at the beginning of the month, a strip of coastline from the Wash to Land's End had been restricted so that no one, neither civilian nor soldier, could move in or out without a high priority pass.

One of the two officers, wearing the single star of an American brigadier-general, peered at a sheet of paper in his hand. '"Slapton,"' he read. '"Unspoiled beach of coarse red gravel, fronting a shallow lagoon and backed by grassy bluffs. Nearby village evacuated."' He looked up and stared towards the shore. 'I guess it's not so goddam unspoiled now, Linus,' he said. 'Not after the first wave hit it yesterday.'

Colonel Linus Iremonger, the second officer, turned. 'How'd it go, sir?'

'Okay.' Brigadier-General George Orme shrugged. 'The air force was late and everybody was scared in case they hit the infantry as they went in. But it went okay on the whole, I suppose. It's easier tonight. All the back-up wave has to do is go in and unload as if it was the real thing.'

He stared at the shore. 'I guess we don't appreciate what the British are putting up with, with these rehearsals,' he observed. 'Now that the blitzes have stopped, the poor bastards have got *us.*'

Iremonger grunted. Certainly, the Luftwaffe had been driven from the sky in this part of the English Channel and even he was aware of the sense of relief the British felt after enduring the bombing ever since 1940. Now the Luftwaffe was restricted only to desperate snap reconnaissances to discover the route of the invasion and, though recce planes were said to be still getting in over the Thames estuary, west of Dover nothing was ever allowed to approach the build-up of shipping in daylight. When they came at night, the barrage threw up such a weight of steel they were forced inland, to drop their bombs on coastal towns in raids that were mere fleabites compared with the blitzes of 1940 and 1941. There was little talk nowadays about bombing – as though the British preferred to put it from their minds – and, like Orme, Iremonger knew that the growing number of American troops – with their demands on transport, space and the younger female population was taking its place with them as Number One Problem. Not unnaturally, the Americans resented it because they considered they had arrived to save the British from defeat and expected their due toll of admiration, gratitude and tolerance for their different approach to things.

It was something which appeared to worry Orme a great deal.

'If we win this war,' he went on, 'it'll be as much due to the endurance and good temper of the British civilian as it will to the strength of our army. Travel restricted, communications restricted, whole areas of the countryside restricted. God knows what the poor bastards will find when they come back after it's all over. Doors kicked in, windows smashed, belongings gone, unexploded bombs and shells and Christ knows what.'

The leaden sea heaved and the mist seemed to thicken with every minute that passed, so that it was barely possible to see the ships to port, starboard and astern. The danger of collision had increased enormously and the voice of the destroyer's British captain came harshly over the creaking of the vessel and the surge of the water. 'Warn all look-outs to be on their toes! This is supposed to be only a rehearsal and we don't want trouble.'

Wisps of sea smoke lifted off the undulating surface of the bay, the mist lying like a grey wall between sea and sky. Out of it the superstructure of a landing craft materialised briefly to port, floating in mid-air as though detached, with its lacing of halyards and aerials. The two Americans stared into the darkness, worried, anxious that nothing should go wrong. With the resources in ships stretched to the limit, they daren't think of the risk of damaging any of them in an exercise.

Irritatedly, Iremonger brushed at the damp which was gathering in tiny globules of moisture on his coat. It came from the wet West Country mist which had so often plagued their rehearsals, blurring the horizon, dimming the view of ships and shore; damp, clammy and grey, like ghostly fingers pawing through the darkness, chilling the body and depressing the soul.

'England,' he said disgustedly. 'Goddam weather's always the same here! If it's not raining, you can't see a thing.'

He tucked his head deeper into the collar of his coat, cold, bored, hungry; wishing the war were over and he were back in the States; wishing the invasion had come and gone; in particular, wishing that this specific exercise, Exercise Tiger, were finished and done with.

'I hate these goddam rehearsals,' he growled. 'Nothing ever happens.'

This time, however, something did.

Almost as though to contradict him, as he spoke there was a flash of fire astern of them, a red glow through the mist and spray, and his head jerked round as the thump of an explosion came across the water.

'What the hell was that?' he said.

Orme was staring with his glasses, trying to penetrate the darkness. 'That's a ship,' he said.

The glow in the distance seemed to be increasing. Then another came, further away, and they heard the hammer of weapons.

'Those guys are firing,' Iremonger said.

'I didn't think they were playing craps,' Orme observed dryly.

Iremonger's voice became louder. 'What the hell are they up to? They're not supposed to be firing yet.'

Orme was staring through his glasses again, his head cocked, listening. 'That's a Spandau,' he said sharply.

'Here?'

'I was in North Africa before they sent me here. I know what they sound like.'

As Iremonger turned to look at Orme, he became aware of sudden activity on the bridge above him.

'Port ten! Full ahead both!' The captain's voice barked an order and the officer of the watch repeated it to the engine room. Immediately the deck began to vibrate. The ship heaved as it leapt forward like an excited horse, the eager rumble of its engine room blowers giving it a living animal sound. The bow wave rose, the stern sank, and a plume of white foam lifted fanlike in its wake.

As the vibration increased, Orme and Iremonger stared at each other, puzzled. Then the hammering of gunfire started again, jerking their heads round once more, thumping against their ears. Over the noise of the sea they heard shouts. They were faint, almost like the mewing of herring gulls on the wind, but even so it was possible to distinguish in them a note of fear, panic and bewilderment.

'What the hell's happening over there?' Iremonger snapped. 'Where the hell did they get a Spandau?'

'For Christ sake, Linus—' Orme's voice was harsh and angry '—they didn't! That's a German gun and I expect it's a German who's firing it.'

Iremonger stared at his companion, startled. From the bridge someone shouted and he took a staggering step sideways and clutched for a handhold as the destroyer heeled unexpectedly.

As the ship burst through the murk at full speed, a motor launch, also turning at top revolutions, appeared in front of them. The bow of the destroyer swung, jerked almost, and the launch slid past.

'Jesus H. Christ!' Iremonger said. 'That was goddam close!'

The destroyer was swinging now round the stern of a lumbering landing ship wallowing at low revolutions in the heaving sea. A gun banged astern, making them jump, and the ship swung again, laying over on her beam ends as she turned. Then, over to port, they saw a landing craft low in the water and men dotting the misty surface of the sea around it.

'That goddam thing's sinking!' Iremonger said.

The landing craft was burning and men were jumping from it into the water. Further away they could see the second glow, brighter now. Tracer shells whipped by like little slots of light sliding past on rails out of the mist, and the ship's guns began to bang again, firing into the slots of light which sped through the superstructure. There was a crack and a flash above their heads that made them duck. Flakes of paint fell on them and, as they raised their heads, the ship swung wildly again, one engine going astern to drag her round. Not far away, in the beam of a searchlight, they saw a small boat on fire and sinking.

'That's an E-boat!' Orme snapped. 'The goddam Germans have got among the convoy!'

'Here? Right off the English coast, for Christ's sake?'

'For God's sake, why not? It's the one thing they've been trying to do ever since they heard we were coming!'

The burning boat was flat and square and carried the number 151 on its bows. As they watched, a man jumped from its stern, then there was a flash as the petrol tanks blew up with the ammunition. The boat seemed to disintegrate in a coiling cloud of black smoke, and the air was suddenly full of splintered planks of wood, pieces of metal, and parts of human bodies. Burning fragments began to rain down on the destroyer.

'Get that boat away!' the destroyer's captain shouted from the bridge. 'There are men in the water there!'

The davits whined and the boat dropped, full of shouting men wearing lifejackets. A few minutes later it was back alongside the ship.

A searchlight came on and the two Americans watched, aghast. The landing craft in the distance was just beginning to roll over. They saw the stern lift then slip quietly beneath the waves, leaving the sea covered with scattered debris and the bobbing heads of yelling men laden down with equipment.

'Those guys are drowning!' Iremonger shouted furiously.

As he spoke, several small launches appeared, rushing in among the bobbing figures, scrambling nets over the side, their crews busy with lines and boathooks to haul the dripping, gasping soldiers aboard. Other vessels were moving towards the second stricken landing ship and they could hear guns thudding away in the distance.

The destroyer's boat was bumping against the ship's side now, and the sailors were pushing at a German, clad in canvas trousers and a white jersey, his soaked cap still on his head, its wet ribbons stuck to his cheek. As he reached the deck, a petty officer grabbed him and dragged him over the rail so that he sprawled in a pool of water. Immediately, he was hauled to his feet and slammed against a bulkhead.

'Get those other men up here,' the captain yelled.

'Sir—' it was a beardless young sub-lieutenant who shouted back, '—they're all dead?'

The captain turned to the officer of the watch. 'Have 'em hoisted aboard, anyway,' he said. 'Let the sawbones see 'em. Get that boat in. Fast. There's a war on.'

Iremonger stared over the side at the sailors bent over the sprawled figures in the boat, at the German who was now being pushed along the deck, and then across the water to where ships' boats, cutters, DUKWs and other small craft dotted the water among the bobbing heads where the landing craft had disappeared.

'A war on?' he said in an awed voice. 'By God, there sure is!'

2

London was grey under the racing scud of cloud. After four and a half years of war, the buildings had a weary look, dark, heavy and scarred with bomb splinters from the blitzes. The people had the same shabby look about them. Their clothes were drab and too well-worn, so that the few Americans in the streets looked like wealthy relations in their well-fitting uniforms. Here and there, eagle-eyed American military policemen waited in twos in the entrances of buildings, their white helmets, spats, belts and pistol holsters bright against their dull clothes. Their British counterparts, in their uglier, less comfortable uniforms and clumsy red-topped caps, eyed them with a faint resentment for their better conditions and rations and the success they undoubtedly enjoyed with the girls.

Watching from his window four storeys up from the street, Major Cuthbert Pargeter was frowning. On the other side of the desk, another man stood with his eyes on him. 'Murder's always awkward,' he was saying doggedly. 'And when it's connected with the invasion of Europe it's doubly awkward.'

Pargeter turned. He was a slightly-built man, young, pale-faced and oddly intense. His eyes were pale too, like his hair, so that everything about him had a neat but curiously anonymous effect.

'You don't have to tell *me*, Superintendent,' he said.

The superintendent's burly shoulders lifted in a shrug and Pargeter took out a cigarette, offered one to the superintendent and sat down.

The policeman produced a light and sat down opposite him. 'I think we're in a hurry on this one, Major,' he suggested.

Pargeter nodded. 'I think we are,' he agreed. 'And they sent you to me because it was army, not civilian. Right?'

Mollified by Pargeter's failing to rise to his own bad temper, the superintendent nodded. 'Bit more than that,' he said. 'It's murder and that's what I deal with. I brought in that Canadian who killed that kid in Essex—'

'So I've heard,' Pargeter said. 'Jolly good show.'

The superintendent was almost beginning by this time to like Pargeter, because praise came rarely from his own superiors. 'But this is different,' he said.

'Why, Superintendent?' It hadn't escaped the policeman's notice that Pargeter never failed to give him his title, something the army persistently failed to do.

'The murdered man was a British officer.'

'There've been other murdered British officers.'

'This one had been hanging about the American camps in Devon, doing a lot of talking and asking questions. That area's been sealed since April 2nd, as you know. And on the night of April 27th and 28th there was a rehearsal of Slapton Sands. The Germans got among the landing craft.'

'I heard that.'

'Down there now, security's so tight nobody wants to know us. So I've been told to turn over everything I've got to your department. It's in your lap, Major. The Americans are making it too hard for us. They're keeping things so secret down there, they're having to spy on each other to find out what's happening.'

Pargeter's thin nose gave an audible sniff. 'What makes you think they won't make it hard for *me*?'

'At least you've got the War Office behind you.'

The superintendent shrugged and Pargeter sighed. 'Better tell me what you know,' he said. 'Motive for a start.'

The superintendent gestured. 'Well, his wallet was found beside him – empty. But it wasn't robbery because his watch was still on his wrist and it was a valuable one.'

'Name?'

The superintendent pushed a file across. 'It's all in there. Everything we know. Name of Dunnaway. Captain Arthur Clarke Dunnaway. Pay Corps. He was supposed to be stationed up here in London. So what was he doing down in Portsmouth?'

'Is that where he was found?'

'On a bomb site near the docks. For a man who was stationed in London he seems to have spent a lot of time moving about. His unit says he was an accountant and his job was to check accounts. There's been a lot of fiddling with funds – there always is, of course – but his work had nothing to do with the Americans and he seemed to spend a lot of his time in hotels and he always seemed to be in the company of American officers.'

'Homosexual, do you think?'

'That's as far as I'd got when I was told to hand it over to you.'

'Any suggestions as to where I should start?'

The superintendent shrugged. 'Down there,' he said. 'We've checked here in London. It's in the file. Before he was called up into the army, he had a job with a firm of accountants in Woking. Thirty-three years old. Degree from Cambridge as well as his accountancy letters.'

'Sounds bright.'

'I think he *was* bright. He must have been. Immediately he joined the army, he was posted to London. He didn't do initial training like everybody else, but went straight to the War Office.'

'Do *they* have anything on him?'

'They say he was an accountant. Full stop. They say they know no more about him than we do. Because of his ability, he was given a sort of roving commission and had been on the move round the country ever since. He didn't seem to do a lot of accounting.'

'Oh?'

'There was a team worked with him. A lieutenant, a sergeant and two men – all Pay Corps.'

'Do *they* know anything about him?'

'No.' The policeman stubbed out his cigarette. 'His men seemed to do the nose-to-the-grindstone stuff while he just wandered about talking to people.'

'Sometimes that's a good way for a detective – any sort of detective, even an accountancy detective – to work. As I'm sure you've found out more than once yourself.' As the superintendent shrugged again, Pargeter leaned forward. 'Home background?'

'Nothing very unusual. Father was a top civil servant who'd retired but returned to work in 1939. He was killed with his wife in the blitz in 1940. Dealt with foreign affairs, it seems. The son did very well at school and his degree was in European languages.'

'Was it now? Which?'

'French, Spanish – and German.'

'Married?'

'No.'

'Girl friends?'

'None we've found. Seems to have been a loner.'

'Wonder what American officers had, that our people didn't have.'

'Money, I expect.'

'Or information. Where was he last heard of?'

'Plymouth, April 24th.'

'I'll start there. Who's the American I should contact? There must be one.'

'Chap called Iremonger. Colonel Linus C. Iremonger.'

'Who's he?'

'Security.'

'I'll go and see him.'

The superintendent grinned unexpectedly. 'You'll be lucky,' he said.

3

'One hundred ninety-seven sailors; four hundred forty-one soldiers. That's a lot of men, Colonel. That's a lot of men to die in something that wasn't the real thing!'

Colonel Iremonger looked round at the speaker, his mouth twisted sourly. The other officer had come down from London and, since he was a logistics specialist and unlikely ever to risk his own neck in battle, the comment had a bitter flavour for Iremonger.

'They weren't even trying to get ashore on French soil,' the officer went on. 'They were trying to get ashore here. On Slapton Sands! And nobody was shooting at them. Except, that is, those goddam E-Boats. And six hundred thirty-eight men is a lot of dead men, especially since most of 'em were engineers who're going to be badly missed when the real thing comes up.'

Colonel Iremonger scowled and turned away to stare at the dead man at his feet. He was an officer, lying in a pool of water left by the receding tide, face down in the sand, still wearing a lifejacket and still carrying the equipment that had not given him a chance when he had found himself swimming for his life.

Iremonger lifted his head and looked at the steep slopes of the Devon and Dorset hills, purple under the low cloud, then he turned to the sergeant who was kneeling by the corpse. 'Got his name, Weinberger?' he asked.

'Yessir.'

'Ticked him off?'

'Yessir.'

'How many's that make?'

'Six, sir.'

Iremonger frowned. He was a short burly man with a blue emery of beard on his square chin. He looked like a boxer and though, like all Americans, he wore a well-cut uniform, his somehow didn't seem to fit him and looked as though his muscles were bulging out at every angle. His eyes were hot and dark and angry.

He lit a cigar and straightened up. Along the tide line in the easterly wind were other groups of men, mostly Americans but also a few British and Polish who'd been brought in to help, grouped about sprawled figures lying on the sand. There was a huddle of jeeps higher up the beach, an ambulance and several covered lorries. Another group of men was busy lifting a corpse wrapped in a blanket into the back of one of them.

'Nearly seven hundred men,' the logistics officer went on with the persistence of a terrier at a rat-hole. 'For God's sake, that's a pretty high rate even for a shooting war, let alone an exercise! Seven hundred, Colonel! Seven hundred!'

Iremonger took his cigar out of his mouth. 'Listen, son,' he said with ill-concealed impatience. 'For Pete's sake, stop saying that! You sound like a professional mourner. If we have no more than seven hundred dead when we go into Europe, I don't think anybody'll complain, except the guys who're dead. Now shut up and go away. I've got things to do. Important things.'

The logistics officer's eyes flashed; then he gestured at the dead man. 'More important than this?' he demanded.

'Yeah!' Iremonger's jaw stuck out. 'More important than this. Much more important than this.'

The logistics officer turned away, affronted, and went to find someone who was more prepared to listen to his indignation. Iremonger stared after him; then he realised the sergeant kneeling by the corpse was waiting for him. He turned and clicked his fingers. The sergeant handed him a waterproof packet he'd taken from the inside pocket of the dead man's blouse and he pushed it into a canvas bag he held.

'Four to go,' he said half to himself. 'Four to go.'

–

The wind was still cold, whipping along the broad stretch of sand, full of dampness and chill. Along the tide line, as Iremonger and his sergeant moved towards them, men were collecting lifebelts and equipment which had been washed up by the sea.

'How many have they found, Sergeant?' Iremonger asked. 'At the last count.'

'Pretty well all of them now, sir,' the sergeant said.

'Except the four we want.'

'Think the Germans got a tip-off, sir?'

Iremonger's eyes narrowed. 'They were certainly prowling around looking for *something*.'

'What's General Bradley think, sir?'

Iremonger chewed his cigar. 'What do you think he goddam thinks?' he snorted. 'He was at sea like I was and didn't even know what had happened till he was told. He knows what we're up against. It was the general who insisted on a thorough count being made.'

'Why, sir?'

'Orders from the high altar. We've got to account for everyone who's missing.'

'A dead man's a dead man, sir.'

'I guess these are different.'

A jeep detached itself from the group of vehicles higher up the beach and headed towards Iremonger. The man beside the driver was Orme, the brigadier-general who had been aboard the destroyer with him.

Iremonger lifted his hand in salute and Orme nodded in reply as he climbed out.

''Morning, Linus,' he said. 'How are we doing?'

'Four to go, sir,' Iremonger said. 'We've just picked up number six.'

'I don't have to tell you how important it is that we account for every one of them.'

'No, sir, you don't.'

'You know why, of course?'

'Some of it, sir. They're Bigot officers.'

Orme took Iremonger's arm and drew him aside beyond the hearing of the sergeant and the driver of the jeep. 'Know what Bigot officers are?' he asked.

'No, sir. I have their names, ranks and numbers but I guess I *don't* know what they are.'

'I'll tell you,' Orme said. 'With the invasion, the usual top secret classification was considered inadequate for the more critical details, and these were placed under a super-secret classification known as "Bigot". Officers authorised to have access to such plans had special clearances which entitled them to be known as "bigoted". Ten of them were lost on Exercise Tiger and every one of them knew the invasion plans.'

'All of 'em, sir?'

'All of 'em. Most people – me, for instance – know bits. A little here and a little there. We each know our own particular area and our own particular job. These guys knew the whole lot and they had their documents with them.'

'The plastic packets, sir?'

'Sure. The plastic packets. They were the guys who knew where everything fitted, how everything co-ordinated, times, places, numbers, how we're going to get ashore, where we're going to get ashore, how we're going to whip the Germans, and which way we're going to go when we break out of the beachhead.'

Iremonger whistled. 'That sure is some responsibility they were carrying,' he said.

'Exactly. There were ten German E-boats and we only sank one, so, for all we know, one of the others might have picked up survivors, one of them one of our Bigot officers. He might have been dead but it wouldn't matter either way because most of them had enough documents on them to blow the whole show. We therefore have to know whether they were picked up or not because, if they were, the whole goddam plan for the invasion's on the line.'

Iremonger frowned. 'Will it have to be changed, sir? That sounds one hell of a job.'

'Not impossible, Linus.' Orme shrugged. 'Difficult, but not impossible. The point is that if the Krauts *did* pick up one of these officers, then things *must* be changed. If they didn't, we'd be wiser to leave them as they are. That's why we have to account for every goddam one. Changes now could ruin the whole shebang, because we don't really have time this year to set up anything different.'

Iremonger chewed on his cigar. 'Well, we're doing what we can, sir. I've been working with the Limey navy at Plymouth on currents and drift, getting their advice on where to look. They're just beginning to appear in numbers. I guess we'll find them all in the end.'

'If the Germans didn't find them first.' Orme turned back towards the jeep. 'Keep me informed, Linus.'

'Sure will, sir.'

Orme began to climb into the jeep; then he stopped and turned. 'Oh, one thing,' he said. 'There's a British officer waiting to see you when you've finished for the day. He's Security same as you, so you'll maybe have something in common.'

Iremonger doubted it. He hadn't so far discovered that he had *anything* in common with the British. Their goddam country was too small and the British were stuffy, slow and lacking in what he called git-up-and-go.

'Guy called Pargeter,' Orme said.

'Is he going to work with me?' Iremonger asked.

'No, Linus. He's following a line of enquiry of his own. It just happens to cross ours, that's all.'

'I'm busy, General,' Iremonger objected. 'Can't he wait?'

'No, Linus, he can't. I know you're not very fond of the British but you might remember occasionally that they were fighting this war – in the front line – for two years before we came into it.'

'If they'd been ready, they'd not have got in the mess they did.'

'For God's sake, Linus, we didn't do so damn well ourselves at Pearl Harbour! And you might not have noticed all the housewives queueing up with their ration books for food. Have you seen American housewives queueing up for food? We've invaded their country. American privates earn three times as much as the British. An American staff sergeant's pay equals a British captain's. And a lot of that dough's invested in chasing British girls – even British *wives*. It's a tribute to their civility that they endure us with good will. So see this guy, Linus, and give him what he wants.'

–

Since bodies had been found along the whole coast from Start Point as far east as Lyme Regis, Iremonger had established a temporary headquarters at Dawlish on the coast south of Exeter, which was about half-way between the two extremities of his search. It was a room in a set of offices belonging to the town council and his equipment consisted of little more than a table and a telephone, with two or three men to man them. The officer cradling an ash plant and waiting on a stiff-backed chair as he returned looked English enough with his pale hair and eyes to make Iremonger feel ill, and he knew at once that he was certainly not his type. Iremonger's types were all burly men, strong-drinking men handy with their fists, headlong men who knew where they were going. The Englishman was slight, quiet and colourless, and

Iremonger decided sourly that he probably hadn't even started to shave.

The Englishman rose and offered his hand. To Iremonger it felt like a warm dead fish, and maliciously he grasped it and squeezed hard. To his surprise, the Englishman squeezed back with equal vigour and the two of them stared at each other, their hands locked, each trying to sum the other up.

'Pargeter,' the Englishman said quietly. 'Cuthbert Pargeter.'

Oh, Jesus, Iremonger thought. Cuthbert!

'Iremonger,' he growled. 'Linus Iremonger. Linus C. Iremonger.'

'I'm investigating the murder of a British officer,' Pargeter went on. 'A Captain Dunnaway. He seems to have had a lot of friends among your people. He was always with them.'

'Yeah? What can I do?'

'Probably nothing. Just making my number with you, that's all. Mustn't tread on any toes, y'know. Might have to ask for a little help.'

Iremonger looked quickly at the Englishman, suspecting a leg pull, but there was no hint of amusement on the solemn face and he noticed suddenly that, in spite of the narrow head, Pargeter's face had unexpected sharp planes and angles and that there seemed to be a bursting energy about him.

'I'm pretty goddam busy,' he said. 'Involved with the invasion.'

'Pretty busy myself,' Pargeter pointed out mildly. 'And *I'm* involved with the invasion, too.'

'I thought you said murder.'

Pargeter blinked. 'At the moment we're wondering if the feller was a homosexual. You'll be aware that homosexuals are always pretty tricky. Chatter too much and all that. Lay themselves open to blackmail.'

'I know that,' Iremonger growled. 'I was a policeman before I got into this outfit.'

'So I heard.' Pargeter blinked. 'The general told me. He also told me what you were doing and why you weren't in the office when I first called.'

It seemed to Iremonger that the general was a bit too quick to shoot off his mouth.

'How many have you found?' Pargeter asked.

'More than half. Around four hundred.'

'I meant Bigot officers.'

Iremonger scowled. 'Nine, now,' he said. 'Why?'

Pargeter blinked. 'Occurred to me that our friend, Captain Dunnaway, might have been blackmailed into passing on information. *If* he was a homosexual, that is, and if he *had* any information.'

'About Exercise Tiger?'

'Hadn't it occurred to you, Colonel?'

Iremonger hadn't so far linked the dead British officer with the disaster on Slapton Sands but he was quick to cover up. 'Yeah,' he said. 'It had occurred to me.'

Pargeter gave him a smile and, despite his instinctive dislike for anything British, Iremonger found himself dazzled by it. It had such a special quality of charm, he even wondered if Pargeter practised it in front of a mirror, to get things he wanted.

'How did it happen?'

Iremonger scowled and, reaching for a file, handed over a sheet of paper and started to read from the folder

"'Troops embarked for final rehearsals,'" he began, "'from the same ports as for the invasion. On the night of April 26–27, they proceeded through Lyme Bay with the mine-craft sweeping ahead of them as if crossing the Channel. Commander-in-chief, Plymouth, threw patrols across the mouth of Lyme Bay consisting of two destroyers, three MTBs and two MGBs. Following a mock bombardment, landings were made during the morning of the 27th and unloading continued through the day and a follow-up of eight LSTs was expected at night.'"

Iremonger paused in his reading to draw breath. "'When that second convoy was manoeuvring in Lyme Bay about midnight,'" he went on, "'with one escort vessel only, HMS *Azalea*, the other having been damaged and returned to base, flares were seen. It was supposed at first that they were part of the exercise; but at about 0130 on the morning of April 28, gunfire broke out astern and all vessels went to general quarters. We were being attacked by ten German E-boats out of Cherbourg, which had slipped past the naval patrols without being recognised. At 0204, LST 507 was struck by a torpedo, all electric power failed and it burst into flames. When the fire got out of control, the survivors abandoned ship. A few minutes later, LST 531 was hit by two torpedoes, burst into flames and, within six minutes, rolled over and sank. At 0228, LST 289 opened fire on an E-boat, which retaliated with a torpedo hit. A dozen men were killed but the LST managed to make port under her own power. For about half an hour the five landing ships remaining afloat exchanged fire with the E-boats which were also engaged by the British destroyer. All but one escaped by the use of smoke and high speed. One – numbered 151 – was

hit and blew up. HMS *Azalea* picked up one survivor.'"
Iremonger paused. 'I was aboard HMS *Azalea*,' he said.

Pargeter sat staring at his feet for a while as Iremonger finished. 'Nasty,' he commented.

Iremonger scowled. He had long since privately laid the blame at the door of the Royal Navy. In his heart of hearts, he wasn't sure that he was being fair, but he was a headlong man and he didn't often stop to think of fairness.

'Somebody slip up?'

'Christ knows,' Iremonger said. 'Mebbe someone was depending too much on radar while the Krauts were using Mark I eyeballs, and when one of the destroyers had to turn back with engine trouble, it wasn't thought necessary to replace it.' He scowled. 'We've identified the Germans – they came from the 5th and 9th E-boat flotillas at Cherbourg.' He indicated the paper he'd passed over. 'You have the casualty figures there. Most of 'em came from the 4th Combat Engineer Battalion and they're going to be missed when we land in France.'

As Iremonger became silent, there was a knock on the door and Sergeant Weinberger put his head round.

'Number ten's turned up, Colonel,' he said. 'A Polish unit with the British Second Army east of Lyme were brought in to help and they've just reported it.'

'Is it complete?' Iremonger asked. 'Papers there?'

'Far as I can make out, sir. I told them they weren't to touch a goddam thing. They said they hadn't. It's at the Weymouth end of the bay and there'll be a jeep load of Snowdrops waiting outside Lyme Regis to guide us to it when we arrive. They're fixing lights, screens, and all the necessary vehicles.'

Iremonger gave a sigh of relief. 'Well, thank God for that,' he said. 'Tell 'em in the office to inform the general. He'll want to know. Then have the jeep brought round. I'm going over there.'

As the sergeant's head disappeared, Pargeter reached for his cap and walking stick. 'Mind if I come, too?' he asked.

Iremonger minded very much, but he remembered the general's warning. 'I guess I can't stop you, buster,' he said ungraciously.

4

It was a difficult drive to Lyme Regis, less because of the distance than because of the number of vehicles on the narrow roads.

The whole coastal area seethed with shipping and, as it grew dark, they could see the little shipyards along the creeks, many of them new, bristling with the naked struts and ribs of vessels. Ships even grew in the streets and workshops, prefabricated parts being hurriedly put together round steel skeletons, so that ship-building had almost become a cottage industry.

Sitting in the back of a jeep driven by Sergeant Weinberger at a lunatic speed between the convoys of lorries, Pargeter stared around him, a frown of irritation on his neat features. First there had been the Czechs, the Poles, the French, the Dutch and the Norwegians, and the British had grown used to them all in time, but now indignity had been heaped on them until they had reached breaking point. There were now a million and a half Americans to bear them down with their weight, and to guard the secrets of the invasion the last straws had been loaded on to British backs with the restriction of the postal services and the sealing off of the southern coastal areas. As it happened, only doctors and those on essential business had been able to move for some time anyway. With petrol cut to nothing, the only transport available was a bicycle or one's own two feet, and no one wanted to use those with the roads' death-traps under the endless convoys moving about at breakneck speed. Houses in the narrow villages of the west shuddered as they went past, sometimes knocking off the corner of a building or killing a dog, sometimes even an unwary child; and to make movement easier, the Americans had even hacked away the corners of the winding lanes that Pargeter loved so much. This was his corner of England and it annoyed him that a set of foreigners, with no intention of enduring England for one minute longer than they could help after the war was won, should destroy its beauty so that they could travel at their usual frantic pace.

Aware of Iremonger's disapproval of him, he tried to make conversation.

'Been a good spring,' he said.

'Yeah.'

It was hardly an encouragement and he fell back once more on his own thoughts, glancing upwards as a flight of aeroplanes appeared suddenly over the hills to his left and hurtled towards the sea. The skies had not been quiet for months. Kent, Sussex, Hampshire, Dorset, Devon and Cornwall were crowded with lorries, tank transporters and bulldozers, all heading south or south-west to the ports. So many streets had become one-way in the little towns that employers were having to give their workers an extra quarter of an hour to get home for lunch, and work in schools had to stop because of the noise of tanks grinding up hills. Practising American troops assaulted the same hills again and again, and in every sandy combe mines and bombs erupted in spouts of black smoke, flame and sand as men leapt from their assault craft. Everything was assembled to simulate reality except death.

A convoy began to pass in the opposite direction, tyres whining on the tarmacadam, each vehicle giving a breathy 'whoosh' as it disappeared. They were filled with American servicemen, all waving and yelling at the females on the pavements, whether they were thirteen, middle-aged or pushing prams. If the invasion didn't come soon, Pargeter thought, Great Britain would sink with the weight of people crammed into it, and, without doubt, the south would be the first to go under. Warehouses overflowed and all double-track roads had had one track closed so that it could be packed with lorries, tanks, cars, jeeps and guns. From the coast where huts and tented camps dotted the fields, the supply and service tails stretched back as far as the Midlands. Hundreds of private properties, farmlands, even whole villages, had been taken over despite the legal difficulties. Everything had been pushed aside, the law as easily as red tape, for the sole end of the coming invasion.

He became aware of Iremonger's scowl and tried again. 'Amazin',' he offered, 'that Jerry's never seen any of all this.'

Iremonger grunted. 'The day the Krauts get past our air force,' he said, 'will be a gala day.'

'*Our* air force, too,' Pargeter reminded him quietly, deciding he didn't like Iremonger very much. 'They had a bit to do with winding up the Luftwaffe.'

They passed through Exeter as it began to grow dark, then out by the coast road towards Sidmouth, Beer and Seaton. As they roared down the hill into Lyme, a jeep with four American MPs was waiting for them. As

Sergeant Weinberger drew to a stop, a corporal climbed out.

'Hi, Colonel,' he said. 'Glad to meet you.'

The police jeep led the way towards Bridport where it turned right. After a while the road became narrower and, beyond Abbotsbury, as they turned right once more, finally ceased to be tarmacadamed. Eventually, bumping over the rough surface of a farm lane, they came to a gate. Beyond was utter blackness. The jeep stopped and the police corporal appeared alongside Iremonger.

'Guess we walk from here, Colonel,' he said.

As they climbed out, Iremonger noticed an ambulance and a black police van in the shadows under the trees. The road to the beach was steep and uneven and they stumbled in the darkness with only their torches to guide them. Over to the east they could hear the rumble of aircraft and the distant thud of bombs and see the weaving fingers of searchlights behind the dark shadow of the Downs.

'Portland Bill,' the corporal said. 'After the landing craft, I guess.'

The road to the beach grew more difficult as it grew more steep, but at last they dropped the final few feet to a stretch of sand and shingle and followed the corporal to where they could see a faint light in the distance under the loom of the cliffs. There were two policemen, a Provost lieutenant and a few soldiers with rifles. As they came to a stop, someone turned up a gas lamp.

'Make it quick, Colonel, if you can,' one of the policemen said. 'We wouldn't like to attract some prowling night fighter.'

The body was lying on its back, sand in its open mouth and on its eyeballs, its skin the colour of putty. One hand clutched papers in stiff fingers.

'This how he was found?' Iremonger asked.

'That's what I understand, sir,' the provost lieutenant said. 'When we arrived there was a Polish officer who'd been fetched by one of his men, the guy who found him.'

'Where is he now?'

'He's gone, sir. I understood that this – whatever it is – was to be kept quiet.'

Iremonger nodded and bent over the dead man. He was a lieutenant-colonel and, oddly enough, he still wore glasses, gold-rimmed ones that had slipped down his grey, sanded nose. Weinberger cut off his identity discs.

'Colonel Greeno, Harry, sir,' he announced, glancing at a list in his hand. 'And that's the last, so I guess we can now all go home.'

'Amen to that.' Iremonger eased the bundle of papers from the stiff fingers and glanced at them briefly. 'Must have been trying to get rid of them when he went down for the last time,' he said.

They saw the body carried up the hill towards the police van; then the canvas screen which had circled it was folded up and taken away. As the vehicles began to move down the lane towards the main road, the provost lieutenant suggested that he find them a meal and Iremonger agreed.

'Thanks,' he said. 'It's going to be late when we get back.'

The Provost lieutenant had his headquarters in Charmouth and when they arrived a sergeant looked up.

'Lieutenant, sir,' he said. 'Would that be Colonel Iremonger with you?'

'Yeah,' Iremonger said. 'It would. Why?'

'Nothing, Colonel. It's not you I want. Would there be a Major Pargeter with you, sir? A British officer, sir? I was told there would be. There's a message for him. It seems they've been trying to contact him since early this evening.'

As Pargeter pushed forward, the sergeant handed him a slip of paper. 'You're to ring that number, Major,' he said. 'They didn't leave no name.'

Pargeter glanced at the number. 'No,' he said. 'Shouldn't think they would.'

The sergeant pushed a telephone forward and, as Pargeter picked up the receiver, he turned a handle and nodded. As Pargeter asked for his number, they all became silent, waiting, listening, wondering what was going on.

'Yes.' Pargeter seemed to stiffen to attention, Iremonger noticed with disgust, as if he were speaking to a senior officer. 'That's right, sir. I'm still on the track of Dunnaway.' The telephone crackled and his eyebrows shot up. 'Where, sir? Right, I'll go at once.'

He put the receiver down, rubbed his thin nose with the handle of his stick then turned to Iremonger and gave him his special smile.

'Got to leave you, old boy,' he said. 'Fun and games seem to be hotting up. Another chap's been done in. Essex this time. This chap was fond of Americans, too, it seems.'

5

Essex seemed to be as cold as Devon and Dorset, with the wind coming strongly from the north.

To avoid delay, Pargeter persuaded an army supply barge to give him a lift across the Thames from Sheerness to Southend-on-Sea. A big ship lay near the shore and the sergeant in charge of the barge cocked a thumb at it.

'Ammo for the invasion,' he said laconically. 'The civvies are scared as hell the Germans will bomb it. We keep telling 'em it's not ammo but they don't believe it.' He grinned. 'Neither would I.'

At the other side of the river Pargeter borrowed a car and a driver from an Intelligence unit and obtained directions. 'First US Army Group's up there,' he was told. 'Patton's lot. Mind you don't get trampled underfoot.'

When Pargeter reached First Army Group's area, however, it seemed a strangely nebulous outfit. The Canadian 2nd Infantry Division, whom he'd seen drilling in the fields of Kent, was supposed to be under its wing, too, yet the camps in Essex seemed virtually empty.

'Old Blood and Guts was down checking everything,' an American top sergeant in an almost deserted tented camp near Chelmsford informed him. 'Complete with side guns and bull terrier. Your guy, Monty, was here, too.'

'When?'

'Tuesday, sir.'

Pargeter lifted an eyebrow, because on Tuesday Montgomery had been at a conference on security in Surrey which he'd attended himself.

'Patton down here often?' he asked.

'Ain't seen him myself, sir. But I'm told he's around a lot, visiting the camps.'

'Which camps?'

'All the camps.'

'There don't seem to be many men in them.'

The sergeant's face was blank. 'There ain't, sir? I heard they was full of guys.'

There was a curious absence of willingness to assist but, despite this, Pargeter managed to find a detective inspector in Colchester who seemed to know a few facts. The murdered man was an Ordnance Corps lieutenant called Jacobson. He was a Jew but, this apart, seemed to have quite a few things in common with Captain Dunnaway, the man found in Portsmouth. Like Dunnaway, he seemed to be a lone wolf, with a job which allowed him to travel about the country. Based on Dover, he'd been sent to Essex to investigate missing ammunition but had then disappeared until found on the mud flats of West Mersea. The inspector had made a few preliminary enquiries and had discovered that like Dunnaway he had had a university background. He also had a knowledge of explosives and weapons, while, with a French mother and a father in the wine trade, he had spent enough of his life in Alsace to become a linguist.

'Which languages?' Pargeter asked, knowing roughly what the answer would be before it came.

'French and, because Alsace was German until 1918, German and Dutch. He was looking for an American, I gather.'

'Which American?'

'No idea. But there are a lot here belonging to First United States Army Group. Under that chap Patton.'

Pargeter frowned. 'I've seen none.'

'They're all around.'

'Where?'

The inspector looked uncertain. 'Well, anyway, that's what I understood. I must admit I haven't seen 'em myself, come to think of it, but there are several Yank aerodromes around. There's one near here – at Chiteley. There's a railway line that supplies it.'

'What with?'

'Spare parts. Bombs. Food. There's always an ammunition train standing in the siding for when the level in the bomb dumps goes down. When it does, they move it up to Colchester and from there portions of it are shunted around to local stations for the dromes. As it gets split up and disappears, they shunt another into Chiteley. The bomber boys have been busy lately with the second front and the scheme was devised so that there'll never be a shortage of bombs. Endless belt sort of thing; the war's getting a bit like that these days, isn't it?'

Pargeter's eyes were narrow. 'Who told you all this?' he asked.

'One of the American officers. You can meet them any night in the pub at Chiteley. It's full of bomber crews.'

Returning across the Thames to Dover Castle to make further enquiries about Jacobson, Pargeter learned that the Guards Armoured Division were also in the area, together with two other armoured divisions, while American infantry divisions were in Ipswich and Folkestone. In Intelligence, he managed to sneak a look at train schedules and routings; certainly the railway had carried into the area a great many British and American troops, their routes and numbers clearly marked, and the roads appeared to have been full of lorry convoys. Indeed, he thought, there seemed to have been a remarkable amount of casualness about 'secret' and 'top secret' documents.

'This the jumping-off spot for the invasion?' he asked.

The officer he asked shrugged, blank-faced. 'Well, there's a lot of wireless traffic. And I've seen landing craft, hangars, loading ramps, gliders and armour.'

As Pargeter drove back along the coast, he was thoughtful. Off Dungeness there were several vast constructions of concrete and steel protruding from the Channel, evidently resting on the sea bed, as big as vast blocks of flats. They looked as if someone had picked up part of the city of New York and dumped it offshore, or as if some vast factory had risen from the water, and he could only assume they were part of the preparations for the coming invasion.

Back in London, he tossed his cap on to his desk and sat down, staring thoughtfully at his blotter. After a while, he reached for a cigarette and rang a bell. It was answered by a girl in the uniform of a Wren second officer.

'Anything happened?' he asked.

Second Officer Elizabeth Wint produced a lighter and lit his cigarette. 'No,' she said. 'No enquiries either. Any moment now somebody's going to decide we're surplus to establishment and send us back to the war.'

Pargeter went on sitting quietly for a moment, studying a notebook he had taken from his pocket and tossed on to the desk with his cap. Then he looked up.

'Remember a naval officer in Plymouth in February getting knocked on the head and being dumped in the sea?'

'Vaguely.'

'Do we have a file on it?'

Second Officer Wint crossed to a steel cabinet by the door. 'The police decided he was gay,' she said. 'Been chasing Americans, they thought.'

'That's what I understood. Let's have the file.'

Elizabeth Wint fished inside the cabinet. She came from the same class as Pargeter himself. Moneyed, privileged, beautiful, well-bred and not-too-clever, she had a flat at Dollis Hill and they'd been carrying on a desultory affair for some months now.

She laid the file in front of him. It was marked 'Jensen, Lieutenant-Commander Hector, RNVR'.

Pargeter opened it. The circumstances and the background were surprisingly like those of Dunnaway and Jacobson. Jensen had been a paymaster-commander in the Regulating Branch of the navy with the job of examining ships' books. This had taken him along the whole south coast of England and in the months before his death he, too, seemed to have been working with the Americans. What he had been working on seemed vague, however, and Pargeter wondered if he, also, had had a fondness for American officers.

The coincidences were too great to be ignored. 'Wonder if there's a mass murderer about,' he mused. 'A different kind of Ripper – like that chap in 1942 who killed all those prostitutes in air raid shelters.'

Second Officer Wint pulled a face. 'These weren't prostitutes. They were men.' She glanced at the files. 'Not particularly small men either.'

'Makes 'em vulnerable. If you're expecting affection, you're hardly in a position to resist a knife in the gizzard.'

He turned over a sheet of paper on the file in front of him. 'Lecturer in Modern Languages, Durham University, 1935 to 1939. Author of *Germany Wakes, National Socialism in Bavaria* and *The Hitler Regime*.' He gestured at the empty chair on the opposite side of his desk. 'Sit down, Liz,' he said.

Second Officer Wint pulled up a chair and, lifting one elegant black-stockinged leg, she crossed it over the other. Pargeter studied it approvingly. 'Fancy dinner tonight?' he asked.

'On service rations, who wouldn't?'

'I can find somewhere.'

'And then?'

'The usual.'

'I'm a glutton for punishment.'

Pargeter's stiff face didn't smile. 'Let's get back to business,' he said, tapping the file. 'Homosexuals? Or were they genuine officers doing their job?'

'They seem to have been pretty fond of the Yanks.'

'I thought that was the privilege only of women.'

'Well, they do have smart uniforms and bulging wallets and they *are* eager to please.'

'They're also pretty eager to get people like you into bed.'

Second Officer Wint smiled. 'They try hard,' she agreed.

They seemed to have drifted off the subject again. Pargeter brought it back with a jerk.

'You heard of that affair at Slapton Sands?' he asked.

'It drifted up the line. Was it bad?'

'Around seven hundred men.'

'Whew! Think the Germans got wind of what was happening?'

'I'm beginning to. Suppose our friends and were being blackmailed into passing on information?' Pargeter paused, studying his fingers, then he looked up cheerfully. 'I think I'll go and see my friend Iremonger again,' he decided.

Colonel Iremonger was no more pleased to see Pargeter a second time than he had been the first.

'How in hell can *I* tell you if the guy was making love to American officers?' he demanded furiously. 'They didn't tell me! And, for God's sake, I've got something better to do than chase 'em round the south of England to ask 'em what they get up to in their spare time.' He stared hard at Pargeter, convinced as he had been from the beginning that he was lazy, stupid and privileged. An intensely patriotic man himself, he considered Pargeter, like most British, to be too damned casual by a long way. Iremonger was a man who could stand with his hand on his heart in front of the Stars and Stripes without a second thought, but he guessed that Pargeter, like many Englishmen, would be faintly embarrassed even to stand up for the National Anthem.

'It's not part of my job,' he growled.

'It might be,' Pargeter said blandly.

Iremonger swung round in his chair and stared at Pargeter angrily. 'You got something I haven't got?' he demanded.

'What makes you think that?'

'You're smiling like the cat that ate the canary.'

Pargeter's smile disappeared abruptly and his face became so blank that to Iremonger it looked as though it belonged to someone else who'd gone away and left it behind.

'Probably,' he said.

'Well, come on, give!'

Pargeter made a little shuffling movement as though he were shifting his position inside his uniform. 'I discovered,' he said, 'that the gentleman I'm interested in was around Slapton just before Exercise Tiger took place. It led to a few thoughts.'

'Such as what?'

'Such as you've probably got something *I* haven't got.' Pargeter's smile returned. 'It would seem to me that you and I might work together with some measure of success.'

Iremonger didn't relish the idea and he sat back, frowning, to light a cigar as big as a torpedo. None too willingly, he offered one to Pargeter who declined gracefully. Iremonger eyed him warily. Pargeter was wearing a wooden expression now and suddenly he began to suspect that under the po-faced façade he was a lot smarter than he looked.

'*Azalea's* survivor,' he said. 'The guy from the German E-boat that sank — a guy called Emil—' he moved the papers on his desk until he came up with the correct one — 'Emil Puttkamer, Able-Seaman Emil Puttkamer — he said everybody on board knew they'd had orders to pick up officer survivors. Note that: not enlisted men, officers. My guess is that they were after the Bigot guys and it sure as hell gave Security a fright when they found there were ten of 'em missing.' It had also, he remembered, led to

44

the suspicion that the Germans hadn't just *stumbled* on the rehearsal.

Pargeter rubbed his nose. 'Any idea who could have tipped 'em off?' he asked.

'These guys of yours who were murdered?'

'It had to come from higher up than that.'

Iremonger sighed. 'Mebbe we *ought* to work together a little.' He made the suggestion ungraciously because he wasn't sure that working with Pargeter was going to be anything but a chore, but he was intelligent enough to realise it had to be done. 'Where do we start?'

–

Both Iremonger and Pargeter were a little startled to find themselves in double harness. For the life of him, Pargeter couldn't imagine that they'd ever find anything in common. Iremonger simply resigned himself to a month or so of misery. Pargeter, he decided, probably drank milk.

They agreed – mutually and with relief – that they should cover different fields. Iremonger was to ask around the units which had taken part in Exercise Tiger. Pargeter was to ferret around in Essex and among the corridors of Whitehall. Within a matter of days, he was back in Iremonger's office.

'Know anybody called Fox?' he asked.

Iremonger stared at him, chewing one of his monstrous cigars. 'There was a guy back home in Nebraska,' he said, blank-faced. 'Name of Champlin Dilwara Fox. Snappy name. He was a half-breed who used to collect trash.'

Pargeter blinked at the sarcasm. 'I'm talking of an American officer,' he pointed out coldly.

'Then why not say so?' Iremonger scowled. 'No, I don't. Why?'

'My murdered officers seem to have one or two common denominators. One of them a chap called Fox.'

'How do you know?'

'Detective in Essex picked up a name and I checked back. That chap, Dunnaway, in Portsmouth, I was investigating, and another chap earlier in Plymouth were also interested in a chap called Fox.'

'How do you know?'

'Asked the officers they met.'

'Find out anything?'

'He seems to be an American officer. At least he wore American uniform.'

Iremonger chewed at his cigar for a moment. 'Think he's some sort of agent?'

Pargeter gave a small shrug. 'We needn't persuade ourselves that there *aren't* German agents around,' he said. 'London have had their eye on two or three, I gather, but, as far as I can learn, most of 'em were arrested before they had any chance of doing any harm. I think the tip-off about Slapton Sands came from a senior official in the Foreign Office who was on loan as senior liaison officer to your people. His job was to sift information for senior American officers. His wife's an ambitious type with money who's looking for a title for her husband. She's got a big house in north Hampshire and makes a practice of inviting allied officers to spend week-ends there. Away from the pressures of duty. We all suffer from them.'

Iremonger glanced sideways at Pargeter. He looked as though he'd never suffered from pressures of any kind in the whole of his life and was taking great care that he wasn't going to in the future, and Iremonger was suddenly reminded of a paragraph in the booklet on the British which he'd been given as he'd sailed from New York for Europe. 'The British are reserved,' it had said. 'But don't be misled by soft speech and politeness. They can be tough.' He glanced again at Pargeter and decided that it probably applied to him.

'Sure,' he growled. 'Pressures are hell.'

Pargeter smiled. He looked like a sleek tom-cat. 'Our Foreign Office gentleman had had a paper on the Slapton rehearsal through his hands and probably talked too much to one of his wife's guests. That week-end – the week-end before Slapton – they were all Americans.'

'And the guy in London? The Foreign Office guy?'

Pargeter smiled. 'He's been removed from his job and sent to Birmingham with the Ministry of Supply. I imagine his wife's not very pleased because it means the end of his promotion and the next step would have carried a knighthood. She'll now remain plain "missis" to the end of her days.'

7

Two days later, Iremonger appeared in Pargeter's office. When Pargeter arrived, he was drinking coffee with Elizabeth Wint and obviously enjoying the experience. The harshness in his manner had gone, and he even appeared to have produced a certain amount of charm.

Elizabeth Wint smiled. 'Colonel Iremonger dropped in with some information for us,' she said.

'So I see.'

Iremonger rose and beamed at the girl. 'Thanks for the coffee,' he said. 'Next time I'm up, I'll remember to drop a can in for you. Might even run to a pair of nylons.'

Pargeter held open the door of his office for him, his face blank and disapproving, and as Iremonger took the chair opposite his desk, he extracted his cigarette case and offered it to the American.

'You married, Iremonger?' he asked.

'Me?' Iremonger knew what was running through Pargeter's mind. 'I'm not the type to be hemmed in by out-of-date inhibitions like that, Cuthbert. Why?'

Pargeter shrugged. 'Nothing,' he said, deciding he'd better keep an eye on Elizabeth Wint. 'What's this information you've got?'

Iremonger made himself comfortable. 'This guy, Fox. In 21st Army Group there are thirteen Foxes. There are also three in the navy and four in the air force. I talked to 'em all. There are also one hundred and ten enlisted men of various ranks with the name.'

'What did they have to say?'

'They'd never heard of Dunnaway, Jacobson or Jensen.'

'Telling the truth, d'you think?'

Iremonger's expression seemed to indicate that it was an insult to suggest that an American could tell a lie. 'That week-end party you talked about,' he said. 'There were six Americans there. None called Fox. I talked to them all. Five I'll vouch for. The sixth is our guy.'

'Go on.'

'Guy called Julius Weddigen. Lieutenant-commander, USN. He's a medic. Psychiatric branch. His job's to go the rounds and tell the guys what to do if they're wounded when the invasion starts, how good the medical services are, and how quick we can get 'em back to safety if they're hit.'

To Pargeter it seemed a strange psychology for an invasion – the British army was busy telling its troops they were immortal and that it was the Germans who were going to die.

Iremonger was still talking. 'He was at a party,' he said. 'A different party. There were British, Free French, Poles, Czechs, Americans. He was heard shooting his mouth off about Slapton.'

Pargeter was silent for some time then he looked up.

'This chap Weddigen,' he said. 'Would it be a good idea to check all the people who might have heard him?'

Iremonger stubbed out his cigarette. 'I did. Personally. All the Americans and all the British. The others were a bit harder. I don't speak their languages. It seems our friend, Weddigen, actually mentioned talking to a guy called Fox.'

'My Fox?'

'I guess now he's probably *my* Fox, too.'

'Have you found him?'

Iremonger frowned. 'No, I haven't. But as it was a pretty casual party and people took their friends and a bottle – you know the sort – that wouldn't be so goddam strange, would it?'

'Was he British?'

'According to the report I got, Weddigen thought he was American but he later wondered if he was right. I guess he's still wondering back in the USA because, like your Foreign Office guy, he's been demoted – and posted home for opening his big mouth too wide. He also wondered if he was a Pole or something, acting as a liaison officer. I guess the truth is he didn't know what the hell he was. It was a warm night and they took their jackets off and there was a lot of hooch and girls. And in any case, there aren't any Poles with us except at top level. They're all with your people at the other side of England.'

Pargeter stubbed out his cigarette and lit another – not so much because he wanted one as because it helped to take away the smell of the cigar Iremonger had now lit.

'Wonder if any of my murdered officers had met your friend Weddigen, or his friend Fox?' he mused.

Iremonger studied him. 'What's on your mind?' he asked.

'They were all introspective types. All quiet. All linguists. All with free and easy jobs. All with strange friends—'

'Americans,' Iremonger pointed out indignantly.

'Strange for Englishmen.' Pargeter corrected himself quickly. 'And I've discovered there's no suggestion of homosexuality about any of them.'

'A guy doesn't trumpet that sort of thing about.'

'A guy certainly doesn't trumpet that sort of thing about,' Pargeter agreed. 'But one might expect that out of the three of them, somewhere there might be some hint of it.'

'What are you getting at?'

'Perhaps they *weren't* homosexuals? *Or* spies. Perhaps, like us, they were looking for our friend, Fox.'

Iremonger looked through narrowed eyes at Pargeter. 'It's an idea,' he said grudgingly.

Pargeter frowned. He looked like a schoolboy who'd just won a prize, but there was nevertheless an air of aggressive maleness about him, an air of ancient wisdom that belied his youthful manner. At that moment his face wore a disapproving look that amused Iremonger, and he seemed angry.

'It's my belief,' he said grimly, 'that there are people around who aren't playing square with us. I think it's time someone did.'

8

The man who met them at the Ministry of War was a faceless sort of individual – pale, uninteresting-looking, plump and spectacled – but he appeared to know what he was talking about and when Pargeter put his ideas about the murdered officers to him, he rubbed his nose, said 'Wait just a moment,' and vanished from the room.

'Just a moment' turned out to be an hour and a half, during which time Pargeter and Iremonger sat trying to sum each other up. By now, Iremonger was beginning grudgingly to admit to himself that Pargeter wasn't such a fool as he looked, while Pargeter was conceding that, even if Iremonger's manners didn't come up to his own impeccable standards, at least he moved fast when he started.

By the time they were beginning to wonder what to say next, the pale-faced man returned. 'You've been summoned to Widewing?' he said.

'What the hell's Widewing,' Iremonger demanded.

The pale-faced man didn't blink. 'General Eisenhower's headquarters,' he said. 'Bushey Park. He's recently moved there. More than likely Tedder, Montgomery, Leigh Mallory, Bradley, Ramsay and Bedell Smith are there as well. You're moving into exalted circles. For most of us, those people are so high up they're out of sight.'

A car was laid on and, as it moved off, Iremonger, who'd been sitting in silence, suddenly lifted his head. 'Second Officer Wint,' he said.

Pargeter turned, a small knowing smile on his face, and Iremonger went on earnestly. 'She's enough to make a man make last stands.'

Pargeter smiled. 'She'll be pleased you've noticed.'

'She got any boy friends?'

'Why? Think they might kick your teeth in?'

'I'm serious. Has she?'

'Only me.'

'You engaged to her?'

'No. Of course not.'

'You sleeping with her?'

'Seemed a good idea. Especially to her. Suspect there've been others, of course. Sex is an occupational hazard in war-time.'

'Does she mean anything to you?' Iremonger persisted.

'How can you tell whether someone means anything to you until you lose them?'

'Think she might?'

'Does it bother you?' Pargeter said, stiff-faced.

Iremonger shrugged. 'Hell, no,' he said. 'She seemed a nice dame, that's all.'

'Suspect she's shameless.'

'Yeah?'

Pargeter nodded and the discussion was dropped.

The car was now passing endless caravans of drab army trucks loaded with war supplies, huge dumps of stores and strings of murderous-looking tanks parked nose-to-tail just off the pavements with heavy guns, ammunition caissons and other military hardware. Headquarters was a sprawling hutted camp in a wide park where the grass had already been worn thin by tramping feet. There seemed to be staff cars everywhere, and they were escorted inside the building by a full colonel and passed on to a slim blunt-faced officer who introduced himself as General Bedell Smith, Eisenhower's chief of staff.

They were shown into a room where four men were standing at a table and immediately they recognised them as General Omar Bradley, Air Chief Marshal Sir Arthur Tedder, Admiral Sir Bertram Ramsay, and Eisenhower himself. Eisenhower turned as they entered, gestured towards a door and they followed him into an inner office. Bedell Smith took up a position with his back to the door.

'Gentlemen,' Eisenhower said, and there was no hint on his grave face of the wide smile that had won everybody, both civilians and servicemen alike, to his side. 'I've had you brought here deliberately. In just a few moments, you'll be taken to see General Hardee, of Intelligence, who'll put you in the picture. But you're here first because you've gotten yourselves involved in something that reaches right to the heart of what we're doing. I just want you to be fully aware of the importance of it, to stress to you the need for absolute silence and secrecy, and to let you know that if there are difficulties you're to come right back here to me.'

They were both feeling a little dazed as they were led by Bedell Smith out of the room and down a corridor. The room they entered was part of another large suite and General Hardee looked more like a professor, with heavy horn-rimmed spectacles and a deceptively quiet voice. He waved them to two chairs which had been set ready for them.

'Okay, gentlemen,' he said. 'Let's get down to it. First off, no note-taking. What I tell you stays only in your heads.'

He sat back in his chair, offered cigarettes and lit one himself. 'Right away,' he said, 'let me congratulate you. You've reached a point in your enquiries that we've been trying to reach for some time, so under the circumstances, we're dropping everything in your lap. You're to turn over everything you're engaged on to someone else and concentrate solely on this. I suggest you make your base at Portsmouth so that you'll be handy both for this place and invasion headquarters, which will eventually be set up down there. You'll be given another officer – a Frenchman who speaks Polish, Czech and Slovak, with a little Hungarian and Ukrainian on the side to take care of any odds and ends. Okay, so far?'

Pargeter and Iremonger glanced at each other, aware that for better or worse they were finally tied together. They nodded towards Hardee.

'Slapton Sands,' Hardee went on. 'Captain Dunnaway, Lieutenant-Commander Jensen and Lieutenant Jacobson. As you've guessed, they *were* connected, but, as you also seem to suspect, Dunnaway, Jensen and Jacobson were neither homosexuals nor informers for the Germans. They were British agents who'd been on to a German spy we've been seeking since January. I need hardly point out that he's obviously very clever and clearly ruthless.'

Neither Iremonger nor Pargeter spoke.

'We have reason,' Hardee continued, 'to suspect that Dunnaway, Jacobson and Jensen were all close on his tail when they were killed and, since you seem to have picked up the trail from them, from now on it's *your* responsibility.

It'll be a great deal easier than briefing someone else, and the less people who know what's going on the better.'

Hardee leaned forward, resting his elbows on the table. 'Now listen carefully, gentlemen, because you're going to hear some secrets which must never be repeated outside this room. You could read them all in a book we have, but anyone who's instructed to read that book is locked in a room until he's finished – even if it takes days – because it contains the strategic plan for Overlord, which is the code name for the invasion of France. It covers everything we've been doing for months already, up to the actual day of invasion and months afterwards. It shows the whole shebang, until we reach Germany itself and gives the estimated times and dates of each move. But, since it takes so long to read and you've not that much time, I'll fill you in myself. You'll need to know what I'm going to tell you to do your job properly.'

Hardee smiled. 'I don't have to stress that you've both been checked and re-checked,' he went on. 'And that you're expected to keep your own counsel and not discuss with anyone but each other what I'm going to say – not even with the French officer who'll be attached to you. Least of all with him, because we've already had too much cause to believe that de Gaulle's people are a little careless with security. If you wish to talk together, I suggest that you borrow a boat from the navy and talk in the middle of Portsmouth Harbour. Understood?'

He sat back and grinned suddenly. They smiled back at him, at ease. Then his face grew harder and they wondered what was coming.

'I'm stressing all this,' Hardee went on, 'because there have already been a few scares. Some of 'em were sheer coincidences – most of 'em to do with newspapers, and not all British newspapers either, because our American correspondents sometimes have big ideas about their own size and consider that the date of the invasion's of prime importance to the folks back home. There have been other leaks. One idiot actually posted our plans by mistake to his sister in Chicago and the parcel burst open in the mail office there. Another guy left a brief-case in a train. Fortunately, the porter who found it had the horse-sense to take it straight to his boss. Then a gust of wind blew a dozen documents through an open window in Whitehall and only eleven were recovered. The twelfth was handed in later by a civilian who didn't leave his name, and we've had to assume he's an honest man and a patriotic Britisher.'

Hardee paused. 'Even American generals aren't above reproach,' he went on soberly. 'One's already been rocketed by Ike and another's been demoted and sent home for guessing at dates at a party. A British officer, who told his parents what he knew, found himself being interviewed by our Security people because his parents had more sense of responsibility than he had. There've been other scares, too, but so far we feel confident nothing's leaked across the Channel about the date and place of the invasion. Slapton worried us some, of course, but, with the recovery of all the bodies carrying Bigot papers, we feel that even there nothing leaked out.'

Both Pargeter and Iremonger were tempted to glance at each other, but they felt somehow that such a movement might suggest they were types who would discuss later what they heard; so they both kept their faces expressionless and their eyes towards Hardee.

Hardee paused again. 'For your information,' he went on, 'the exact date of the invasion's still to be decided, but, as you can guess, it has to take place when the tide will be low enough to expose the beach obstacles Rommel's been erecting, and around dawn to enable follow-up troops to land on another low tide before darkness. We also need a late rising moon for the paratroops and glider-borne units to get in, and there are plenty of other considerations – among which, of course, will be good weather and a calm sea, which we can't predict.

'These are the main considerations, and since you could easily work it out for yourself from what I've said, I can tell you with the Supreme Commander's approval that a provisional date's been fixed and it isn't far away. You can be sure, of course, that the Germans have worked that out too. In fact, we're pretty sure they have. In other words, they know we're coming, all right. They even know roughly when.' Hardee smiled and ended in a flat voice. 'The only thing they don't know is *where*.'

9

During the silence as Hardee stopped speaking there was a knock on the door and tea appeared, carried by an American WAC sergeant.

'We have American coffee at eleven,' Hardee said, 'and British tea at five. It makes for good relationships.'

He smiled and remained silent until the WAG had vanished again. Then he picked up his cup and gestured to them to do the same.

'Fortunately for us—' his voice, as he started to speak again, was pitched low, almost as though he thought they might be overheard '—German Intelligence is in disarray at the present time. Himmler's been trying to extend his influence by taking it over, so we're being considerably helped in our countermoves by the sycophantic rubbish his people are putting out to lull Hitler into believing – as he wishes to believe – that all's well. What's more, to bring Hitler to his senses and kill the rubbish the SS are feeding to *Führerhauptquartier*, German Intelligence have deliberately been inventing allied divisions that don't exist in the hope of making him afraid and more realistic. You needn't know how we know, but we do. They claim we have fifty-five divisions available, and there are even hints that there may be seventy-five or even eighty-seven. As you probably know, we have nothing like that number, but there's no reason why German GHQ shouldn't go on thinking we have, and they're already bringing their propaganda machine into high gear with stories of hospitals in England being emptied ready for casualties from the second front.'

Hardee paused to sip his tea and shift the papers on his desk. When he continued there was a malicious glint in his eyes. 'We've encouraged them to believe we're going to a variety of places,' he said. 'For instance, there's a big discussion going on in the newspapers about a landing on the Riviera and we hope it's diverted a few divisions down there because, when we go, there must be not only enough manpower and equipment but an excess, so that our blow can be neither parried nor avoided.'

Again Hardee paused. 'We've been bombing inland France for months – to the north of the invasion area. The Germans think it's because we're going north, but in fact it's to seal the invasion area off from the rest of the country. Meanwhile, British operatives in neutral countries have been enquiring in bookshops for copies of Michelin Map No. 51, which covers the Pas de Calais. You can be sure the Germans haven't failed to notice this. To make confusion worse confounded, we've also striven to give the impression that the invasion might also arrive in Holland. Dutch documentary films are noticeably being made in London, Dutch-speaking wireless operators have been hired, postcards and photographs of the Netherlands have been advertised for, and Queen Wilhelmina was persuaded to broadcast to the Dutch that their ordeal will soon be over.'

Hardee finished his tea and lit a cigarette – slowly, as if to give himself time to think before going on. 'Crates of carrier pigeons have also been dropped by parachute in north-west France and Belgium,' he said. 'Only five or six birds have come back and the information they brought was largely useless, but, as we thought they might, the Germans found some of the crates and, plotting the drops, noticed that they were all north of the Somme and the Amiens-Abbeville line, which once more indicated the Pas de Calais. A signal we picked up which indicated that von Rundstedt also believes we'll invade by the shortest route was used to bolster up these views. In all this, we're helped by the fact that almost every one of their agents in England have either been arrested or "turned round" so that they're now sending back to Berlin exactly what we want them to send. However, we do suspect there are still two uncaught – one of them in the south watching the build-up for the invasion and one over in the Eastern Counties keeping an eye on the bombing offensive.'

Hardee hesitated, frowning. 'More of that in a moment,' he said. 'The Germans' firm belief in our extra divisions and the fact that they think they're all in East Anglia ready for the crossing to the Pas de Calais area ties in very nicely with the information we have that they've built sites up there for the launching of pilotless aircraft for the bombing of London – what they call V-weapons – so that the Pas de Calais once more would seem the obvious place to invade.'

As he stopped, Iremonger and Pargeter were silent, then Iremonger drew in a deep noisy breath.

Hardee smiled. 'As you also seem to have discovered, we've gone along with German thought and filled all those empty camps in the south-east of England with a phantom army group – Army Group Number One – and we've even put General Patton in command. Since he's senior to General Bradley, it would be natural for the Germans to assume that he *would* have an army group, and it's a card we must play for all its worth.'

He paused to light another cigarette and glance at his notes, Pargeter was aware that Iremonger was looking at him and, as he turned his head, he saw Iremonger give him a nervous smile as though he, too, were awed by the secrets that were being laid bare to them.

Hardee sat back, blew a few puffs of smoke and started again. 'Fortunately,' he said, 'since we have command of the air, Luftwaffe reconnaissance only occurs when we allow it to, and where they *are* getting through is only in the east. They're *not* getting through in the south and west, and what they're seeing in the east are dummy ships and landing craft and dummy army units. Even the people living in those areas believe there are troops and planes there.

'False airfields have been set up, movements of landing craft have been taking place ostentatiously in the North Sea, balloons are drifted over Nazi outposts to give the impression of forces moving about the northern channel, and buoys with special electrical apparatus inside are floated down to simulate large fleets on the German radar screens. To encourage the deception, the bomber boys have been smashing German radar installations to the south but have left those in the north untouched, and in the meantime we keep the cookhouse fires in Kent and Essex stoked up so they can see the smoke. We expect Army Group Number One to pin down the German XV Army Group for some time after D-Day, and I dare wager when we go ashore they'll strip Brittany, southern France, Norway and Denmark for reserves, but keep their divisions opposite the Pas de Calais intact in case we're only feinting.'

Hardee seemed to have finished, but he turned over more sheets and looked up with a smile. 'You're getting a heavier briefing than some generals,' he admitted. 'But we *have* to make it all work. Otherwise a lot of lives are going to be lost. Which is why your job's going to be to find the man who killed Dunnaway, Jacobson and Jensen and told the German navy of Exercise Tiger at Slapton. If he finds out that Army Group One exists only on paper, the obvious conclusion he'll draw is that we *must* be going to Normandy and since that's where we *are* going, gentlemen, such information would be disastrous if it went to the Germans. Any questions?'

'One obvious one, General,' Iremonger said. 'This agent you mention: Do you have *any* information on him?'

Hardee reached into a drawer and drew out a brown file which he laid on the desk in front of him. He smiled apologetically. 'It isn't much. The only reason we think our man might be your Fox is because he's not a civilian recruited by blackmail but a professional German officer who worked in Austria before the Anschluss, and in Prague before they went into Czecho-Slovakia. He also speaks excellent Polish and was in Warsaw when it fell. After that he's believed to have joined Polish officers as they fled from Poland in 1939. He reached Egypt that same year and eventually England.' Hardee took out a photograph and laid it in front of them. It showed a German officer complete with high-peaked cap, fly-away breeches, polished boots and stiff collar.

'Ebert Klaus Reinecke.' Hardee tapped the file. 'Also known as Hans-Heinrich Müller; Franz-Karl Dittli; Adolf Matajec; Jan Chlebowski; Jean-Pierre de Leone; Walter MacMaurice; Padraic Seamus O'Shea; Arthur Jones; and Thomas John Dent.'

'He gets around some,' Iremonger commented.

'Born Hanover, 1902. Joined army in 1918, aged 16. Decorated in World War I with Iron Cross, second class, and three months later with the Iron Cross, first class. So he's not short of courage. Seconded to Intelligence in late twenties. Employed in Austria, Czecho-Slovakia and Poland. Gained a Knight's Cross outside Warsaw. The rest you'll find in there.'

Pargeter glanced at the picture. The German officer's features were thin and indeterminate and he appeared to be laughing and pointing at the camera. Hardee leaned over the desk. 'When we go into France,' he said, 'we have to expect heavy casualties – perhaps even *very* heavy casualties – but we must do everything in our power to keep them within bearable proportions. It seems to me, therefore, that as of this moment, our German friend is probably the most dangerous man in England and that you have a very formidable task.'

Part Two

From a Check to a View

1

Hardee worked fast and a large detached house at the north end of Portsmouth, filled up to an hour or so before with American officers, was set at their disposal. Sergeant Weinberger and four men, two of them British because Pargeter had insisted that they should not all be American, had occupied it, and tables were erected and telephones installed.

Despite his slight frame and apparent casualness, Pargeter was possessed of the physical keenness of a demon, and the fact that they had their headquarters straight and ready to roll by evening was entirely due to him. Sergeant Weinberger looked at Iremonger in a daze.

'Does that guy always spend as much energy as this on living, Colonel?' he asked. 'Because, if he does, he sure as hell deserves to die young.'

Iremonger grinned. A fair man, he had to admit that Pargeter *was* pretty fast off the mark.

'Major Pargeter, Weinberger,' he said, 'like God, moves in a mysterious way, his wonders to perform.'

Weinberger scratched his head. 'He sure is a funny little gadget, Colonel.'

The description seemed to fit Pargeter's neat frame.

'I shouldn't underestimate him, all the same,' Iremonger warned. 'He's tougher than he looks and when he moves into top gear he's a lulu. He also has a great deal more natural cunning than appears on the surface so when he wears his please-may-I-leave-the-room look, just watch out.'

The first evening in their new headquarters was quiet and Iremonger was reading the paper, grinning all over his face. 'Hardee certainly shoves things along,' he said, tossing it to Pargeter.

On the front page was a picture of an American general complete with staff, six-guns and bull terrier, addressing a group of American soldiers. 'General Patton talking to GIs during a tour of inspection of East Coast camps,' the caption said. 'The troops are to be visited tomorrow by the King.'

Sergeant Weinberger, who had appeared with an armful of files, leaned over Pargeter's shoulder to look. 'Your goddam newspapers have gotten so small you could fold 'em up and get 'em in your wallet,' he observed. 'How do they get everything into four pages?'

'We're noted for our terseness,' Pargeter said.

As Weinberger vanished, rebuffed, Pargeter pushed forward the folder Hardee had given them. 'Reinecke,' he said.

Ebert Klaus Reinecke, the file revealed, was the only son of Karl Reinecke who as a major in 1916 had been awarded Imperial Germany's highest award for gallantry, and as a major-general in 1940 had been killed at Sedan, one of the few senior German officers to die. His grandfather was a Colonel Heinrich Reinecke, who in 1870 had been one of the first soldiers to see Paris as the Prussian armies had arrived to invest it.

'Our Reinecke,' Pargeter went on, 'seems to have had a flair for languages – including English – and was ordered – note that, *ordered* – by the General Staff to join Intelligence. He became a field worker.'

'That the lot?' Iremonger asked.

'Not quite. Married three times. First time in 1930 to a woman who died in childbirth, leaving a son. Second time in 1934 to a Viennese girl who was killed in a motor accident in 1938. Third time in early 1939 to Sabina-Christina Grubovius, an actress. Last-heard-of rank was lieutenant-colonel.' Pargeter frowned. 'Know what Reinecke means?' he asked.

'Do you?'

'German's one of my languages. It means "Reynard", "Old Cunning", "Brer Fox". Probably explains why he calls himself "Fox" in English.'

As they talked, there was a knock on the door and, as it opened, Elizabeth Wint appeared. Pargeter's jaw dropped.

'What the devil are you doing here?' he asked.

'Just been posted,' she smiled.

Pargeter turned to look at Iremonger, who was grinning all over his face. 'I was told we had to have female staff for typing, filing, and so on, and since American dames are so goddam pushing, I guessed mebbe we ought to have an English one.'

While Pargeter was still staring, the telephone rang and Iremonger disappeared to his office. Pargeter turned and looked at Second Officer Wint.

'Rather fancied a posting to the American forces,' she explained cheerfully. 'After all, no American walks, and they don't expect their lady friends to walk either.'

'They're all sex mad,' Pargeter said coldly.

She was infuriatingly unperturbed by his annoyance. 'Not really. Mind—' she shrugged – 'I have to admit that if a girl adjusts a stocking in a cinema, every American in the place turns round. But they're lavish with their Luckies and Camels, and at dances at American bases you get ice cream, coffee, doughnuts, *and sugar in bowls.*'

Pargeter sniffed. 'They're completely naïve and quite gullible. Every prostitute in London these days claims to be Free French when they're neither free *nor* French. What's more—' he ended in a bleat of indignation as though this last were the most heinous of their crimes '—they monopolise the taxis.'

She smiled. 'Do you want the truth?' she asked.

'Why not? A little old-fashioned truth is always welcome.'

'Right. I like them.'

They were working up to a monumental row when Iremonger slammed down the telephone next door and appeared in the doorway, scowling. 'That was Security,' he snarled. 'They ran a routine check on those papers we took from that guy we found on the beach at Abbotsbury – Colonel Greeno, the last of the Bigot officers. There were fingerprints on 'em. *Fingerprints that weren't his.*'

–

Frowning deeply, Iremonger stood at the window, his hands thrust deep into his pockets. His cigar was out but it rolled round in his mouth as he chewed fiercely on it.

'That guy Greeno was the only one of those Bigot officers who'd taken the papers out of the packet,' he was saying. 'It would have to be *him* some bastard found, holding the goddam things in his hand.'

Pargeter blinked. He wore a bland urchin look as if he knew exactly how things were shaping. '*Why* was he holding them in his hand?' he asked.

Iremonger turned. 'What do you mean, why was he holding them in his goddam hand?'

Pargeter's thin pale face was expressionless so that he looked like a small boy having his teacup read by a maiden aunt and determined to catch her out by giving nothing away. 'Up to now,' he said, 'it was no business of mine. Now it is. I came out of France at Dunkirk and I also escaped from Greece in 1941, so I've seen quite a few drowned soldiers. But I never saw *any* of 'em holding anything in his hand. When a man's drowning, he lets go.'

Iremonger frowned. There was something curiously smug about Pargeter. It implied experience against his own lack of experience, a knowledge of war against his own lack of knowledge, and a sort of sly delight in proving to people that he wasn't such a fool as he looked.

'What the hell are you getting at, you narrow streak of Limey whitewash?' he growled.

Pargeter shrugged. 'Can't imagine why he had 'em in his hand at all,' he said. 'After all, what did he think he was going to do with 'em? Strike a match and burn 'em? In the sea?'

His eyes changed and became as hard as flint. 'Somebody *found* that body, Iremonger – somebody who was *expecting* to find it. Like the E-boats, he was looking for it and he took those papers out of the plastic case, and studied them, and when he'd finished, he stuffed 'em in Greeno's hand because he didn't have time to get 'em back in the packet. He had to leave them there

73

because, otherwise, we'd have known they'd been found and there'd have been an immediate alarm.'

He set out the facts in such a neat way Iremonger felt dim-witted. He scowled because he knew Pargeter was right. 'There were only Americans and British on that beach,' he said slowly.

'And a few Poles. I think we should make enquiries about who found Greeno. In fact, it seems to be a job for our French interpreter friend. Has he arrived yet?'

'Sergeant Weinberger said he'd seen him. A goddam count, no less.' Iremonger sounded bitter. 'I seem to be surrounded by all the riff-raff of European aristocracy here.'

—

The Polish unit was part of British XXX Corps and was stationed on the edge of the New Forest just outside the American zone. The French interpreter, Lieutenant Count de Rezonville, chattered all the way there. He was tall, devastatingly handsome, incredibly rich, and spoke English to Second Officer Wint with a charming set of mispronunciations that Pargeter suspected were deliberately put on to attract girls.

'You 'ad better call me 'Enry,' he told them. 'My name, of course, is Louis-Henri-Benoni, but that, I think, is perhaps too much for Anglo-Saxons.'

The Polish commanding officer, a colonel with an unpronounceable name, produced the man who had found the body of Colonel Greeno. After four years attached to the British army he could speak reasonable English and there was no need of de Rezonville.

'Yes,' he agreed. 'I find this gentleman.'

'Anybody else there at the time?' Iremonger asked.

'No, sir. I am alone. There are other soldiers on the beach but they are much far away from me. I swim much – for the muscles, you know – and I know the tides. They are very different from Gdynia where is my home until the war. But I think the tides will make the body where I find him, so I look. And so I find.'

'How did you find?' Pargeter asked.

The Pole opened his eyes wide. They were a brilliant blue and surrounded by dozens of tiny laughter lines. He grinned, 'I look, sir. With the eyes.'

Pargeter grinned back and it occurred to Iremonger that he and the Pole seemed to be hitting it off very well. 'No,' he explained. 'How was he when you found him? On his side? On his back?'

'Oh! I understand, sir. He is on the face. I show.' The Pole was entering into the discussion with enthusiasm, and he now flung himself to the floor to demonstrate a body lying facedown on a beach, one hand underneath him, one hand flung out in front.

'Like that?'

'Yes, sir. Just like that.'

Pargeter glanced at Iremonger. He seemed to be suggesting that perhaps Iremonger had questions of his own. 'Go on, Cuthbert,' Iremonger growled unwillingly. 'You're doing okay.'

'What happened then?' Pargeter turned again to the Pole.

'I fetch the officer.'

'Which officer?'

'I do not know his name. He is also searching alone. He say he will stay by the body, while I go and call others. We are a long way from other peoples. Perhaps nearly almost a mile. I run and shout. Others come.'

'And the dead American?' Iremonger said.

'He is still there, of course.' The Pole looked startled. 'He has not got up and walk away.'

'No.' Iremonger frowned. 'How is he lying now?'

'The same. On the sand.'

'No, for God's sake! On his face still?'

'Oh, no!' The Pole smiled at his error. 'He is like this.'

Once more he flung himself down, lying on his back, his arms outstretched.

'So the officer you fetched had turned him over?'

'I think so, yes.'

'And the papers he held in his hand? Had he them in his hand when you first found him?'

'I don't know. This hand is underneath him. So.'

The Pole was about to hurl himself to the ground yet again when Iremonger stopped him. 'Quit doing that!' he said. He turned to the Polish officer. 'Can't you tell him to stop doing that?'

The Polish colonel smiled. 'He is enthusiastic, this one.'

The Polish soldier was looking hurt and it was Pargeter who restored his good humour.

'And the officer?' he asked. 'This officer you called, the man who stayed with the body while you ran for help. Who was he?'

The Pole smiled. 'I don't know,' he said cheerfully. 'He do not belong to my outfit.'

2

The square-topped cap hanging behind the door, with the khaki mackintosh and officer's greatcoat, had an obviously foreign quality about it. It didn't belong in that narrow little room which was somehow as English as it could be, with a pair of faded towelling curtains at the window, left behind when the house had been requisitioned for the army. It belonged to a wider land than the narrow Hampshire village where the house was situated, redolent of plains and horses and even fluttering lance pennants; tall, spiky with arrogance and oddly eastern Europe.

The room was no more than twelve feet by seven and barely provided enough space for a bed and one man's equipment. It had only a small window; it had once been a bathroom, but the bath had been removed because now everyone used communal ablutions. Since it was at the back of the house facing north and the sun never penetrated, it remained chilly and cheerless even on the brightest day.

The man who occupied the room was a tall man, strongly-built, handsome, assured and arrogant-looking. It had not been difficult to acquire the room because no one else wanted it, and it was too small to be shared. With his kit piled against the door – as if he were reorganising it for the day of the invasion – he was assured of complete privacy and could do whatever he wished without fear of interruption.

Sitting on his bed with the black-out thrust into the small window, he studied the wet prints he'd developed. The camera that had taken the photographs was an excellent one but, without an enlarger and no means of getting to one, he was having to decipher the writing the picture showed with a powerful magnifying glass.

The pictures were good, however, and apart from a little blurring along the edge, they were clear and quite readable, despite the faded ribbon of the machine which had been used to type the original message.

> '**BIGOT**. *Top Secret.* Supreme Headquarters Allied Expeditionary Force. Office of the Assistant Chief of Staff, G–2. Shaef/2DX/INT. G–2 estimate of the use of Ultra in the assessment of German Enigma signals before, during and after Operation Overlord. (Based on information available up to 15 April. Amended by Shaef 2DX/I/INT. of 20 April.)

> '*Object*: The object of this paper is to estimate the usage of Ultra to anticipate from Enigma signals enemy moves against Operation Overlord.

> '*Assumption*: That enemy dispositions in FRANCE and the LOW COUNTRIES are as shown on the attached map (Appendix A) and that the moves outlined in the attached list (Appendix B) can be assumed from the present assessment of enemy signals. A close

78

watch on Enigma signals and the use of Ultra intelligence should confirm whether such moves are being initiated...'

Eyes narrowed, he stared at the prints, reading carefully. His photography, with troops only a quarter of an hour away, had had to be hurried. The sun had been out and it had been difficult to prop the sheets up at the right angle to do away with the shadows; but he'd managed it successfully, though without time to replace the sheets in the plastic packet in which he'd found them.

There were fifteen sheets altogether and the inference was obvious. The allies were intending to invade Normandy at the beginning of June and thereafter to draw German armour towards their left at Caen, which they expected to capture on the first day, while their right broke out and headed for Cherbourg which they expected to fall by the end of the month to provide the major port that was so essential for the build-up of supplies. The frequent references to 'towing', 'Mulberry' and 'caissons' made it clear what the concrete objects were that had been seen off Selsey and Dungeness, and that the allies were taking their own harbour across with them until Cherbourg fell. There was no reference to the Pas de Calais, and the allies were plainly gambling that the VI flying bombs being assembled in that area would not be fully operational before the attack could be swung north towards them.

He sat back, staring at the prints. They seemed to confirm something he'd suspected for a long time – that the allies had long since broken the German cipher system and were able to read and assess German signals without difficulty. Surely, here in his hands, was the explanation for the Luftwaffe's defeat in the Battle of Britain which, it now appeared, was less due to the courage of the British pilots than to the foreknowledge the allies had had of German plans. How else could it be explained? Or Alamein? Or Sicily? Or Rome? Or the U-boats which, for nearly a year now, had been fighting a losing battle?

In his hands he held a summary of allied plans for the invasion, so vast they were terrifying. The whole of England was packed with men – among them Poles, Czechs, Dutch, French, Danes, Norwegians – all of them hating the Germans, all of them waiting to go home. It had been Hitler's biggest mistake to antagonise so many nations at once because it was obvious Germany couldn't hold the whole coast of Europe in strength; and in Normandy, it seemed, the allies had probed a soft spot.

The man on the bed frowned. He'd already learned that the famous Atlantic Wall, on which the Germans were relying for the defence of Fortress Europe, was largely a fraud. The Atlantic Wall, they were saying in Berlin, was so tight not even a louse could creep through; but the reports he'd heard were that any amateur swimming club on a day out could penetrate it without trouble. In places it was so thin it resembled a fragile length of cord with a few small knots at isolated places, most of them in the Pas de Calais area. To his certain knowledge, Normandy was poorly defended, and only an earlier warning he'd sent, springing from an intelligent guess at possibilities, had set Rommel frenziedly improving on them.

Now, in his hands, he held the confirmation that his guess had been correct. At first he'd imagined that Normandy was to be the site of a diversionary attack to draw troops from the Pas de Calais. Now he was certain that the diversionary attacks, if there were any, would *not* be in Normandy. Normandy was to be the site of the main assault.

His face, intelligent and intense to the point of nervousness, changed. He was a lonely man who didn't mix much. A few of his brother officers assumed his silence was because he had taken the tragedy of Poland to heart. They believed he had a family there but they never heard him talk of them. Though it was safer that way, it was also lonelier. He seemed to have been alone for so long now, never able to talk to other men on level terms because his fears weren't their fears, his loyalties not their loyalties, so that he sought only the company of undemanding women and the shared comfort of a warm bed. Women allowed him to relax and satisfied the desperate sexual need he felt for his wife.

He looked at the photographs in his hand again, suddenly feeling lighter-hearted. What he held could virtually end the war and take him home. By using the knowledge that the allies had broken their cipher system, German intelligence could load the information contained in their radio messages to lead the allies to disaster. And if the invasion failed, they would never be able to mount another for years – if ever. They would have no choice but to seek terms, and then – if anyone in Germany had any sense – the Reich would demand peace and see they got it.

He thrust the thought aside as he realised that the first and most important thing he must do was send a warning to OKW headquarters in France. His role had changed. His original task as leader of a team of saboteurs had swung long since to collecting and collating information. Now it had changed again. For Germany he had probably become the most important man in Britain. Krafft in Essex, the sole survivor of his sabotage team, was doing a good job and could be left to carry on with the information he'd fed him, but he knew he wouldn't last long because he was far too reckless. As for himself, it had been pure chance that the Poles had been called out to help look for the Bigot officers; as soon as they'd been told to search particularly for field officers he'd known it was important, and the enormous secrecy the Americans had shown had convinced him he was right.

He glanced once more at the photographs in his hand. Then he thrust them into his pocket and, pulling a sidepack from among the pile of equipment, he hurriedly began to throw things into it.

It seemed to be time for him to move on.

3

'Those papers,' Pargeter said. 'When you found them, were they wet or dry?'

Iremonger frowned. 'Damp,' he said. 'But that could have been the goddam mist that was everywhere at the time. They certainly weren't saturated and they sure ought to have been, oughtn't they? As a matter of fact, I thought about it afterwards, but decided the guy must have got them out of the packet after he reached the beach, and then died of exhaustion or exposure – somethin' like that.'

As the jeep headed back to Portsmouth, Iremonger sat frowning at the road unfolding ahead and the constant procession of American army lorries.

'Did you read the papers?' Pargeter asked.

'No.' Iremonger's frown grew deeper. 'I just saw the top of the first sheet. It said "Bigot". In pretty big letters. Then "Top secret". Also in pretty big letters. Then "Supreme Headquarters, Allied Expeditionary Force. Office of the Assistant Chief of Staff". Then underneath in ordinary typing it said "G2 estimate of the enemy build-up against Operation Overlord". Something like that. I also noticed the second sheet. Same heading, but this one said "G3 directions for manoeuvring, D1-D2, with instructions to be followed on break-out from beach-head".'

'See any names?'

'Cherbourg, Lorient, St Nazaire, Brest, St Malo and Rennes. There were more, I guess, but I'd been instructed not to read the papers, so I didn't. I just couldn't help seeing some of the goddam stuff.'

It was Pargeter's turn to frown. 'If this bloody Polish officer wasn't a Polish officer at all, but our friend the Fox,' he said, 'then it means that the Germans will be getting information of where the landing's going to take place and where we'll be heading after we break out from the beachhead.'

Iremonger remained sunk in gloom. 'We'd better have a check made on all ports and all airfields,' he growled. 'Even small ones. In case the bastard tries to get out of the country.'

'We'd better also set up a round-the-clock check with radio detectors and arrange for all service operators not involved in transmitting or receiving to listen out in case the Fox tries to transmit.'

'Yeah.' Subtly, Iremonger noted, the man they were seeking had become not 'Fox' but 'The Fox'. It was a title that suited him because he had the same shadowy cunning as a fox, remarkably slippery, and vicious if trapped. 'I'll go see Hardee,' he went on. 'He'll fix it. Any operator not actually working a channel could be looking for him and arrange to jam anything suspicious. In the meantime we'll contact all Polish units attached to the British XXX Corps.'

–

Within two days they had discovered the name of the Polish officer who had found the body of Colonel Greeno.

'Kechinski,' Pargeter said. 'Captain Taddeus Kechinski, 20th Polish Recce Regiment, follow-up troops attached to the 50th Division. Stationed in the New Forest, and called in to help find the bodies of American soldiers lost on the night of April 27 to 28. The police saw his identity card.'

'And the guy himself?'

'Arrived in England early 1940 via the Middle East, together with other Polish officers. Background: Reserve officer. Married with one child; present whereabouts of wife and child not known. Has since not been out of England. Interested in photography.'

'How interested?'

'If he was interested enough to possess a good German camera he could have photographed those papers in the quarter of an hour it took that Polish soldier to fetch help.'

'He sure could. Let's go see this guy Kechinski. He might be a contact of the Fox.'

Pargeter's pale eyes gleamed. 'He might well *be* the Fox,' he said.

–

Kechinski's unit was stationed near Ringwood and it took them two hours to reach it because of the volume of traffic on the road. In every field there seemed to be scattered lines of men assaulting some imaginary object, and in every wood and copse hutted and tented camps sprawled. It was becoming difficult to believe that anything else existed but the need to land troops on the coast of France.

The Polish reconnaissance regiment was billeted in a village, some of the men in tents, some in huts, some in private houses. The colonel's office was in what had once been the church hall, a battered tin hut whose floor still showed traces of the French chalk that had been scattered there for weekly dances.

The colonel was unable to identify Kechinski from the photograph Hardee had provided. 'This is a mere boy,' he said. 'Probably in his early twenties. Kechinski was around forty.'

'Forty-two, in fact,' Pargeter said as the Pole shrugged. 'This was taken some years ago. Could it be him?'

'It could. On the other hand, equally it could not. I don't know.'

'Where is he now?'

The colonel shrugged again. 'Not here. He has just left us. He was suffering from neuralgia. I think it is to do with not knowing what has happened to his wife and child in Warsaw. He reported sick a week ago and was admitted to hospital at Winchester. I had him driven there in my own car.'

Iremonger scowled. 'Then he must have gotten out again,' he growled. 'Because on April 30th, he was on the beach at Abbotsbury near Lyme Regis in Dorset.'

For a moment they were silent then Pargeter spoke. 'Would there be a photograph?'

The colonel shook his head. 'I think not. He was a keen photographer himself and had an excellent camera which he said he'd taken off a dead German in Poland, but he wasn't very interested in portraits. There is a group photograph, of course.'

The photograph was a long one of two or three hundred men in lines, piled in tiers one above another like stacked cards. The colonel smiled. 'A prize for anybody who manages to identify himself,' he said. He jabbed a finger. 'That is Kechinski.'

The face he indicated was no larger than a little finger nail and was none too clear. Even the face of the colonel didn't look like that of the man in front of them.

They compared the two photographs they now possessed and there seemed to be no relationship between them. The new one showed a man who had become thickset with the years, strong-looking and stern-faced.

'Could be two different guys,' Iremonger said.

The colonel shrugged. 'In a unit photograph,' he said, 'one doesn't have to be handsome. Just present.'

Pargeter cleared his throat. 'Colonel,' he said. 'What else do you know about Kechinski?'

Holding his cigarette between finger and thumb in the arse-about-face fashion that so intrigued English girls, the colonel raised his shoulders in another shrug. 'Not much,' he said. 'He joined us from a unit in Scotland. A good officer. Very useful. He spoke French, English and German, in addition to Polish. Sometimes even, I thought he spoke them better than he spoke Polish. He had been on the staff of General Sosnowski for a period.'

'And General Sosnowski?'

'Attached to the staff of General Bucknall, XXX Corps.' The Pole smiled. 'I believe *they* will be spear-heading the British half of the landing.'

–

'This guy Kechinski knows more than is damned well good for him,' Iremonger said angrily as they hurtled back towards Portsmouth. 'Probably the direction, the date, and any contacts we might have with the French Resistance.'

'If he studied those papers Greeno was carrying,' Pargeter said, 'he even knows what happens after we're established on French soil.'

As they breasted the hills behind Portsmouth, they could see the Solent so packed with warships, transports and landing craft, it seemed in parts almost possible to walk across to the Isle of Wight without getting the feet wet.

'Jee-sus,' Iremonger said in an awed voice. 'How can those guys on the other side *not* know what's coming? Do you know, there are fifty-four thousand guys just establishing and maintaining the installations for the assault forces and another four thousand five hundred just cooking for *those* guys, to say nothing of another four thousand doing nothing but watch security.'

'Let's hope one of 'em's turned up Kechinski,' Pargeter said.

A subtle change had come over their relationship. Iremonger was not so hostile and Pargeter not so painfully prepared to be patient. In the few days they'd been together, they had discovered an odd phenomenon: they worked well in company, sparking ideas from each other in the way an ideal police investigation team did. Neither was prepared yet to admit more than that, but they *were* prepared to accept each other's intelligence.

As it happened, however, they drew another blank at the hospital at Winchester. It was full of men who'd been injured during training, but Kechinski had discharged himself the night he'd arrived.

'He just disappeared,' the sister in charge of the ward told them stiffly. 'He left a note, with an address in Wales, where he said he was going to join his unit.'

'In Wales?'

'That's what he said. He said he'd heard the invasion was finally coming off and, because of that, had found that his neuralgia had disappeared. You'd be surprised what this invasion's done for people like the Poles, Dutch, Czechs and Free French. For four years they've been hanging around in England, suffering from the mopes. The worst danger they laid themselves open to in some cases was venereal disease.' The sister had obviously made a great study of wartime psychology and was full of enthusiasm. 'The hospitals for nervous cases and cases of depression were packed with them because they were homesick, deprived of action, and parted from their families. Since it became known that there'll be an invasion this year the wards have emptied. Kechinski was just another.'

Iremonger looked at Pargeter. 'That's what you think, Sister,' he said grimly. 'This guy's illness was just a goddam ruse to be away from his unit without anyone being suspicious. And he hasn't returned to his unit in Wales because his unit isn't in Wales. It's in the New Forest.'

4

'The guy could be anywhere,' Iremonger snarled.

'More than likely in London,' Pargeter said. 'You can hide better in London than in the New Forest.'

'Well, we've got to goddam find him! And, first off, since he seems at one time to have masqueraded as a Yank called Fox, and he's probably doing it again now, I guess we'd better look up the list of American deserters. Let's go see the Provost boys.'

The Provost boys had a formidable list of soldiers, from major down to private, who had decided they didn't like the war enough to be part of it, and had quietly opted out, vanishing into the back streets and living on stolen ration cards and rations.

'You have to accept, of course,' they were told, 'that some of 'em might no longer be alive, because some guy might have swopped identities with 'em a touch forcibly.'

The list was extensive and, since nothing was known of what had happened to the owners of the names, it left them still in the dark as to the identity Kechinski had adopted.

'We'd better get in touch with the police,' Pargeter suggested. 'And ask them to keep a look-out, too. Then we can check on canteens, servicemen's clubs and officers' clubs.'

'Rainbow Club? American Red Cross?'

'*And* the French Club in St James's, the Polish Club, the Czech Club and all the other foreign clubs, because we don't really know what nationality or rank he is at the moment, and he seems to speak all the necessary languages. We could also search bomb sites and air raid shelters and try the women's voluntary services and detention centres, and request the navy and the merchant navy to search ships – especially those heading for neutral ports.'

Pargeter frowned in a self-dependent absorbed manner, indifferent to the grin spreading on Iremonger's face. There was an infuriating complacency about him but Iremonger had a feeling that he knew exactly what he was doing. 'The police'll co-operate,' he said, 'because they're at it all the time and, without a ration card and an identity card, nobody can live any other way but rough.'

'This guy won't be living rough,' Iremonger said.

'No, he probably won't,' Pargeter agreed. 'But we can't take a chance. And, just in case he tries to make a dash for it, we'd better warn bobbies in coastal villages to put the request round that all small boats be immobilised by the removal of oars, rowlocks or whatever starts their engines.'

Iremonger studied Pargeter. 'You ever a cop, Cuthbert?' he asked.

Pargeter sniffed, suspecting sarcasm. 'I was on the officer reserve and I was called up in 1939.'

'How come you ended up in Intelligence?'

'They didn't know what to do with me.'

'Why not?'

'Got shot.'

'Where?'

'Backside.'

'I mean, what country?'

'Oh!' Pargeter permitted himself a small grave smile. 'North Africa. Why?'

'Just wondered. You seem goddam efficient.'

'I've done it all before.' Pargeter blinked and got back to the subject. 'We also make snap raids on the clubs and pubs and canteens, and get troops confined to camp for snap kit inspections.'

'What the hell for?'

Pargeter smiled. 'To check on 'em. No one'll worry. They're having them all the time with the invasion just round the corner. De Rezonville can handle the foreigners. In the meantime, we get Liz Wint to contact Kechinski's last unit before the one in Ringwood and see what they know about him.'

As they were talking, the telephone rang. It was the detective inspector Pargeter had questioned in Colchester about the murdered Jacobson.

'That chap you were investigating,' he said.

'Go on, Inspector,' Pargeter encouraged. 'I'm all ears.'

'Seems he was asking a few questions about a chap out Chiteley way. Chap called Isaac Hatcher.'

'Was he now?'

'Yes. So I did a bit of asking around for you, and it seems this chap Hatcher was seen in the pub at Chiteley talking to an officer.'

'What sort of officer?'

'The landlord thought he was a Pole. He was in British battledress and beret but he had that funny metal badge on it they wear. Is it what you're after?'

'It is indeed, and I'm obliged to you, Inspector. It sounds very interesting.'

'I tried to find out who this Hatcher was.' The inspector sounded pleased with himself. 'But there's no Isaac Hatcher in Chiteley and when I asked at the other villages around, there wasn't one there either.'

'This might make you jump, Inspector,' Pargeter broke in. 'But your friend Hatcher might well be an enemy agent.'

'He might?' The inspector sounded startled.

'He might indeed. Like your Polish officer. What else do you know?'

'Not much. But I did find out that this Polish officer was around here on and off until recently. Till they put the restrictions on, I reckon. I traced him to the George in Colchester. He had a camera and he borrowed a bicycle from the porter and said he was going to take photographs to take back to his wife in Lodz. The porter particularly remembered the name because he comes from Lodsworth in Sussex and they exchanged a few words about it.'

As Pargeter put the telephone down, there was a thoughtful expression on his face. 'I think you're going to be busy,' he said to Iremonger. 'I think I've just picked up the trail of our Polish friend again.'

Iremonger was none too willing to let Pargeter disappear just when his organisation was beginning to move, but he was also astute enough to know that Pargeter didn't stick his delicate nose into things unless they had the sweet smell of certainty about them.

'Better tell me about it,' he said.

Pargeter smiled. 'Do you want poetry readings or facts?' When Pargeter had finished, Iremonger scowled and lit a cigar. 'You'd better get over there,' he agreed. 'Liz Wint can take over here. She seems to know what ticks.'

Pargeter was about to turn away when he paused. Iremonger looked up.

'Liz Wint,' Pargeter said. He looked like a little boy up before the headmaster.

'What about her?' Iremonger asked cautiously.

'She's a nice girl.'

'Yeah. I've noticed. Also very sexy.'

'Not exactly a mind like quicksilver, though.'

'A girl with legs like that doesn't need a mind like quicksilver. What are you getting at?'

'She's very impressionable.'

Iremonger grinned. 'You reckon?'

'And I know Americans. Most of them think a mistress is a sort of caste mark – like a big car.'

Iremonger's grin widened. 'You'd be surprised,' he said, 'at the number I've heard at parties telling a girl that Americans mate young to have children, again in middle age for love, and finally in old age for companionship. It's a line a general can use as easily as a green lieutenant.'

'It won't wash.'

Iremonger smiled. 'You'd be surprised,' he said.

Pargeter gave him a dirty look as he disappeared, and the American pressed the bell. His heart skidded about a little under his shirt as Liz Wint appeared.

'You always busy in the evening?' he asked.

She smiled. 'Sometimes I manage to fight myself free.'

Iremonger grinned. 'You're a pretty girl. I like looking at you. Mind me saying so?'

She smiled again. 'Work it into any conversation you like.'

'How about a meal tonight?'

'On service rations, why not?'

Iremonger's smile widened. 'Poor old Cuth,' he said. 'I wonder how he'll get by.'

Liz Wint gave him a sharp look. 'Have no fear,' she said. 'He'll manage. His family have had centuries of practice.'

The detective inspector was waiting for Pargeter when he arrived in Colchester, and promptly offered transport in the shape of an elderly Morris. It chugged a bit and the cold wind blew in round the celluloid side-curtains of the canvas hood.

'I've found out a bit more about Hatcher,' the inspector said. 'He was known in the local pub at Chiteley, but everybody knew he didn't live there and always assumed he cycled out from Colchester. He kept to himself and liked to sit and listen.'

'I bet he did,' Pargeter observed. 'Especially if the place was full of talkative American bomber crews. Any idea where he is now?'

'Not the foggiest.'

There were a few Liberator bombers in the air as they drove between the flat Essex fields. 'From Asham,' the inspector pointed out. 'That's the aerodrome near Chiteley.'

Over the drum of the car, they could hear the noisy revving of an engine. Then, sharp and staccato, the sound of a machine-gun firing at the practice butts came on the wind across the low hedgerows, so that Pargeter, remembering what Hardee had told them, wondered whether the force at Asham was merely a token group to keep the locals guessing.

As they drew nearer the sound, the inspector indicated a row of ugly, red-brick cottages. 'Chiteley,' he said.

There was a train among the trees in the distance and, automatically, with an expert's eye for detail, Pargeter counted the waggons – nineteen of them. A few American airmen with lorries moved alongside them, watched by local girls in flowered dresses.

'There was a big raid yesterday,' the inspector said. 'Fortresses. Magdeburg, I heard. That's Asham taking what they want, and then the train'll move off in bits up to Wattisham, Rattlesden and Bury St Edmunds. There'll be another one in tomorrow.'

He stopped the car opposite the cottages, and what happened next was almost like a scene from a film. One moment Pargeter was watching the villagers talking at their doors and a postman moving down the street with his sack on his back, followed by a dog, then the whole thing came to a stop as if someone had switched off the projector. It was totally unexpected and happened without the slightest warning, and he knew at once that he was standing on the edge of a catastrophe.

There was a terrific jolt that seemed to shake the whole countryside. Then, as he was whirled away by a tremendous hurricane of air, he saw a massive ball of orange flame enveloping one of the railway waggons in the distance. As it swept up, each of the other waggons exploded, almost in unison. The earth quaked and he caught a glimpse of men tumbling and staggering as the ground rose skywards in a coil of dense black smoke, beneath which gushed nineteen separate pillars of flame. Then the long roar of the explosions blended and reverberated into one long blast that stunned him and – awakening the whole countryside north of the Thames and rolling across Essex, Suffolk and Norfolk – hurtled out into the North Sea.

As the sheet of flame climbed skywards, red hands clawing at the heavens, Pargeter found himself in a dry ditch where he'd been flung.

Tremendous waves of noise beat against his ears so that it was like being tied to the clapper of a great bell. A roar like sustained thunder was going on around him but, as he tried to shout, his mouth felt full of cinders, and he was surrounded in inky cotton wool which was rolling up into the sky. Enveloped in a terrific heat, he felt he was asphyxiating in the pall of black smoke and the smell of burnt explosive. Great steel wheels were hurtling through the air like bombs and he saw another orange pillar of glittering flame soaring up.

It was like looking into the muzzle of a blow lamp, and he felt his body lifted again and again and slammed back into the ditch. The trees over his head billowed and swirled and burning fragments came down like glittering bats. Spout after spout of black smoke leapt up, joining with one another like some dark evil forest until it was all obscured in a widening and rising smudge. Pieces of wood and metal, planks and timbers, kept showering down, and he could hear the thuds as they struck the ground; then finally the corrugated iron sheets began to arrive, twisting down like leaves in autumn, slicing backwards and forwards.

As he realised it was all over, he staggered to his feet. Everything – trees, houses, fences, people – seemed to be on fire. Bodies smouldered where they'd been flung by the flash and the blast. As his eyes fell on a bloody torso and the white face of a corpse, he couldn't understand why they were dead and he was alive.

The car in which he'd arrived lay on its side in the field and there was no sign of its hood. Then he saw the inspector climbing out of the ditch further on, and together they started running.

'I thought it was an air raid,' the inspector panted as he joined Pargeter. 'Then, when the ground shook, I thought it must be an earthquake instead.'

A cloud of greenish-ginger smoke was still rising and spreading like a mushroom. Chiteley was flattened, houses leaning against each other like a half-collapsed pack of cards, their roofs in the road in a torrent of fallen slates and bricks. The zone of destruction seemed to stretch for a mile in a vista of shattered bricks and crackling flames. Not a roof remained anywhere. The village was nothing more than a group of half-standing walls and charred stumps of chimneys, its inhabitants still dazed by the colossal explosion that had taken place. Only a lost bewildered dog sniffing at the body of a man propped against a house, his face wearing a surprised look, the front of his scalp raised up like a ridiculous quiff, seemed to be still alive.

Then the survivors began to appear, in a state of shock, staggering, weeping, grasping at Pargeter and the inspector as they helped to pull them clear. Dozens more lay beneath the wreckage of their homes and stunned men were scrabbling in the debris to drag them out. They looked like beaten animals, utterly demoralised.

By the railway track, it was even more ghastly. There were bodies everywhere, some with their garments and hair still on fire. A weeping American airman, dreadfully burned about the face and hands, moaned softly. 'It was the train!' he said. 'It was the goddam train!'

Where the train itself had been was only a charred wasteland. Every tree for hundreds of yards had been stripped of its foliage and most of its branches so that they stood up stark and straight like a lot of poles. The grass was scorched and the track was bent and twisted as if some giant hand had wrenched it up. On the spot where Pargeter had seen the waggons was a deep crater in which rested three separate sets of bogey wheels and the remains of a lorry. Railway huts had been flattened and shelters reduced to twisted sheets of iron. There was no vestige of a road, only heaps of rubble and huge craters.

A few other unhurt people were arriving by this time. They all looked as blank as Pargeter and the inspector, because none of them knew what to do. Then a soldier appeared on a motor cycle, his face shocked, and the inspector grabbed him by the arm.

'You seen any telephones that work on the way here?' he demanded.

The despatch rider shook his head. 'Shouldn't think there are any for more'n a mile,' he croaked. 'The wires are down all the way.'

The inspector stared at him wild-eyed. 'That thing got a pillion?'

'No. But you can sit on the carrier.'

'Right.' The inspector turned to Pargeter. 'If anybody comes along, tell 'em where I am. I'm off to find a telephone that works.'

–

Pargeter was still there when daylight came the next day. By this time, men from the USAAF base were tramping past, their haggard faces showing what they'd seen. Squads of British engineers, pioneers and infantry, rushed to the spot during the night, were occupied in clearing the place up, though by the look of it Chiteley would never be tidy or green again. An explosives expert had also arrived with a Security man, and Pargeter showed his credentials.

The explosives man was a sour-faced Scot given to keeping his own counsel, and it took some time to persuade him to talk. 'Aye, it was sabotage,' he said unwillingly. 'There was no reason at all why it should go up. The weather couldn't have been more normal and it was being handled properly. I'm no' sure how many tons of bombs there were until I see the documents, but I gather there were several separate bangs.'

'There were nineteen,' Pargeter said. 'I saw every one. How was it done?'

'It's no' difficult wi' a train full o' bombs,' the explosives expert said dryly. 'A charge, a detonator, and a fuse. It would need a long time-setting, mind, or he'd have gone up wi' it.'

'He might well have,' the Security man said. 'A body was discovered on the edge of the wood. An identity card in the wallet says it belongs to Isaac Hatcher, a farm worker, of Chiteley, but no Isaac Hatcher's known in Chiteley and the identity card's one of a batch stolen in London last year.'

5

It was dark when Pargeter returned to Portsmouth, and there were searchlights over Portland Bill. The control room was empty except for Sergeant Weinberger, who was doing the telephone stint, sitting with his feet on the desk, reading a western. As Pargeter appeared, his eyes widened because Pargeter's normally immaculate battle-dress was torn and stained with oil and dirt and what looked like blood, and he was wearing a borrowed cap that was too large for him and rested on a deep bruise that spread from his eyebrow down one side of his face.

'Jesus, sir,' Weinberger said. 'You been in a fight?'

'Sort of,' Pargeter said. 'Where's Second Officer Wint?'

'She went off with Colonel Iremonger, sir. What happened? That ain't your hat.'

As Pargeter headed for his office, the telephone rang and Weinberger yelled, 'Major! It's for you!'

Pargeter took the call with an expression of irritation on his face. As he listened, the expression changed to one of gravity. 'Yes, sir,' he said. 'I'll tell Colonel Iremonger at once.'

He put the telephone down and smiled bleakly to himself. 'Sergeant Weinberger! Did Colonel Iremonger leave a telephone number?'

'Yeah, Major. He did at that.'

'Ring it, will you?'

'He won't be there now, sir.'

'I think he might.'

Iremonger was fast asleep when the telephone went, and he sat bolt upright, startled and angry, to snatch at the instrument.

'Yeah?'

'We have a call for you, sir.'

Iremonger's head turned. Second Officer Wint had pulled the pillow down over her head and was keeping her eyes tight shut.

It was Pargeter on the line. Iremonger had guessed it would be. 'Hello, Iremonger,' he said. 'Sorry to disturb you.'

Iremonger glanced again over his shoulder. 'Thought I'd have a night out,' he said. 'Found a bottle of whisky. Decided to sleep it off in a hotel instead of fighting the black-out. What the hell do you want?'

'The lid's blown off,' Pargeter said. 'Churchill's got to know about the Fox.'

'How, for Christ's sake?'

'Bushey Park told him. Eisenhower apparently decided that they couldn't keep him in the dark for ever. He says we've got to put a watch on all aerodromes, ports and fishing villages, and all units have been told to carry out investigations into all their officers, while lists of deserters have to be checked, and snap raids and equipment inspections have to be made.'

'For Christ's sake, we're doing all that!'

'I know.' Pargeter sounded smug. 'I don't think we need do it again. I think he's quite happy now he's blown off a bit of steam. You can go back to sleep now. But I thought you'd like to know.'

The telephone clicked abruptly and as Iremonger put his own instrument down, he glanced round. The pillow had been lifted.

'He knows?'

'He sure does,' Iremonger snarled. 'And I dare bet the bastard rang up just to make me feel guilty.'

—

When Pargeter appeared next morning, Iremonger was already in the office, sitting with his feet on the desk, reading the signals that Weinberger collected for them from Fort Widley.

'Big air raid Portland Way last night,' he said gruffly. 'Goddam noisy.'

'Yes. I saw it.' Pargeter bent over his desk, his expression coldly polite. He was wearing his best uniform, Iremonger noticed, but his eyes glittered and he started to whistle 'The British Grenadiers' to himself in a shrill dedicated way as he moved about the room, so that Iremonger was pleased to see he was human enough to have a temper and that he'd been able to rouse it.

As Pargeter glanced over his shoulder, his face wore its po-faced schoolboy look. 'Were you with Liz Wint last night?' he asked.

'Yeah. Took her to dinner. Mind?'

'Not really. Free agent. All the same, bloody bad manners.'

'Why?'

'Supposed to be friends.'

'Who? *Us?*' Iremonger lowered his feet with a bang. 'I'd never have known it. You limeys always did have a goddam funny way of showing your affection for your American cousins. Sometimes I feel like something the cat dragged in.'

Pargeter's whistling had a dogged note about it now. There was no hint of the sly amusement that irritated Iremonger, so that he scowled, disconcerted as he usually was by Pargeter's offhand manner. Then, as he glowered, Pargeter turned his head and for the first time Iremonger noticed the bruise down the side of his face.

'Hello, hello,' he said cheerfully. 'Some guy been handing them out? You been chasing somebody's wife?'

'No.' Along with his best uniform, Pargeter seemed to have donned a martyred air. 'I got it near Colchester.'

'I heard an ammunition train went up round there. Did *you* blow it up?'

'No. It blew *me* up.'

'It did!' Iremonger sat up abruptly. 'Were you there?'

'Right on the spot.'

'Christ, Cuthbert, I'm sorry! I was only kidding you along! You know that. Any damage?'

'Not to me.'

'I heard there were a lot of people killed. What was it like?'

'Bit dodgy,' Pargeter said with a monumental under-statement.

Iremonger stared, and of the two it was Pargeter who was the more composed. Iremonger scowled at him, baffled.

'Well, for Christ's sake, say something!' he snapped.

'What about?'

'For Sweet Jesus' sake, there's just been a disaster! I know there has because I've been in touch with Eighth Air Force over a deserter who turned up. And you were there and appear with a face like a goddam choirboy and say only that it was a bit dodgy. For Christ's sake, it was more than that! People have been killed and, if I know you, you probably won yourself a VC or something rescuing a lot of 'em from under their houses. It's the sort of goddam nosey-parker thing you would do. For Christ's sake, give!'

Pargeter blinked and seemed to summon up his reserves of imagination for an honest sustained effort that might produce a picture of what had happened. 'Well, it *was* a bit messy,' he said. 'Spoiled my uniform and all that.'

Iremonger stared at him angrily, then decided there was no point in pursuing the matter. Pargeter would tell him in his own good time, and until then he'd have to grin and bear it. He pushed a message flimsy across.

'Snowdrop patrol called,' he said gruffly. 'They've got a guy they think we could be interested in. Found him in a bombed-out house, living rough. He's a deserter from the Eighth Air Force. They say we've only to telephone and they'll fetch us at once. Feel up to it?'

Pargeter seemed to have recovered his equanimity at last. 'Oh, yes,' he said, as though he were accepting an invitation to a party. 'Let's ring.'

The Provost car arrived within minutes.

'Jesus, that's fast,' Iremonger said.

As they looked through the window, they saw a huge American open De Soto just pulling to a standstill and, as the doors opened, four white-helmeted military police swung on swivelling seats, to be all out of the car within a second, all holding their weapons at the ready.

'Christ on a bicycle!' Iremonger said.

He turned to look at Pargeter, who was wearing a small supercilious smile under his black eye. Iremonger glared at him. Then, grabbing for his cap, he plunged outside.

'What in the name of the great jumping Jehosephat is this?' he demanded of the lieutenant in charge.

'Three Platoon, 4th Company—'

'I said "what"? Not "who"! What in the great goddam was all that performance for?'

The lieutenant smiled. 'Just a little thing I thought up, Colonel.'

'And the swivel seats?'

'For speed, Colonel. We exist for the apprehension of military criminals.'

Iremonger stared at him in amazement, aware of Pargeter standing just behind him.

'What you'd call an exaggerated sense of security,' Pargeter murmured. 'Even when you people collect your regimental pay, you have a convoy of jeeps full of armed men. *Our* paymasters manage to do it with nothing but a brief-case and a bicycle.'

Iremonger glared and turned again to the lieutenant. 'For Christ's sake,' he said, 'you're in Portsmouth, England, not Chicago, Illinois. If you go on like this you'll have the British rolling round in the aisles laughing at you.'

They rode across the city in the back of the huge car, Iremonger faintly embarrassed and aware of the lieutenant's stiff disapproval. At Provost headquarters the lieutenant led the way inside. In a small room guarded by two white-helmeted, white-spatted military policemen armed to the teeth, a small unshaven soldier with spectacles and wearing a mixture of uniform and civilian clothes sat huddled on a chair, watched intently by a sergeant, also armed to the teeth.

Iremonger stared at him. 'You expecting this guy to fight his way outa here?' he demanded.

The lieutenant's nostrils went white. 'No, Colonel,' he said stiffly. 'But he admits to murder.'

'Does he now? Who of?'

'A comrade, sir. Another deserter. We've found the body just where he said it was.'

'And you think this might be the guy we're looking for?'

'It could be, Colonel.'

'Grow up, son.' Iremonger turned away disgustedly. 'The guy we're looking for is a *soldier*.'

-

It was a statement that was full of contempt and, though neither of them bothered to verify it, they were both certain that the wretched shivering man in the cell, a technician with a history of homosexuality and neurosis drafted into the army against his will, could never have done the things they knew the Fox had done.

When they returned to Portsmouth, de Rezonville was waiting for them. He was sitting on Elizabeth Wint's desk chatting to her, and he stood up, smiling.

Second Officer Wint pushed a signal flimsy across. 'Your Polish unit,' she said. 'I found it. It's now under training in Kent. They say they've never had an officer called Taddeus Kechinski on their strength.'

Iremonger scowled. 'Oh, charming,' he said. 'Bloody charming!'

Another flimsy floated across the desk. 'Also, a signal from Bushey Park. There will be *no* freezing of troop movements.'

Iremonger's jaw dropped. 'We haven't asked anybody to freeze troop movements.'

Pargeter blinked. 'I have,' he said.

Iremonger stared at him. 'You have? With the invasion imminent? Christ, you've got a nerve!' He looked at Liz Wint. 'Was it a signal?'

'No, a telephone call. They were what you might call "rather formal".'

'I guess they were at that.'

De Rezonviile smiled. 'One other thing,' he said. 'The police at Southampton 'ave telephoned. They 'ave someone they think we might be interested in.'

'Have you questioned him?' Iremonger demanded.

De Rezonviile shrugged. 'I do not know what questions to ask,' he said. 'I do not know what we're looking for.'

Iremonger jerked his head at Pargeter. 'Come on, Cuthbert,' he said. 'This time, we'll take our own transport.'

–

The man in Southampton, wearing the uniform of a British major, had aroused suspicions at an officers' club where he'd been staying, because of his youth and the fact that he wore campaign decorations only an old soldier could have won. Instead of being a major, he turned out to be merely a sharp-witted second-lieutenant with a background of dubious enterprises as a civilian. His suitcase was found to be filled with nearly half a million clothing coupons.

'Thinking of kitting yourself out?' Pargeter asked dryly.

For a while nothing further happened. The results of Pargeter's snap raids came in. A few deserters and men who had been absent without leave had been arrested, but nobody who couldn't be firmly identified. Camp searches revealed nothing either, beyond a lot of missing equipment and two girls in the food store of an American unit in Devon. It seemed they had been there for two months, sleeping on army palliasses and eating unrationed food in return for services rendered to the cookhouse staff.

Iremonger scowled, frustrated. 'Nothing but goddam petty criminals,' he said.

He glanced at Pargeter, looking smooth and unruffled and urchin-like at his desk with his fading black eye. 'Don't you ever get impatient, you bastard?' he demanded.

Pargeter shrugged. 'For us, it's been a long war.'

They had the photographs of Kechinski blown up in various sizes from blurred to fuzzy and studied them, trying to imprint his face on their minds; and for another twenty-four hours examined what evidence they had on him. But the Pole seemed to have no friends, no enemies, nothing; the sort of faceless figure that sinks into the background. They did discover from his last unit near Ringwood, however, that he'd been carrying on a sporadic affair with a Wren officer in Southampton, a pretty blonde girl who was none too willing to talk. In the end, she admitted the affair, somewhat shamefacedly because it seemed her friends had teased her that she was unwise to trust a Pole.

'They were right, too,' she agreed. 'Because one of the other girls here knew him as well, and I knew there'd been a girl in London.'

'When did you last see him?' Pargeter asked.

'Mid-April. About then. We were travelling on the train together. I was going to Brighton on pass. He got off at Chichester. He was going to see some friends, he said. Then I got a letter to say his unit was going further west somewhere and I've never heard another word from him, though I did hear he'd also been having an affair with a woman called Harvey in Lyme Regis.'

'Would there be a photograph?'

Without a word she fished in her shoulder bag and produced a snapshot of herself with a grim-faced officer in uniform. 'That's him,' she said bitterly. 'Taddeus Kechinski. Tad the Pole. He didn't seem very pleased when it was taken.'

'Can we keep it for a while?'

The Wren gave a wry smile. 'You can keep it for ever,' she said. 'I don't think it's going to be much use to me now.'

They had the photograph blown up at the nearby RAF station at Boscombe Down and compared it with the one they'd obtained from Kechinski's unit. It wasn't much better, but the angle was different so it was one more small step in the right direction.

'At least we know now how he looks from two angles,' Iremonger said. 'I wish we knew something about him.'

'We know one thing,' Pargeter pointed out.

'What, for God's sake?'

'Women. He needs women. We know of seven he's been with. He's been married three times, and then there's the girl in London, the Wren, the friend she mentioned, and now this woman in Lyme Regis. Perhaps it's his Achilles' heel.'

'Having dames is an Achilles' heel?'

'He's not been near his wife since 1939. That's a long time for a married man to remain celibate. There *are* men who need women. Perhaps he's one, and one of 'em might know where he is now.'

6

The tall officer in the square-cut cap with the grey metal badge descended from the train at Chichester. As he left the station, the streets were full of uniforms – sailors from the landing craft filling the creeks of Chichester harbour; airmen from the neighbouring aerodromes of Goodwood, Tangmere and Ford; artillerymen manning the ack-ack batteries that held off the persistent German recce planes; and the infantry, tankmen and engineers gathering in enormous numbers in the Downs for the invasion.

The city had avoided much of the shabbiness of the war but after five years there was little in the shops and what there was, was heavily disguised as luxuries. There were a few people waiting at the bus stop but none of them looked twice at the officer. Men with strange uniforms had been a common sight in England since 1939.

The bus was already full when the Fox climbed aboard, pushing among the women carrying their shopping, the sailors and soldiers returning to their billets, and the few Americans who talked to everybody within reach on the understanding that silence on a public transport could only be bad manners. The bus lost a few of its passengers en route but it was still well-filled as it rolled into Selsey. The place was quiet in the late evening, drab and ugly in its wartime dreariness.

It was a long way from dusk as the Fox started to walk out of the town. The roads were full of soldiers and their girl friends walking arm-in-arm through the summer evening. Here and there, under trees, couples clutched each other in agonising embraces, aware of the unreality of life with the invasion and the possibility of dying just round the corner. When it was finally dark – and, with double British summer time, he had to wait a long time for it – he headed back to the town. Half-way down the High Street he turned left into a road of indifferent houses, some occupied by soldiers, some empty. Keeping to the shadows of the tall macrocarpa hedges, he slipped into an opening which had once contained a gate and, making his way through the neglected garden to the rear of the house, he took out a key and opened the back door. As he closed it behind him, a cut-out switch on the jamb brought on the light and he stood blinking in a shabby kitchen giving on to a narrow hall. A man poked his head round the angle of the stairs; a small, pudgy man, pasty-faced with unhealthy violet sacs beneath his eyes. His hair was thin and plastered to his skull. He wore an old tweed jacket and a Fair Isle pullover which had worn to a hole over his stomach.

'Oh,' he said. 'It's you.' He gave a little snigger. 'You get nervous, just waiting.'

The Fox began to speak in German but the little man made a warning gesture. 'In English. You never know who's listening.'

'They don't listen to *you*.'

'No. But I've been here since 1933. Have you got something?'

'Yes.'

'The invasion?'

The Fox smiled. 'Yes.'

'What!' The little man in the Fair Isle jumper grinned. 'I don't believe you! You're doing well. You'll have heard that Krafft made good use of that ammunition train in Essex that you found for him.' He paused. 'Too good. He blew himself up.'

'He was always careless.'

The little man frowned and shrugged dismissively. 'We'd better get on with it,' he said.

Taking a torch from a shelf by the door, he began to climb the stairs, checking the black-out as he went. The house had a stale cabbage smell and the furniture was as shabby and uncared for as everything else. In the back bedroom the little man pushed the bed aside and, rolling back the worn carpet, raised one of the floorboards with a knife. More floorboards followed, and, by the light of the torch, he lifted two square attaché cases from between the joists and opened them. A coil of wire appeared which he unrolled and began to hook behind nails knocked at intervals into the picture rail, extending it through the door, along the landing and round the front bedroom.

Then, sitting on the floor, he pulled a morse key towards him and sat for a moment staring at the paper the Fox had handed him.

'Where did you get this?' he asked.

'From the American I found at Abbotsbury.'

The little man read slowly. The Fox had made his message both clear and concise, but the little man went painstakingly through it a second time before putting on a pair of earphones and drawing the morse key nearer. Then he looked at his watch and started to tap out the letters of the address. The reply came at once and he began on the cipher groups of the message itself.

He had sent only the first few words, however, when his ears were filled with a sudden high-pitched howling that completely drowned the signal. For a moment, he sat listening. Then his eyes narrowed, and he cautiously began to tap again. Once more the howling came, now shatteringly loud in the surrounding stillness.

'Jamming?' the Fox asked and the little man nodded.

'Have they jammed you before?'

'No. Never. I got your message about the ammunition train through to Krafft without the slightest trouble.'

For a moment they looked at each other in silence. After two more attempts to transmit had each produced only the same immediate and ear-splitting reaction, they could no longer doubt what it meant. Quietly, without panic, the little man switched off the set and slowly began to uncoil the aerial.

'They've found me,' he said. 'And whoever they are, they're suspicious of what I'm sending.'

'When *can* you send it? Tonight?'

'Not a chance!'

'Tomorrow?'

'Not a hope. They're on to me. I've suspected for some time that they've been watching this place. If I try to send they'll take bearings on me and have me at once. I can't risk that. I've got to clear out. Now that Krafft's gone there's only me left. You'll have to find a different way of getting your stuff across the Channel. How about via Ireland?'

The Fox frowned. 'There's a communications ban on Ireland. The embassy in Dublin's closed to us.'

'Pity Krafft's gone.'

'What about his transmitter?'

'No idea where it is.'

The Fox was deep in thought. He had long since considered the possibility of failure. 'There *is* an alternative,' he said. 'Let me have the documents.'

The little man reached under the floorboards and pulled out an army file containing leave passes, railway warrants, movement orders and ration cards, and a set of rubber stamps. Selecting a railway warrant, a movement order form, identity card and ration book, the Fox began to fill them out, but not in the name that was printed on the name tag inside the collar of his mackintosh. He worked carefully, occasionally stopping to look at his watch and listen. When he'd finished, he looked up. 'I'd better go,' he said.

'I'll clear up here,' the little man said. 'Leave it to me. There's plenty of time. I'm sure they didn't get the chance to put a direction finder on to me. How're you going to get it across?'

The Fox smiled. 'Take it myself,' he said.

By the time Pargeter and Iremonger returned to Portsmouth it was dark and an air raid was in progress. There was a smell of burning in the air, and from down the street came the sound of fire engines grinding forward over the rubble in low gear.

Pargeter edged the jeep forward, the tyres crunching on broken glass as if they were driving over frozen puddles. Compared with the blitzes of 1940 and 1941 the raid had been a trivial affair, but people had been killed and houses destroyed. A small car had been thrown among the ruins of a wrecked building and a woman's hat lay on a splintered door just behind it. By the light of the flames, they could see the all-too-familiar view of rooms, ready for living in but minus their front walls like a stage set. In some, by a trick of the blast, everything had been sucked out except the pictures which still hung neatly and perfectly straight.

When they reached their headquarters, Sergeant Weinberger was sitting in the cellar with two of the British soldiers on the staff. It smelled of damp and mice but Weinberger had a bottle and they didn't seem too downhearted.

'Where's Second Officer Wint?' Iremonger demanded.

Weinberger shrugged. 'She went off when she'd finished.'

'And Lieutenant de Rezonville?'

Weinberger gave a small secretive smile. 'He went with her, sir.'

Pargeter was pleased to see that it was Iremonger's turn to look disconcerted. 'That goddam Frog,' he growled.

Weinberger offered them mugs into which he splashed whisky from his bottle. 'You get what you wanted, sir?'

'No,' Iremonger growled. 'How about here?'

Weinberger shrugged. 'We've had a helluva lot of reports on radio activity,' he said. 'Most of 'em from communications officers complaining about wireless operators jamming important signals. They'd been passed on to General Hardee who passed 'em back to us and said we'd better look into 'em. I guess the jamming we asked for's affecting the wrong guys. They all say the same thing: How the hell do we get this goddam invasion on the road if we can't send a signal ?'

'I guess it had to happen?' Iremonger grinned.

Weinberger searched among the flimsies on the desk. 'There's one, though,' he said. 'Might be something. Came from the British Navy. A guy who was handling German messages in North Africa thought he recognised something. The message was jammed.' Weinberger grinned. 'So, I guess, was every other goddam message in the area.'

'When was this?'

'Late last night, sir. Not so long ago, in fact. If you want him, he's at Fort Blockhouse. Which, believe it or not, is a British submarine base.'

—

To get to Fort Blockhouse, they almost had to fight their way into HMS *Vernon*, which was a shore-based establishment. No one in the Royal Navy could imagine why two army officers should want to be inside a naval base, and it took a great deal of arguing with the Regulating Branch and a cold-eyed elderly commander before they were allowed to proceed.

A sailor who looked as though he was about sixteen years old accompanied them to the King's Stairs Landing and a boat ran them to HMS *Dolphin*, the submarine base at Fort Blockhouse, on a spit of land across a narrow strip of oily water. He looked far too young ever to have been to sea himself, but seemed to have imbibed the navy's distrust of less senior services with his mother's milk.

They climbed ashore near a jetty alongside which lay lean grey shapes and groups of smaller boats. There were acid carboys on the quay among the ropes, and a couple of lorries waiting by a party of men struggling to lift what appeared to be a large piece of radio equipment.

A naval lieutenant was waiting for them and he saluted Iremonger's superior rank. 'This way, please.'

They were led into the communications centre where they were promptly offered cups of tea by an extraordinarily pretty Wren officer.

'Are all your Wrens pretty?' Iremonger asked.

They were left to finish their tea – as though the navy considered it impolite to hurry them – then an elderly naval commander with the wavy stripes of the Reserve on his sleeve brought in a petty officer signaller.

'Petty Officer Forester,' he said.

Petty Officer Forester was a very young man whom Pargeter guessed had been called up in the early days of the war and, because he was clever, had risen quickly in rank. He explained what had happened.

'I was in North Africa,' he said. 'Shore-based in Tunisia, monitoring German messages in Sicily before the landing there. You get sort of familiar with 'em and I spotted this one at once. I could have taken the message down but my instructions were to jam it. I did so.'

'Did you get *any* of the message?' Pargeter asked.

Forester smiled apologetically. 'A few groups, sir, that's all. We had 'em deciphered. All I can make out are odd words – "*Warning. Geheimschlüssel gebrochen*…" In case you don't know what that means…'

'I speak German,' Pargeter said. 'It means "Warning. Cipher broken." What time did you pick it up?'

'Twenty-three fifty-seven, sir. And it was from somewhere not far away. Selsey. Chichester. Somewhere like that. It was loud. Our jamming would be loud, too, and if he knows his stuff he'd guess *we* were pretty near. Perhaps that's why he didn't transmit again.' Petty Officer Forester looked at the commander sitting at the desk. 'There's one other thing, sir. I heard the police contacted us a day or two ago about some chap they think might be reporting the ships moving in and out of Portsmouth Harbour.'

'That's right,' the commander agreed. 'Seems he can see from a house in Selsey. They've been watching him for some time. Somebody spotted the sun on his binoculars.'

'It could be there, sir,' Forester said.

'Selsey?' Pargeter rubbed his nose, looked at Iremonger and then at the commander. 'For Selsey, don't you leave the train at Chichester and catch a bus?'

'That's right, you do.'

Pargeter's eyes gleamed. 'Chichester's where that Wren in Southampton said her Polish boy friend dropped her flat.'

Iremonger rose. 'Let's go.'

Pargeter reached for his cap. 'I think we better had,' he agreed. He paused and beamed hopefully at the commander. 'And while we're about it, hadn't we better contact the police there and ask 'em to hold this chap of theirs until we arrive?'

8

It was almost dawn when they reached Selsey. Offshore there was a conglomeration of the same kind of tower-like structures rising from the water as Pargeter had noticed at Dungeness on his way back from Dover, half-submerged block-long objects with ponderous steel arches beginning nowhere and ending nowhere.

'Something to do with the invasion,' the police inspector who met them pointed out. 'Some sort of floating harbour they're going to take across with 'em. Shall we go? We've got your man.' He paused. 'Or at least, we've *almost* got him.'

'What the hell do you mean?' Iremonger demanded. '*Almost* got him.'

The policeman pulled a face. 'We've been watching him for some time but when we got your message and turned up at the house this morning the bastard dodged us and holed out upstairs. He took a pot shot at my man with a gun.'

'Did he, bejesus? What have you done about it, for Christ's sake?'

The policeman was unruffled. 'I called in soldiers and got 'em to surround the place. They're from an engineer company stationed just up the road. We'd got our hands on everything before he bolted but he must have had the pistol hidden in his clothes because it was while he was collecting a few belongings to accompany us to the station that he produced it.'

'Who is he, for Christ's sake?'

'Chap called Smith. Came here well before the war. Watch repairer. Supposed to be a naturalised Swiss but there's a rumour that his name's Schmidt and he isn't Swiss at all. He was obviously on his way elsewhere. We found a radio under the floorboards.'

–

As they left the police station, the air raid sirens started. 'Oh, Christ!' the policeman said in a weary voice as he climbed into the jeep. 'Another? They're after those things in the sea. Every time they come over, they drop chandelier flares, and there'll be a bloke up there working his Brownie as hard as he can go. They're always talking about them on the German radio. "Invasion," they say. Then there's a lot of loud laughter, as though they think it's funny.'

The air raid turned out to be a false alarm and the all clear was already going as they turned off the High Street.

'Nobody visited him much,' the inspector said. 'He was supposed to be a widower. But we found a copy of *Jane's Fighting Ships* and a pair of German binoculars. You can just see the sea from his front bedroom window.'

There were several policemen and soldiers about the house, keeping carefully out of sight round corners, and a few scared-looking women and old men poking their heads out of doors.

'Is it the invasion?' one of the women asked Pargeter.

'No, madam,' Pargeter replied frostily. 'Not this time.'

The young lieutenant in charge of the engineers seemed eager to rush the place. 'Want my chaps to go in?' he asked.

'You'll get no medals for it,' Pargeter said. 'And I think it's *our* job. How about a pot shot or two at the back bedroom window? While he's replying I'll go through the front door.' The lieutenant seemed delighted at the prospect of letting off his firearms. 'Right, sir.'

'Door open, Inspector?'

The inspector nodded.

'Right.' Pargeter seemed completely in control. He turned to the lieutenant. 'No need to smash the place up. Just a couple of million rounds to make him keep his head down. Break a few windows and take the roof off so he's kept busy wondering where it's coming from, that's all. I'll pass the signal when to start.'

He was about to turn away when Iremonger grabbed his arm. 'See here, Cuthbert,' he said. 'If you're going to tackle this goddam guy, I'm coming with you.'

'Better leave it to me. Done it before.'

'So have I, goddamit! In the States, cops have been busting doors down ever since Al Capone.'

Pargeter looked at him, blinked and nodded. 'All right,' he agreed. 'Better let me go first, though. Count three.'

Before Iremonger realised what was happening, Pargeter had run up to the house and was standing with his back to the wall alongside the open front door. Iremonger joined him at the other side of the door, and Pargeter nodded to the inspector who waved to the lieutenant at the far side of the house. A shot was fired and they heard glass tinkling. There was silence, then two more shots, and finally one in return.

'He's at the back bedroom window.' The lieutenant's message arrived via the inspector.

'Better step it up a bit,' Pargeter suggested.

The inspector passed on the message and the lieutenant waved. There was a ragged volley and a tile fell from the roof followed by more breaking glass. This time the fusillade was answered by a flurry of shots from inside the house, and as they started Pargeter slipped through the front door, and Iremonger heard his boots pounding up the stairs. He forced himself to count three then charged after him.

As he reached the bottom step he heard a cry from the upper floor. He became aware of a black bulk apparently floating through the air towards him, and as it smashed into him, he crashed against the half-opened door behind him. The door slammed shut under his weight and he slid to the floor with the glass from the pane in the door dropping on to his shoulders. Through a daze, he heard Pargeter calling.

'Okay,' he said. 'You can come in now.'

Iremonger was dimly conscious of the inspector and the policemen stepping over his legs, then the weight on him was dragged away so that he was able to sit up. The inspector and the constable were gripping a small plump man wearing a Fair Isle pullover with a hole in the front. Pargeter was sitting at the top of the stairs holding a pistol.

'What happened?' Iremonger asked.

'When he heard me on the landing he came rushing out of the back bedroom. I stuck my foot out and he went straight to the bottom. It sounded like some chap driving a tank down.'

Iremonger rubbed his head. His back felt as though it was probably broken. He looked sourly at Pargeter. 'Where did you learn that goddam trick?' he demanded. 'In the commandos?'

'No.' Pargeter smiled. 'School!' He shrugged. 'It's not our chap.'

The watchmaker was recovering consciousness now and they dragged him into the kitchen and sat him on a stool. As he held his head, Pargeter fished the photographs of the Fox from his pocket and held them out.

'Know that chap?' he asked.

The little man glanced at the pictures. 'No,' he said. 'Never seen him before in my life.'

The inspector reached for the pictures. 'I have,' he said. 'In the town here. Not so damn long ago, either. Pole, I think.'

'That's right. Did he come here?'

'Half the allied army could have come here after the blackout started,' the inspector said. 'We can't see in the dark.' He pushed through the door of the dining room. Two small attaché cases stood open on the table. Inside were a transmitter and a receiver. 'People who want to listen to the BBC don't have that sort of gadget,' he said.

Pargeter swung round. 'Any fingerprints, Inspector?'

The inspector grinned. 'Bound to be.' He nodded towards the fireplace, which was full of ash from burned sheets of paper, and Iremonger knelt, carefully moving the ash with a pencil.

'I've been through it,' the inspector pointed out. 'I found this.'

'This' was a fragment of charred paper, a mere corner of a sheet on which were the words '*Ultra wichtig*...' and below that '*Funkverkehr*'.

'That looks like German to me,' the inspector observed.

'It sure does,' Iremonger agreed.

'"*Ultra*" means much the same in both English and German,' Pargeter said. '"*Wichtig*" means "important". "*Funkverkehr*" means "radio traffic". I think we'd better get the military police to put patrols on all local railway platforms to check for passes.'

'You might be a bit pushed.' The inspector produced an army folder full of stamped railway warrants, leave passes, blank identity cards and ration books. 'He's probably been gone some time and we also found this.'

9

The sun was high over the roofs of Lyme, and beyond the town sombre cliffs stood out to sea, shadowing the long grey claw of the Cobb as it curved away from the land.

'Pretty place.' Pargeter sounded as though he were looking it over with a view to spending a holiday there, and seemed quite unperturbed by the fact that they had so far failed to trace the latest movements of the Fox. Every male passenger on the Southern Railway had been checked, but he had been too quick and had already slipped through the net, so that they had had to start once more from scratch, using the little they had learned about his women friends from the Wren in Southampton.

'Ships went out from here to attack the Spanish Armada,' Pargeter went on. 'And Monmouth landed here in his idiotic attempt to gain the throne of England.'

'Who's Monmouth?' Iremonger asked. 'And what the hell's the Spanish Armada got to do with it? You drive me up the wall, Cuthbert.'

Pargeter smiled. 'I try a lot,' he admitted.

It required only a quick look at the telephone directory to unearth Kechinski's Mrs Harvey. She was a good-looking widow, whose husband had been killed at Dunkirk four years before, and her attitude to the Pole was a very different one from the Wren's.

'My husband's dead,' she said. 'There's no mistake about that. I loved him, too, but you grow lonely. There's been plenty of talk in Lyme, of course, but chiefly from women who're fortunate enough to have their husbands still alive and handy.'

'Did he come often, ma'am?' Iremonger asked.

She smiled. 'Not often. But he always had a full ration book. And that was something I didn't query. One doesn't.'

'Where is he now?'

She managed a twisted smile. 'I heard from one of his friends that he was seeing an American girl, a WAC or a WAVE or whatever they're called.'

'Name?' Pargeter asked. 'Do you have a name?'

'An American name. Copak. Kopek, something like that – Vokac. That was it. Lieutenant Vokac. Is that any help?'

'It might well be, ma'am,' Iremonger said. 'Do you know anything more about him?'

'Nothing apart from the fact that I sometimes thought he wasn't a Pole but a refugee German.'

Iremonger leaned forward. 'Why did you think that?'

'He came here once after they'd been doing an exercise. He was covered with mud and he had a bath. I took his clothes to try to clean them, and a wallet fell out of his pocket and everything was scattered on the floor. There was a letter and it was in German, and I decided he might be a German Jew – or a Socialist or an intellectual or something – who'd found his way into the Polish forces. Quite a few did, I believe. If he'd admitted to being a German, of course, he might have been interned.'

'Or imprisoned, ma'am,' Iremonger said.

The bright smile faded. 'What do you mean?'

'We have reason to believe that your friend, Captain Kechinski, was neither a Pole nor a refugee, but a German agent.'

The woman's face fell but she recovered quickly. 'This'll be a story for after the war,' she said ruefully. 'I should be able to dine out on this one for years. Am I suspected too?'

Iremonger smiled. 'No, but with your permission we'd like to check for fingerprints. Was there anything else that made you think he was German?'

'Photographs. Of a small boy. He was dressed in those leather trousers the Germans wear and there were mountains in the background. I always understood there were no mountains in Poland, only plains.'

'Did *you* ever take any photographs of him?' Pargeter asked. 'For yourself, perhaps?'

'A few when he wasn't looking. He didn't like them.'

The photographs were not very good but they were better than the ones they already possessed. They showed a tall, good-looking man in battledress standing in a garden. Most of them were profiles, though there was one three-quarter front view which was clear and sharp.

'May we have these?' Pargeter asked.

Mrs Harvey smiled, a slightly strained smile now. 'If you could return them,' she said. 'Women are incurably romantic.'

—

The fingerprint experts proved beyond doubt that Kechinski was the man who'd handled the dead Bigot officer's papers. The prints were all over the house and, what was more, they matched the prints found in Selsey.

'At least we now have a better idea what the guy looks like,' Iremonger said. 'Tall, dark and handsome. One for the ladies.'

'Resourceful,' Pargeter reminded him. 'And dedicated. *And* dangerous. Three men are dead to our knowledge, to say nothing of others, perhaps, in Austria, Czecho-Slovakia, Poland and the Middle East.'

They'd already tapped US Army Records, looking for Lieutenant Vokac. But US Army Records had had other things to do and were heavily involved with the invasion.

'For Christ's sake, there are a million and a quarter Americans in this country!' they were told indignantly. 'Do you think we've nothing better to do than chase up some guy who's been screwing a dame?'

'He's been doing more than screwing a dame,' Iremonger snorted. 'He might even have been screwing up the invasion.'

In a sweltering summer heat, they drove to the American Postal Unit at Bushey Park to try another line. To their surprise, Eisenhower's headquarters had disappeared.

'Gone to Portsmouth,' they were told by the WAC captain in command.

'That must mean things are going to start up any time now,' Iremonger growled. 'So hurry it up, ma'am, will you?'

'Okay, okay! Here we are: Vokac. Lieutenant Louise Vokac. Attached to a Harbour Craft Company in Dartmouth, Devon. It's secret. They don't answer the telephone.'

Back in Portsmouth, Weinberger was working himself up into a state of anxiety.

'Sump'n's happening, Colonel, sir,' he announced when they appeared. 'Invasion HQ's switched from London down here. The signal came in while you were away. Southwick Park.'

'Yeah,' Iremonger said laconically. 'I heard. Find out where it is. We'll need to know, I guess.'

They set off west as soon as they'd eaten. The coastal areas were almost impassable now. Specialised troops and armour for the invasion were on the move, and every road and lane was full of lorries, vehicles and guns, every village green crammed with men and machines waiting for the order to move on to the ports. The air stank of petrol and diesel and the rancid smell of sweating men, and the countryside resounded to the tramp of boots and the clatter of tank treads. There was something in the wind. They both knew it. Every man in the army knew it, and there was a tension in the very air they breathed.

'Cuthbert,' Iremonger said gravely, staring round him. 'We've got to nail this bastard before long or we'll be too late.'

Dartmouth was packed with Americans and the whole of the river was full of landing craft. Lieutenant Vokac, who was billeted with other WACs in a large house at Kingswear, was warm, friendly and efficient. Like the woman at Lyme and the Wren in Southampton, she was a blonde.

'Sure I knew him,' she said. 'But not for long. His outfit was posted away almost immediately.'

'Where to?'

'Portland area.'

'What unit was it?'

'He never told me.'

Iremonger frowned. 'What was his job, for Christ's sake?' he asked. 'Liaison officer?'

Lieutenant Vokac stared. 'Liaison officer? Why would he be a liaison officer?'

'He was a Pole.'

'A Pole?' Lieutenant Vokac smiled. 'Jack Kechinski was *not* a Pole. My father was a Pole and I know a Pole. He was like me, a second generation American. He came from Michigan.'

–

'Michigan, for God's sake!' Iremonger said. 'This guy's got more identities than Houdini had escapes.'

There was an awed respect in his voice. Without any doubt, the Fox was a resourceful man.

Lieutenant Vokac had no hesitation in identifying him from the photographs they'd obtained in Lyme Regis.

'Sure, that's him,' she agreed. 'No question about it. But why's he wearing that crazy cap?'

'It's Polish.'

'When I saw him he was wearing an American cap.'

'You sure?'

'Sure I'm sure. Jack Kechinski. I saw his papers, signed by the adjutant of some transit camp north of Southampton.'

'Assigning him to what?'

'From Third Army to First Army.'

'First Army's earmarked for the invasion.'

'Sure is. And, for your information, First Army comprises VII Corps under General Collins and V Corps under General Gerow. And Collins' corps comprises four divisions, except for a few odds and ends, while Gerow's comprises three.'

Iremonger's brows crammed together over his eyes. 'For sweet Jesus' sake,' he said, 'that's a lot of guys to investigate! We need some beef, Cuthbert. I'm going to see Hardee.'

10

Southwick House lay to the north of Portsmouth, an early Victorian mansion set in extensive parkland. A trailer village had been set up in a hazel copse about a mile away, protected from German planes by the trees and from intruders by trigger-happy sentries.

Iremonger's pass got him through the gates but he was immediately taken aside and briefed by an American lieutenant-colonel. 'It's forbidden to walk in the fields, Colonel,' he pointed out. 'Trodden grass shows up in aerial photographs and we can take no chances. All permitted entrance and exit routes are indicated by white pegs or painted lines. You will stick rigidly to them.'

General Hardee listened to Iremonger in silence. Iremonger was dusty and a little weary, and Hardee seemed surprised to see him back.

'We know where he's been, General,' Iremonger explained bitterly, 'but we don't know where he's at now. I guess this is where we have to ask for help. We're going to need the okay to start searching ships.'

Hardee hesitated but he finally nodded. 'You've got it.'

'How long have we got, sir? Before the party starts?'

'I have no authority to tell you that.'

Iremonger nodded. 'No, sir. Of course not. But if things start happening before we've finished, nobody's going to stop for *us*.'

For a while Hardee studied the report they'd prepared for him. Liz Wint had typed it out carefully, listing all the known information, even the scraps of messages they'd picked up through the navy and at the house in Selsey. Then he tossed it down and sat back in his chair.

'It seems,' he said, 'that before anything else happens you're going to have to learn even more of our secrets. You're very privileged, I might add, because soon you'll know as much of the damned plan as Ike himself.'

He wrote a name and address on a piece of paper. 'I think you should see this man,' he said. 'And pass on what he tells you to Major Pargeter, so that if anything happens to you, *he'll* know what's going on. I'll telephone ahead and you'll be told everything.'

'About what, General?' Iremonger asked.

'You'll find out when you arrive. Better burn that address when you've got it firmly in your head.'

–

The address was in Bletchley Park fifty miles to the north of London. The house was near the main road and handy for the railway, large and ornate and entered by a pretentious porch. It was surrounded by spacious lawns with the usual cedar trees, and a number of huts had been erected round it. The man Iremonger saw was a senior air staff representative and – like the man they'd seen in London, like Hardee, like so many others he'd met – someone who wouldn't arouse anyone's interest.

'Ultra,' he said. 'I have permission to tell you about it.'

'It's a *thing*?' Iremonger asked.

The man behind the desk smiled. 'In this context, Ultra isn't an adjective meaning "terrific" or "superior". It's a code name for a cipher-breaking system we've developed through the possession of a secret German signalling machine. We've had it a long time and most of our senior officers – army, navy and air force – avail themselves of it.'

Iremonger sat in silence, wondering what was coming next.

'In 1938,' the speaker continued, 'a young Polish mechanic employed in eastern Germany found himself making what he judged to be a secret signalling device, and he took careful note of the various parts he and his fellow workmen were using. Later, since what he was working on came under top security, he was sacked and sent back to Poland, but with war clearly on the way, he contacted a British agent and was smuggled to Paris where he made a large wooden mock-up of the machine he'd been working on in Germany. It didn't take long for our backroom boys to identify what he was making as an improved mechanical cipher machine known as Enigma. It became pretty obvious that, somehow, an original machine had to be obtained and, eventually, one was.'

Sitting back, the man behind the desk thought for a moment as though weighing up the secrets he was divulging. 'It worked on a system of electrically-connected revolving drums,' he continued. 'Around them were placed the letters of the alphabet. When a typewriter fed messages into the machine they were so proliferated by the drums, it was estimated that a top team of mathematicians might take a month or more to work out all the permutations necessary to find the right answer for a single cipher setting. The Germans had therefore considered that their cipher was completely safe.'

There was a long pause then the dry voice went on monotonously. 'By the spring of 1940, however, our cipher experts had worked out how to use the machine to decipher messages that we picked up, and, with the aid of teams of experts from each of the three services, we were able to decide what was happening in the darkness across the Channel. In the end, the precise composition, strength and location of the enemy's forces was immediately to hand. It might surprise you to know that it helped us win the Battle of Britain, told us of German invasion plans, and enabled us to hold Rommel in Africa. In other words, now that we're winning, it doesn't seem to us in the know here that our victories have all been accomplished by superior arms and strategy. They were won by wits and brains, developed in the years when we hadn't much else to fight with. This operation of intercepting, breaking and putting meaning to enemy signals was code-named Ultra.'

The man smiled and shifted in his chair. 'That's as much as I'm prepared to tell you without a directive from headquarters,' he ended. 'General Hardee said you had problems and needed to know what we did here. Does it answer your questions?'

Iremonger sat in silence for a moment, thinking of the few brief words they'd picked up on Ultra and their implications.

'It starts up others,' he said. 'What would it mean if some German agent here knew we had Ultra and passed it on to German GHQ?'

'I hope to God no one ever does.' The face behind the desk became grave. 'Because of Ultra we can not only counter what the Germans do but can move our troops into the areas from which the Germans have moved theirs. If the Germans knew we had Ultra, it's obvious they'd feed us false messages which would, in effect, do to us exactly what we're now doing to them, and I don't have to tell you how serious that would be. It could mean that when it comes to break out of the beach-head, they could persuade us that certain areas were thinly held when, in fact, they were heavily fortified. It could be disastrous.'

11

The weather was calm and fair and an American band played jazz on the Town Hall steps. But, though everybody tried to behave normally, every now and then, along the main road, watched by women and children and old men, convoys of vehicles went rapidly past like ships on wheels.

The colonel and the other senior officers came and went on unheralded conferences, and the HQ clerks were tantalised by secret papers which they saw but never got a chance to read. Boxes and bales of new equipment kept arriving, and those lorries and vehicles about which there was the slightest doubt were hurriedly replaced. Kits were checked and in a last burst of glorious weather the waterproofing began, the men working with cans of plastic grease, moulding it into phallic shapes and obscene symbols before plastering it over the engines of the trucks.

The last preparations were completed, the last inoculations given, private possessions taken away, unfit men replaced, kits made up, and everybody issued with iron rations and ammunition. The last talks were given. 'June 5th's the date,' they were told. 'But you've no need to worry. All we have to do is go straight ahead, firmly, and without hesitation.'

The colonel was a quiet man not given to rhetoric, but another man came also – a big man with a general's badges – who appeared to have been brought up on Hollywood's idea of a tough soldier. 'This is the showdown, fellers,' he said. 'You're as well trained as any soldiers in the world, and when you get across to the Far Shore you're going to be better equipped and better prepared than any of the slimy bastards you're going to meet because they're only old men and boys. You are going in there to kill the Kraut and that's all you've got to think of from this moment on.'

The lecture left a nasty taste in the mouth, even to men who firmly believed in their own invincibility. In the case of the quiet newly-joined officer it was different. He wasn't sure what to believe. A weak resistance might be probed by a single determined man, yet a weak resistance could also allow the Americans to advance so fast he wouldn't be able to cross the lines as he planned.

The preparations continued. The trucks were marked with huge white stars, and on the nearby aerodrome airmen were painting white stripes on the wings and fuselages of aeroplanes. Essential stores arrived, and rumours came thick and fast. At one detention centre, it was said, men were making crates for supplies and at another coffins for the enormous casualties that were expected.

The order to move came at midday, and in the evening they paraded by their vehicles. Smoke pots were lit, as they'd been lit on previous occasions for exercises, but nobody knew whether it was to persuade the people in the houses around that this was just another exercise or to hide the fact that they were leaving.

At mid-morning the next day, led this time by a policeman on a motor cycle, they reached a public park near the coast. The grass was flattened and the scarred ground dusty. The area was surrounded by double lines of barbed wire and patrolled by sentries, and immediately became known as Stalag Luft III. They parked their trucks inside and made their way to the tents which had been erected for them. The men spread their blankets, not talking much. Every road around them was full of vehicles and guns. Columns of soldiers kept marching past, dusty and heavily laden. The officers drew commando knives, binoculars and maps while the men ate, slept, and played poker and craps. A squadron of tanks rattled past, camouflaged sheets and nets for night bivouacs lashed above the tracks with drums of oil, petrol and kit. Nearby, a tearful wedding group was arguing with the MPs who were not prepared to let the bridal car cross the line of march.

To keep them all busy, baseball games were started and footballs thrown about. In a marquee there were models of the French beaches for them all to see, and, having seen them, no one was then allowed outside the wire. The tension that had been felt for some time continued to mount and the jokes were all a little forced. The food was bad and they were overcrowded and uncomfortable, and there were never enough latrines or washing facilities and always huge queues. Their money was changed into francs and the jeeps and lorries were packed. New notices were erected outside the wire – '*Do not loiter. Civilians must not talk to troops*' – and the people outside hurried by, pretending not to see them.

That evening they were told the plan and what they had to do, and the change was electric. The suspense was succeeded by a wave of relief, and the evening meal was riotous. A church service was held and the people in the houses around could hear the sound of hundreds of men singing 'Eternal Father, Strong To Save' coming from beyond the barbed wire. The men seemed unusually well-behaved and very pious, but it didn't stop a lot of them getting very drunk on smuggled whisky. The following morning, while it was still dark, they were marched to the docks.

After an hour's marching, they halted and squatted on the pavement to eat their rations, and women with tears in their eyes kept appearing with jugs of tea. The other side of the street was lined with tanks and jeeps, whose crews were washing and shaving in water begged from the householders. The day had a sultry warmth so that, loaded as they were with equipment, they were sweating in their helmets and battledress.

There was another long wait, and a soldier trained as a sniper began to use the telescopic sight of his rifle to watch a girl's bedroom window and relay the salacious details to friends. There were constant rumours – 'The ship's sunk', 'They don't need us', 'They've already landed in the Channel Isles' – and a Catholic padre heard confessions in the back of a lorry. Past the end of the road they could see another column of men moving alongside the rusty barbed wire rolls of the old coastal defences.

The long pause gave them time to think again. They had accepted everything but now they were wondering, and doubts came. Despite the humid warmth, the day was grey with mist, and as they marched to the shore the Channel lay before them, cold in the indifferent light. Three Fairmile motor launches crowded with men and equipment began to move slowly out to sea, and in front of them was an unforgettable panorama of ships and craft, stretching as far as the eye could see, with above them a network of silver barrage balloons. Most of them had the British patchwork camouflage but others wore the neater shading in grey-blues that the Americans favoured.

The harbour was laid out in three lanes with large mooring dolphins so spaced that three LCTs could tie up at the same time and swing with the wind and tide. Beaching craft moved constantly to and fro, from shore to ship and back again, and soldiers and vehicles were arriving in a constant stream, the hardmaster and his men handling them like traffic policemen at rush hour. Ships and destinations had been fixed long before by code letters prominently displayed, and loads of ammunition and men waited at every junction to join the southward stream. Each LCT took about half an hour to fill, topping up with fuel and water at the same time, and soon they were standing in lines to go aboard. On one of the barges a dockworker was struggling to repair damage caused by a collision, kneeling with his mate and his welding apparatus on an improvised staging of planks, ropes and fenders against the flat side of the vessel, on which the tanks had been moved to lift the hole above the water line.

Eventually, the call came to move again. The waters of the harbour were already being churned up by a tangle of wakes as smaller vessels began to leave and turn into a long line that uncoiled towards the Channel. The men tried to make themselves comfortable on the crowded decks and go to sleep. Some didn't bother and simply played cards.

The sky was sad and quiet and curiously ominous, the water like shot silk, the air soft and misty and full of unexpected breezes. The Fox walked on the deck, keeping to himself. As he leaned on the rail, he saw other ships, also grey and edged with the same khaki fringe along the rails.

Staring at the land with narrowed eyes, he wondered just what was to become of them all. The men around him muttered quietly – chiefly of women or drink or baseball and football scores. Meals were served, the officers in shifts in the saloon, the men using their mess tins for stew and tea which had been cooked ashore. Afterwards, they all stood along the rail again, staring at the shore and the iridescent water alongside.

The CO called a conference after they'd all eaten and they gathered together in the saloon of the ship with the sergeants. Maps were produced, exactly the same as the ones they'd been studying for some time, but this time the maps had names on them, and opposite the names, 'Dog', 'Easy' and 'Fox', he saw the French towns of Vierville, St Laurent, Les Moulins, Colleville, Grand Hameau, Ste Honorine and Port-en-Bassin.

As the conference finished and they went on deck again, he realised that the ship was moving into the river and that a wind had got up from nowhere to put a popple on the water. Girls in Wren uniforms manning small boats around them were waving, their cries of 'Good luck' coming thinly across the water. Everyone was quiet and tense, uncertain what to expect. A few still played cards; a few sang softly to themselves.

A man standing by the incendiary bin which had been placed on deck for burning unwanted papers, letters and documents, sniffed the increasing wind, his eyes worried.

'I hope to Christ it's not a rough crossing,' he said sadly. 'I can be sick in the bath.'

12

Lying straight and narrow in his bed, the sheet tucked up neatly to his chin, Pargeter stared at the ceiling. Second Officer Wint alongside him made little delicate snuffling sleep noises that went with her good looks and her good breeding.

He had long since tackled her about the night he'd rung Iremonger at the hotel in Portsmouth. 'Where were you?' he'd demanded.

Her wide blue eyes had stared up at him innocently. 'Sleeping, of course. Stayed the night with a girl friend.'

He didn't believe her and, knowing he didn't believe her, she smiled disarmingly. 'Would it help if I cried a little?' she asked. 'Quietly? With ladylike tears?'

He didn't argue. He wasn't one to worry about the niceties of what they got up to. War and the likelihood of being killed had destroyed a lot of old moralities. All the same, it was pleasant to feel that, through him, the British Empire was holding its own with the United States of America.

He frowned. There was so little time. The waiting couldn't go on much longer. There were so many men and machines in southern England the coastline seemed to bulge. The pace had noticeably quickened in the last few days and there had been a warning that trains might be unexpectedly and suddenly cancelled, which could mean only one thing. Even the songs of Vera Lynn and Anne Shelton had grown more sentimental of late, and comedians like Tommy Handley and Max Miller were careful to avoid using jokes which, with death just over the horizon, might be in doubtful taste.

It had been a depressing day. The morning's post had brought a letter from his mother to say his sister's fiancé was missing over Germany with the RAF, and during the afternoon a strange American voice had rung up with a message for Iremonger. 'Just tell him that General Orme's dead,' it said. 'There was an accident with a grenade.'

Everybody in the world seemed to be getting killed or preparing to get killed, he decided. As the pace increased, so the accidents increased and men were dying even before they saw the enemy. He had no idea who General Orme was but he assumed he was sufficiently close to Iremonger for it to make some difference.

A lorry ground past outside, and he moved restlessly, wishing the thing could be over. The tension couldn't last for ever. Before long, nerves would start to get frayed and if something didn't happen soon people who so far had managed to avoid grumbling would start wondering what the hell it was all for.

Another lorry ground past, then another and another. He held his breath and heard shouting outside. He had heard lorries in the night before, but now there was something in the urgency of the voices that convinced him that this time was different.

Crossing to the window, he looked out. The hotel stood at the bottom of a long curving slope and a long line of lights twinkled on the hills. The whole of England seemed to be on the move.

–

As Iremonger had set off on his return journey from Bletchley, he had found himself impeded all along the route by the lorries moving south. Some of them, he noticed, had barbed wire strung along their sides and sometimes a notice, 'Do Not Talk To The Troops'. At first it puzzled him, but then he saw a convoy stopped by a village green and sentries keeping away the girls and the children who had swarmed round as usual with their cries of 'Any gum, chum?' Immediately, he knew what it meant. He was witnessing the first rumblings of the great avalanche that was to lead to France, the first heave that was being felt in every corner of the British Isles.

The knowledge filled him with awe. Remembering what he had just learned about Ultra, and what he knew of the Fox's knowledge of Ultra, he was horrified to realise they might be too late to stop him. Automatically, he began to drive faster, forcing his way out of the convoy, his hand on the horn button of his car as he screamed alongside the lorries in a cloud of dust tinted golden by the last of the sun.

It was dark when he started to climb the South Downs and, as he dropped down on the other side, he saw lights and the figure of an American soldier waving a torch. There had been an accident on the edge of a village where a lorry rounding a corner a shade too fast had sideswiped a small private car driven by a doctor and, as the soldiers had jumped down to see what had happened, in the dark another lorry had run them down.

There seemed to be injured men and bodies lying all over the road. A harassed village policeman long beyond the age of retirement was struggling to sort out the mess and the doctor from the car which had been involved in the first accident was kneeling over one of the GIs, a pair of broken glasses on his nose. A young officer was trying to organise transport for the injured and had found a tarpaulin which he was helping to stretch over three silent shapes which lay by the roadside, their heavy boots lopsided in the grass.

'Goddam war,' he was saying edgily. 'I wish the lousy invasion was over.'

They all looked strained, and Iremonger realised just how much the coming attack was taking out of everybody. Nerves were on edge; people were jumpy. Every man in the army tried to pretend he didn't care but, despite all the reassurances that all would be well, the thought that when they crossed the Channel the Germans would be waiting for them couldn't be made to remain at the back of the mind out of sight.

It was well after dark when he reached Portsmouth. There was no sign of Pargeter in his room. Headquarters was silent and the man on the telephone was sitting with his feet on a chair, dozing. Iremonger swept the heavy boots to the floor with a crash. 'Where's Weinberger?' he demanded.

The man came to life with a jerk and was on his feet at once, staring dazedly at Iremonger.

'He's asleep, sir, Colonel, sir.'

'Get him.'

Weinberger appeared within two minutes, heaving at his trousers. 'Colonel? What's on?'

'Where's Major Pargeter?'

'Off duty, sir.'

Iremonger's arm flung out. The grind and roar and rumble of vehicles outside seemed enormously loud. The whole house seemed to quiver with it.

'Hear that?' he demanded.

'Sure, sir. Convoys, sir. Military convoys.'

'That,' Iremonger snarled, 'is the invasion!'

Weinberger was sceptical. 'American correspondents think the invasion's only a hoax,' he said. 'I've been talking to one.' Iremonger's pointing finger quivered. 'Listen, you goddam dope! Listen for yourself! What do *you* think it is?'

Weinberger looked shamefaced. 'The invasion, I guess, Colonel!'

'Sure it is! Now get me Cuthbert! He's not in his billet!'

It was quite obvious the telephone had failed to startle Pargeter, as Iremonger had hoped. His voice sounded edgy but he seemed well in control of himself.

'Get your ass down to headquarters!' Iremonger's voice was harsh. 'Things are happening.'

'As a matter of fact I was already on my way.' Pargeter sounded as infuriatingly cool as he always did.

'Then get a goddam move on! I need you! I need everybody. I want every member of the staff, including Second Officer Wint. I dare say you know where she is. Get a burr under your tail. We have to move fast!'

Iremonger slammed down the receiver and lit a cigarette, then he tried to ring Southwick Park, but it was impossible to get through and their very inaccessibility seemed a confirmation of what he had already guessed. He picked up the telephone again to contact an officer he knew in Movement Control at Portland but, this time, though he could hear the number ringing out, there was no reply. Portland appeared to have disappeared into thin air.

He banged down the instrument once more, now thoroughly frustrated and aware that the sound of traffic outside had increased. Jumping to his feet, he went to the door and looked out. There were vehicles as far as he could see in every direction, all full of men and equipment. Military police had materialised from nowhere to see them on their way. He dived back to his desk.

'Weinberger,' he yelled. 'Get hold of Southwick! If necessary, sit on the telephone!'

When Pargeter appeared Liz Wint was with him, looking faintly dishevelled.

'Picked her up on the way,' Pargeter said.

Iremonger gave him a malicious smile. 'Yeah,' he said. 'Of course.'

Weinberger appeared. 'Southwick, sir,' he announced. 'I got 'em.'

Iremonger snatched at the telephone. An unknown voice answered, deep and suspicious.

'Who's that?' it demanded.

Iremonger started to explain but the man on the other end of the wire had clearly never heard of him. 'Get off the line,' he snarled.

'Listen—'

'Get off the line!'

The wire went dead, as, without waiting for Iremonger to say any more, the speaker slammed his own instrument down. Iremonger stared at it for a moment in a fury, aware that like everybody else he was being carried along willy-nilly by the first forward surge of the invasion.

'Goddam!' he said.

He began to shout again for Weinberger and the sergeant, caught up in the excitement as much as Iremonger, put his head round the door, looking worried.

'Where the hell's de Rezonville?'

'He ain't appeared, Colonel.'

'Find him.'

'I've tried, Colonel. *He's* vanished, too, I guess.'

'Godammit, what's happened to everybody?' Iremonger paused and drew a deep breath as he realised he was letting his excitement run away with him. 'Find out what happened to him, Weinberger,' he said more calmly.

'Sure, sir.'

Iremonger reached for a cigar and forced himself to light it slowly. Pargeter was still waiting by the desk. He looked faintly supercilious at all the noise and fuss, as though, if he'd had his way, he would have conducted the war in a much more gentlemanly fashion. Iremonger grinned at him, curiously pleased to see him in spite of everything.

'We're in business, Cuthbert,' he said. 'This goddam invasion's come too goddam soon. We weren't ready for it, and if we're not careful we're going to get snarled up and the Fox's going to dodge us. All the same—' he jabbed a finger '—we have permission to search ships. We better start searching.'

-

The drive to Portland at dawn was a replica of the drive from Bletchley. On every road there were strings of lorries, guns, armour and marching troops. There were no bands, no fluttering flags, no crowds to shout 'Farewell'. Just women offering cups of tea when the lorries halted, and a fervent 'God bless you'. Everybody knew now.

British, Canadians and Americans were rolling southward through the villages and towns, countless columns of troops and convoys of steel vehicles converging on the ports. All night nothing had been heard but the thump of army boots on the paved streets and the "Eft! 'Ight!' of sergeants. All night long there had been the rattle and roar of engines as vehicles rolled in an ever-thickening stream to the water's edge to board the beaching craft on the hards or the transports at the docks. The men threading their way through the assembly areas of tanks, guns and vehicles looked brown and fit and curiously relaxed, like athletes before a contest. There was little sound beyond their boots and the noise of engines and they were not talking, simply smoking and chewing gum to stay awake.

As Iremonger edged the jeep past a British convoy, a whistle blew and the men began to climb into the lorries in an orderly confusion. Iremonger was frowning heavily. The message about Orme, coming on top of the accident he'd witnessed, troubled him. If generals could get killed, what goddam hope was there for people of lesser rank at the sharp end of the army?

When they reached Portland, the fine weather of May seemed to have gone completely and they found they had even less time than they thought. Troops were pouring aboard the ships, and there was tremendous activity with the loading of tank landing craft. There was difficulty even in getting into the loading area, and security police, their helmets glistening in the thin drifting rain that had started, tried to turn them back.

'I have authority to be in there,' Iremonger snapped.

The MP called a sergeant who immediately sent for an officer. The officer stared at Iremonger's authority and didn't believe it.

'How do I know it's genuine?' he demanded. 'I've never seen one of these passes before.'

Iremonger glared. 'Where's General Bradley's headquarters?' he demanded.

'Why?'

'Because I guess if *you* don't know what the hell to do, he will.'

But Bradley had already left to go aboard the cruiser, USS *Augusta*, and there was only a small cadre of officers left to run the place. 'You'll have to move damn fast,' one of them pointed out. 'Every vessel in Portland's supposed to be under way by 0315. And the good Lord help 'em, too,' he ended fervently, 'because the weather forecasts show what looks like the worst gale for twenty years coming in from the Atlantic.'

Their explanations were accepted, however, and a brigadier-general got on the telephone to the loading area. But still nobody wanted to know them.

'For Christ's sake,' a harassed lieutenant-colonel told them, 'we're loading for an invasion! The biggest sonofabitching thing that's ever happened either in this war or any other. The thing's been worked out to the minute. If I halt it to search for this guy of yours, the whole goddam invasion'll be late!'

Every hardmaster seemed to have much the same answer and, since a search at this stage was clearly impossible, they returned to Bradley's headquarters and sent out a signal requesting all units to state if they had a Captain Kechinski with them.

It was well into 4 June now and the first vessels were already heading for the rendezvous area south of the Isle of Wight. When the replies began to come in, they were all the same. No one knew Captain Kechinski. Three Kechinskis appeared – all lieutenants, none of them named Jack, John or Jan, all in their early twenties, and all well and truly vouched for by their colonels.

'Think the bastard's already at sea?' Iremonger asked.

'More likely he's changed his name,' Pargeter said, 'and he isn't Kechinski any longer.'

By the time daylight arrived, what Bradley's aide had said was clear. The forecast in the G-2 Journal looked alarming and the weather map looked like a day in December. Outside, the thin rain had changed to a downpour.

'There'll be a low ceiling tomorrow,' the meteorological officer predicted. 'It'll ground the air force and swamp the landing craft. They should postpone until the 6th.'

'At this rate, until the 7th!'

'They can't postpone until the 7th or every goddam ship will have to come back and refuel. The plan's tied to the moon and a delay could mean next month. And you can't keep all those men aboard till then. It just isn't possible.'

The atmosphere was one of uncertainty, anxiety, and even dread. Every available allied fighting man had been channelled into the invasion and there was a feeling that instead of victory the assault could turn into a disaster. Like a juggernaut, once in motion it could not be stopped, yet suddenly it looked like ending in the most unholy and bloody catastrophe in the history of warfare. With the gale, the chances of success, with swamped landing craft and no air force, looked slender, yet they dared not delay; surprise would be gone because the date and landfall were already the common property of thousands of men.

'Christ,' Iremonger said. 'The weather was perfect in May. Why didn't we go then?'

As they argued, an aide appeared. 'The code word's arrived,' he said. 'It's been postponed for a day – unless it's cancelled altogether, as it ought to be.'

Iremonger's own anxiety matched the more general sense of depression, defeat and anger. Despite the authority to search that he carried in his pocket, he was in fact powerless because no one was sufficiently interested to be helpful. Unit commanders had more on their minds at that moment than identifying an unknown officer. Vessels already at sea were being chased home by destroyers in the grey dawn after a black night during which radio silence could not be broken. By midday they were back and churning it out off Portland Bill, the luckier of them inside the harbour, the men sealed inside their cramped craft for a second day and wearily reconciled to the ordeal of waiting.

The gale showed no signs of abating. The rain lashed the windows and blew the gulls inside out. As the waves continued to mount, senior naval officers in foul-weather gear stood outside staring at the sea, trying to assess chances. For Iremonger and Pargeter it was an impossible situation. A few vessels had been searched but the overcrowding made it impossible to check every man. Even the muster rolls were no help because the elusive

Kechinski no longer appeared to exist under that name, and there was no alternative but to request units to report every officer who had joined within the last fortnight.

It was quite clear by the way signals were answered, however, that no one on board the landing craft and landing ships was very concerned with finding – and possibly losing – some valuable and busy officer at this stage in the game. By evening only five units had reported back, and they had little hope of hearing from many more.

The anxiety was now tense enough to touch. Then, suddenly, there was a gleam of hope. The two low pressure systems which had been causing the gale were amalgamating off the Hebrides in a single low, and the meteorologists began to predict moderating winds and a break-up of the cloud cover.

'They might go after all,' they were told.

Pargeter frowned. 'In that case,' he said, 'we'd better hand over to the United States Army Provost Department.'

Iremonger scowled, smarting under their failure. 'Those stone-headed bastards couldn't find a pig in a sack,' he said. 'I'm going with 'em.'

Pargeter stared at him in surprise, and he went on angrily. 'We're never going to find this goddam Kechinski over here!' he said. 'We're going to have to go over to the other side and pick him up on the beaches before he makes contact with the Krauts.'

'That's impossible!'

'We've got all night to nail the sonofabitch! If we can get Southwick behind us, we can *insist* on units answering our signals. They can't ignore a Supreme Headquarters directive. And if we know what unit the bastard's in, we can get ourselves landed right alongside and pick him up before he does any harm.'

Pargeter studied him speculatively for a moment. Then an unexpected smile lit up his grave features.

'Well,' he said primly, 'they say an old soldier's a cautious soldier, but you'll need somebody with experience to look after you, Linus. Perhaps I'd better come too. Let's go and put it to Hardee.'

13

The weather was still poor. In the harbours ships still tugged uneasily at their anchors and ropes, and seasick pills were still being handed round. Some men had now been aboard for three or four days; the strain was beginning to tell, and the high morale of the first day had slipped. Instead of the need for courage, they remembered only the pep talks that had made them realise they were only statistics in a great gamble – so many would be seasick, so many would drown, so many would be killed.

There were grim faces at Southwick when Iremonger and Pargeter arrived. An Associated Press release had mistakenly announced that allied forces were already landing in France, and there were a great many officers on telephones busily contradicting it or trying to find out how it had come to be issued at all.

There were more than mere false alarms in the air, too, because the windows were still quivering under the force of the wind, and the rain was driving horizontally across the lawns.

'The low up near the Shetlands is filling up,' an American colonel told them. 'We expect lower seas and less surf for two days starting on the morning of the 6th. Since the met boys refuse to predict beyond that, they decided to go. Ships are starting to move out already.' He shuddered.

'And God help those who have farthest to go,' he went on. 'The wind was still at force five when we got the "go ahead", and the goddam plan's supposed to be dependent on calm weather and flat seas.'

Iremonger jerked him out of his gloom with a bark.

'We need a ship,' he said. 'We need to be in this thing.'

'By the time we can get you down there they'll all have left.'

'Then lay on a destroyer.'

'There aren't any spare destroyers.'

'Then find one.'

The colonel glared. 'There are no reserves.'

'Then put us on a battleship.'

'With whose authority?'

Iremonger's jaw hardened. 'General Hardee's,' he said. 'You'd better take us to him.'

—

General Hardee's face was as grim as the rest as he motioned them to chairs.

Iremonger coughed. 'We've pin-pointed him, General,' he said. 'He's with General Bradley's First Army.'

'First Army comprises two corps – around seven or eight divisions,' Hardee pointed out.

'And a hell of a lot of small units, General,' Iremonger admitted. 'But we know he's there, so we have to look for him. We know now what he looks like and roughly where he is.' He laid on the table the blown-up photographs they'd obtained. Hardee put on a pair of spectacles and stood up to peer closer.

'Same man?' he asked.

'Yes, sir.'

'Name?'

'Not Reinecke. Not Fox. Nor any of the others. At the moment he's going under the name of Kechinski. When he was a Pole he was *Taddeus* Kechinski. He's since become *Jack* Kechinski, an American.'

'Can't Records help you?'

'I doubt if he'll be on 'em, General.'

'Movement Control?'

'We'd need to know his unit and we don't, sir.'

Hardee sat for a moment, thinking. 'Searching the invasion fleet's a formidable task,' he said.

'It can be done, sir, if we're given the authority. A lot of people are tensed up and don't want to be distracted from what they're doing. We're getting nowhere.'

'That's hardly surprising.'

'On the other hand, sir, I don't have to tell you how important it is to find him.'

Hardee looked up. 'You do not,' he snapped. 'But you've left it a little late!' There was a hint of annoyance but no more.

'The postponement's helped us, General,' Iremonger leaned forward. 'If we go with 'em, sir, we have another twenty-four hours. And if we have to pick him up on the other side, then we sure as hell will. But we need help to make everybody give us the returns we want.'

Hardee drew a notepad towards him. 'Prepare your signals,' he said. 'I'll give them top priority. But prepare 'em damn carefully because General Bradley's got plenty to think about besides you. You'll be fitted out with anything you want here and put on the destroyer, *Forbes*, which will put you aboard *Augusta*. The replies should be waiting for you when you arrive. By the time you're ready to go, I'll have a loading schedule listing all units waiting for you. It'll show every outfit, which ship they're in and which beach they're due to land on. It'll be up to you, when you've pinned down your man, to see that you're put on the appropriate ship and the appropriate stretch of beach.'

Within minutes they were being rushed to stores to draw the necessary equipment. Fitted out with helmet, lifebelt, pistol, carbine, commando dagger and binoculars, Iremonger felt as if he were strapped inside a cage of harness. When Pargeter arrived, he was surprised to find that all he carried in addition to his walking stick was a revolver in a holster. His only other item of equipment was a navy-blue British-type steel helmet marked with a large white W.

'What the hell have you got there?' Iremonger said.

Pargeter blinked. 'Linus,' he said gravely. 'I'm a British officer and when I go ashore at the other side, I'm going ashore looking like a British officer.' He took off the flat helmet and glanced at it. 'Smart, don't you think? Scrounged it off a civilian storeman who works for you people. He's not allowed out of camp, and he had no money to go the canteen, so he let me have it for half a quid. He's an air-raid warden when he's off-duty here.'

'What about a tommy gun?'

'Got a revolver and a flask of brandy. Should be enough.'

Iremonger frowned; then he grinned. 'I think we'd better have a drink,' he suggested. 'It might be our last chance for a while, and I'm told they've got some good whisky here.'

Pargeter smiled. 'You've found a way to my heart,' he said.

-

Hardee was waiting for them when they returned with a thick wad of paper clipped inside a file. 'Loading schedules,' he said. 'The file also includes a *laissez-passer* to any ship, unit or beach, no matter what's happening. Signed by me and countersigned by Ike himself. I have to rely on you to use it properly. I've been in touch with General Bradley. They'll be waiting for you aboard *Augusta*. Your signal's been sent out carrying the most urgent classification and the insistence that replies are sent without fail and at once. I just hope our man's aboard a ship whose radio hasn't broken down. How long do you need to wind up your affairs?'

Iremonger glanced at Pargeter. 'Got the photographs, Cuthbert?' he asked.

Pargeter patted his breast pocket and Iremonger turned to Hardee. 'Nothing more than a telephone call, sir.'

They headed in different directions. When they rejoined each other, Iremonger was frowning. Pargeter gave him a beaming smile.

'She wasn't there, was she?' he said.

'No.' Iremonger scowled. 'How the hell did you know who I was telephoning?'

'Guessed.'

'Weinberger said she'd gone off with that Frog guy.'

'Yes, she did. I rang her billet. She was there. She was crying.'

'Was she, by Christ? What were *you* calling her for?'

'Same as you, I suspect. To tell her I might be busy for a day or two but not to worry, I'd be back before long. Right?'

Iremonger scowled again and nodded. 'Thought she was entitled to it.'

'Save your consideration,' Pargeter said. 'We left her alone too often and she was never the most faithful of women. She's dropped us both. De Rezonville's been recalled to his unit and he's already embarked and sailed. She was weeping for *him*.'

Iremonger stared. 'That Frog bastard?'

Pargeter shrugged. 'Better-looking than you, Linus,' he said. 'Better-looking than me, too. And, I suspect, a great deal more wealthy than either of us. A woman can make a man appear to be an imbecile in ten seconds flat.'

'Yeah.' Iremonger grinned unexpectedly. 'One thing,' he observed. 'We don't have to worry now about being killed.'

Part Three

From a View to a Death

1

When they reached Portsmouth the weather was still soupy and wet, with low visibility and a chill in the air that made them shiver. The streets were bare and there was a queer stillness everywhere. Now that the fleets had sailed, it was oddly unnerving to see the empty harbour.

Not long before, it had been noisy with military music as commandos had filed aboard their assault ships at the Isle of Wight pier. Now there was a great air of solemnity and secrecy, and the only assault forces left were the torpedo boats which were to dash across the Channel at daybreak. Over the lighthouse on Portland Bill, aircraft – their lights on – were passing in dozens and heading out to sea.

'Just about four years to the day,' Pargeter pointed out, 'since we were kicked out of France at Dunkirk.'

An RAF high-speed launch ran them out to a destroyer waiting beyond the boom. As the coxswain thrust the throttles forward, they rammed the stern of a naval launch cutting across their bows in a hurry.

'Nothing out of the ordinary,' one of the airmen said cheerfully. 'Have to have an accident now and then to make things go right, and we haven't rammed anything for days.'

As they scrambled on to the deck of the destroyer, she put to sea at once. From the bridge, they could see a weathered gun position squatting lonely and silent on stilts offshore, and the concrete blockhouses on the beach behind them.

'After tomorrow,' Iremonger said, 'Churchill can tear 'em all down.'

Pargeter nodded. 'Amen to that,' he said.

After a while they became aware of a dark line ahead and began to make out masts and fluttering flags, and eventually the square shapes of landing craft. Beyond them were troopships with smaller landing craft hanging from their davits. The sea seemed to be full of them.

It was almost dark as they spotted *Augusta* among the other vessels, a rakish beauty among the snub-nosed LSTs with her yacht-like bows and eight-inch turrets. It was hard work climbing up the wooden rungs of the rope ladder from the destroyer's boat, and the great ship was already moving again as they were dragged over the rail.

The cruiser's decks were wet with drizzle. The wind lashed at a canvas curtain across an open steel door, while the radar antenna on top of the foremast washed in and out of the overcast hanging low in the dark sky. Confused by their new surroundings, they followed the naval officer who met them, stumbling over ring bolts and deck projections in the dark. Passing through a dogged-back steel door, they found themselves in a war room that had been constructed on the aircraft deck, a temporary shed-like construction whose sheet-metal walls seemed to buckle and sway as the ship moved. Lights had been rigged up, taped like the face of the clock against the concussion of the guns when they fired. One wall was papered with a

Michelin motoring map of France and next to it there was a terrain study of the assault beaches, bracketed into letter and colour designations. Between them, a Petty pin-up girl lounged on a more alluring beach. There was also a detailed map of the Normandy coast marked with concentric arcs giving the range of enemy coastal guns, and another charting the disposition of enemy divisions in blurred markings. A long plotting table filled the centre space, at which a naval lieutenant traced an overlay of beach defences. On a waist-high shelf along the seaward wall stood a row of typewriters for the journal clerks and log-keepers.

Bradley was wearing a pistol and a steel helmet, and was chatting with a colonel as he stared out at the mist and low cloud and the lessening visibility. The wind was still roaring round the ship at twenty knots and the water of the Channel was lifting in menacing waves.

'There'll be a four-foot surf on the beaches,' Bradley was saying. 'It doesn't look good.'

'*I* think it stinks, sir,' the colonel said.

Bradley turned – a tall, approachable, spectacled Missourian with the face of a professor of history – and greeted them warmly.

'You'll forgive me if I have to throw you on to the mercy of one of my staff,' he said. 'But I have other things to do. Colonel Fitzsimmons here will give you all the dope and there'll be food for you. Is there anything else you need?'

'Only our replies, General.'

'Fitz will fill you in.'

Excusing himself, Bradley turned away to confer with the naval man behind him. They heard the anxious muttering start again among the officers round them, and it made them realise that the fate of the invasion hung not in the big-hulled command craft but in wet-bottomed small vessels where seasick men cowered and groaned.

Fitzsimmons, a lean, lantern-jawed Texan wearing glasses, who looked remarkably like Bradley himself, stepped forward with a sheaf of flimsies. 'There's been a good response,' he said. 'You'll have to accept that those guys out there have other things on their mind right now apart from your problem, but, even so, they seem to be trying. We've sent a repeat request to let them know it's urgent and goddam important, and the replies are still coming in. There are still twenty-odd on the way, so you'd better find something to eat. By the time you come back, we'll probably have the lot.'

They were given steaks and coffee in the officers' ward-room, and when they returned to the war room Fitzsimmons was waiting for them.

'Your signals are all in,' he announced. 'Nine units admit to new officers who've joined in the last fortnight. I've told them to check again into background, age, et cetera. The first of them's already replied. Their new officer's not your man because he's a lieutenant-colonel aged forty-nine and his name's Finkelstein and it seems he looks as though it is, so *he* won't be a Nazi. That leaves eight. You'll just have to wait.'

High above *Augusta's* bridge, a radar antenna rotated monotonously under a woolly sky. In the plotting room an officer bent before a radar screen, searching for the tell-tale pips that signified enemy aeroplanes.

'Nothing at all,' he said.

'Perhaps it's going to be Sicily all over again.'

'You can hardly expect *that* in the crowded Channel. On a clear day an aircraft at ten thousand feet can see Southampton.'

'It's not a clear day, goddamit! I wish it was.'

They waited restlessly. Out of the eight replies they still needed, three more had now answered. Two had no doubt about their new officers, who apparently could be vouched for by other officers in their units. Only one seemed to be in doubt.

'Captain Harry Gavin,' Pargeter said. 'Seventeenth Rangers. On board SS *Mounts Bay*.'

There was a strange silence about *Augusta*, as though everyone was afraid his voice might be heard, but also a sense of quiet exaltation that reached even through the tense anxiety of Iremonger and Pargeter.

Pargeter was standing quietly, wearing a crumpled field service cap, the air-raid warden's helmet swinging from his hand. His face was calm and expressionless, as if he had complete faith in ultimate success; as though, having endured the Nazis for five long years, he was certain now that they were due for their come-uppance.

Another report came in. Once again the unit reported that its new officer was known to them and had been even back in the United States.

'Leaves four,' Pargeter said.

To the south there was a glow in the sky, and for a moment there was a little more nervous muttering.

'It's the light at Cap Barfleur,' one of the naval officers said. 'It's one of the world's tallest and most conspicuous lighthouses.'

'Goddam funny to find it shining like that.'

'Expect the German naval forces need it.'

'I sure hope they're not out and needing it tonight.'

Another reply came in. Once again they drew a blank. The new officer was a man of impeccable background, a well-known attorney whose face was familiar from newspaper photographs.

'Three to go,' Iremonger muttered. 'Four, with the guy in the Seventeenth Rangers they're not prepared to vouch for.'

The next report came in almost immediately. Once again the commanding officer was in no doubt about the genuineness of his officer.

'Two to go.'

The big ship was now slipping past the buoys that marked the swept channel towards the French coast. Only the lonely wind in the rigging and the wash of water along the sides of the ship broke the silence. At 0335 a clanking bell called the crew to battle stations, complete with helmets and Mae Wests. The moon hung misted in the overcast sky, and the wind still lashed the Channel. According to the log it had slackened.

'I wouldn't have noticed,' Pargeter observed.

'The airborne divs must be already down and waiting for us,' someone remarked. 'Any time now.'

Pargeter frowned. 'We're not going to get our replies,' he said.

'Could be their radios have failed,' Fitzsimmons pointed out. He took a look at the heaving sea. 'Maybe, even, the damn ships sank.'

Pargeter looked at the lists Hardee had given them. 'Third Cavalry Recce Squadron,' he said. 'On board SS *Oluma*. Ninth Mortar Unit. On board LST 123. Our man's either with those or he's this chap, Gavin, they can't vouch for in the Rangers, on SS *Mounts Bay.*'

'All in the O-Force convoy, bound for Omaha Beach,' Iremonger said. 'We'd better get ourselves put aboard one of 'em.'

They went to the command room where Fitzsimmons found the position of the three ships. '*Mounts Bay's* nearest,' he said. 'Heading for Dog Red on the right of the attack. We shall be taking up positions soon, so we'd better get you moving. The cavalry recce squadron's with the 18th Regiment on Easy Red. That's right alongside Dog Red, so you'll be able to just nip along. The mortars are on Fox Green, away on the left. I'll fix the boat.'

As he vanished, they heard a faraway roar across the Channel and everybody looked up.

'The heavies!'

Off the starboard bow an orange glare ignited the sky as more than thirteen hundred RAF bombers swarmed over the French coast from the Seine to Cherbourg. An enemy ack-ack battery ashore stabbed blindly into the night and a shower of sparks splintered the darkness as a bomber was hit. A ribbon of fire fell through the clouds from the swelling roar, and they could see the shape of the stricken bomber coming down. As it levelled off near the ship, banked round the stern and exploded into the Channel, a high-speed launch roared towards the spot.

Iremonger looked at Pargeter. He looked cold. His eyes were tired and there was a red tip to his nose, but he still seemed a whole lot calmer than Iremonger felt.

'Think we'll survive this one, Cuthbert?' he asked.

Pargeter's head turned. 'It's my earnest hope,' he said.

Iremonger's next words came without any conscious effort on his part, as though some need for friendship at that particular moment drove them to the surface. 'When it's all over,' he said, 'you should come over to the States and see me in New York. I'd give you a good time.'

For a moment he thought Pargeter was going to cold-shoulder the idea with one of his icy silences, then his face split in the wide smile whose sheer charm always shook Iremonger.

'Why not, Linus?' he said. 'And why not you come and stay with my family in Dorset! I could promise you some good shooting.'

Iremonger's simple heart warmed to him. 'I guess we'll get all the shooting we want on this trip,' he said. He paused, overcome by a feeling of guilt. 'When I first met you, Cuth, I thought you were a bastard.'

Pargeter grinned. 'So did I you.'

'But you're not bad. You know that. You're not bad.'

'Neither are you, Linus, neither are you.'

Iremonger felt much better. It was something he'd needed to get off his chest for some time. Underneath his carapace of hardness, he was a sentimental man who enjoyed being liked. And the fact that he was liked by someone as aloof and prickly as Pargeter pleased him. He felt he'd made the grade and found a friend for life.

Fitzsimmons appeared in the increasing light. 'We've signalled the picket boat away,' he said. 'Are you ready?'

Iremonger glanced at Pargeter and hitched at his equipment. 'Ready as we'll ever be,' he said nervously. 'Let's go.'

2

It was hard to do nothing but stand and wait.

The crossing had been rough, and many of the men had been seasick. It was cold on deck but stuffy below to the point of nausea, and a night sense of strangeness and insecurity came as danger was magnified by the darkness. Many of those who had been worrying about the landing were now longing for it, if only to be off the rolling, pitching ship that imprisoned them.

Huddled on the boat deck, the Fox could smell the fresh tang of the Channel. Over the lash of the sea he could hear the drone of hundreds of landing craft, the sea buffeting against their blunt bows as they headed southwards. Everyone had been expecting bombs, torpedoes, gunfire, mines, E-boats and destroyers, and there was a strange kind of wonder that so far none of them had materialised.

The men about him who were still capable of standing upright, were quiet as they made their arrangements, adjusting the chin straps of their helmets, checking their identification tags, making sure their lifejackets were secure and worked properly. A few of them were eating chocolate because there wasn't much point in being killed on an empty stomach, but others went constantly to the heads to throw up what they'd eaten or to the dispensary for something to settle their insides. The seasickness was worse than the boredom and the fear. Several men had vomited into their helmets, and there had been a fight when a wretched soldier had thrown up into a comrade's lap.

They were all surprisingly serious, but that was something the Fox had found was common to all armed forces before a big event. It had been the same before Warsaw. The jokes died away, but so also did the complaining, and everyone became studiously polite to each other, as though they felt they wouldn't like to be remembered for ill-manners if they were killed, or as if they were afraid of being rude to someone who might not see the next dawn.

All round in the darkness the phalanx of shipping bore down on the coast of Europe. They came in rank after rank, twenty miles across, ten lanes wide, five thousand ships of every description, from fast new attack transports through the whole gamut of rust-scarred cargo vessels, small ocean liners, Channel steamers and hospital ships, to weather-beaten tankers, coasters and fussing tugs. Among them were endless columns of shallow-draught landing ships, great wallowing vessels three hundred and fifty feet long, some of them carrying other smaller craft for the beaching. Ahead of them were the minesweepers, coast-guard cutters, buoy layers and motor launches. The sky was full of barrage balloons, and the cloud ceiling, which seemed to be only just beyond the masthead, echoed with the roar of aircraft as squadrons of fighters weaved and turned. Surrounding the fantastic armada, with its armoury of guns, tanks and vehicles, were the warships; heavy cruisers, light cruisers – many of them with proud records – sloops, corvettes, gunboats, anti-submarine craft, torpedo boats; and everywhere, on every side, the destroyers.

Many of the soldiers were afraid. Some were introspective and talked of things that normally they kept to themselves, admitting their fears and their domestic worries with an unexpected candour. Almost every one of them had written a letter of some kind as he'd waited. A few had books, and an officer nearby held up a Shakespeare he was reading.

'Every time I try to move on,' he said, 'I keep going back to that speech of Henry V's. "And gentlemen in England now a-bed shall think themselves accursed they were not here."'

'The way I feel,' another voice replied, 'I'd be goddam glad to be in England and a-bed.'

Below decks, chaplains were conducting services and talking to men who wished to be prepared in case they were killed. Most were tense, but a few were light-hearted enough to be indifferent. Many of them were green troops, despite being well-trained, and, for all his contempt for the British, the Fox knew that these American soldiers hadn't the same feeling for the invasion as the islanders. They hadn't been bombed and driven out of France. They hadn't seen their homes destroyed and their families killed. And they were a long way from their own country and didn't feel they were liberating themselves or anyone else either. They were largely unwarlike, and the poison of combat was not in their blood; but nevertheless no one wanted to go to sleep in case he missed something.

The night was thick, blustery and black. The heaving Channel was flecked with white and steel grey, while the clouds fled past in tormented, tattered shrouds in a cold sky. The west- north-west wind whipped spume into the faces of look-outs and soldiers alike. The men in the small craft were sick, weary and – like Jonah – wondering when they were to be spewed up on an alien shore, longing to get their feet on dry ground. Those on deck were lucky. They could see what was happening. Those below huddled in a stink of vomit, waiting in a misty limbo of time.

In the distance, tugs grappled with strange tows on a night that was never meant for towing. All round the Fox men huddled against the wind, their faces grey, their eyes dark under the pot-shaped helmets that gave them a strangely medieval appearance. They had been on deck now for fifty hours, and they stared dumbly backwards at the long line of ships unwinding behind them as though paid out from a colossal spool. Above the thunder of the aircraft overhead, they could hear the drenching sounds of the sea and the shuddering stresses of the plates.

No one was allowed to make a noise or shine a light, but no one wanted to, and they kept their voices down as if the Germans could already hear them. Last-minute orders came round, and a few more photographs for them to examine. The Fox thought how ironic it was that he should be about to assault defences that had probably been put up on his own recommendation.

Radio news flashes were passed on to them, and there were a few quickly suppressed cheers when they learned that the allies had entered Rome. There was so much courage around him, it was hard to imagine it all being dissipated, as it inevitably would be within a very short time. The Wehrmacht must certainly know by now, from radar alone, what to expect. His own efforts to inform them of the date and time and place of the invasion no longer had any significance. What mattered now was the information about the Bigot plans and the secret of the Ultra decoding system, which he carried on closely written sheets. He had spent a great deal of time carefully translating and setting out the facts so that even the stupidest lieutenant could grasp their importance at a glance and have the sense to direct him immediately to a superior officer.

The vital thing was for the papers to get through to the German high command. It would be preferable if he were alive to explain them but, failing that, he must get them to the Wehrmacht dead. And if he had to be dead, it must be where his body would be found by his own people. As a guarantee of its being not only found but searched, he had the silver oak leaves of a colonel ready to put on at the last moment if necessary. Finding a dead field officer in their lines, the Germans would be sure to go through his pockets. The search would produce the papers, and his job would be done.

The thought of dying didn't worry him much. He preferred to live but he accepted that his duty, if necessary, was to die. He no longer had any idea whether his wife and child were alive. After the bombing of Hamburg, the British newspapers had been full of the firestorm which had hit the city on several days of night- and day-time bombing, and from the photographs that had appeared he had realised that the district where they lived had been right in the centre of it.

A bell clanged and orders came over the tannoy to assemble at loading stations. He patted his pocket where the papers were, and began to move through the shadowy figures around him to the side of the ship. The deck lights were out and only blue lamps were showing as they grouped near the LCAs hanging from the davits. As they began to be called by name and serial number to their boats, he moved up with the others.

The sky had lightened now until the Fox could recognise faces. Then the day came, murky, grey and majestic, showing up the allied fleet with a fearful grandeur, and he wondered why there had been no interference from the Kriegsmarine or the Luftwaffe.

The tannoy crackled again as a special message from the admiral in command was relayed. 'It is our honour and privilege to take part in the greatest amphibious operation in history...'

The man next to the Fox swallowed, his eyes gleaming whitely under the rim of his helmet. 'Did he say "honour" or "horror?"' he grated.

Outlined against the sky the Fox could see the big battleships sprouting their forests of antennae and, behind them, low in the water and sluggish, the vast convoy of troop-filled transports and landing ships. The mass of vessels seethed with noise and activity, and engines throbbed and whined as patrol boats dashed backwards and forwards and winches whirred.

His name was called and he moved forward, climbing over the rail into the LCA. It was swaying slightly on the davits with the movement of the ship. The men around him, packed tightly against each other, were silent, their faces sombre in the dim light. The tension was enormous and a sergeant tried to break it.

'Say something funny, someone,' he said, but no one did and no one laughed.

The mist was thick but a man pointed and said, 'That's the land.' Nobody believed him but, after a while, the consistent irregularity of the shape ahead proved that it certainly wasn't a bank of cloud. The Fox stared fixedly at it, seeking the landmarks he'd seen on the aerial photographs. At last, almost as if he were forcing them to appear through the murk, he saw a line of houses just above a pale strip which slowly took on the appearance of a stretch of sandy beach.

'Good luck,' someone said. 'Lower away.' The boat slipped down the side of the ship to the water, banging against the hull in the wind. Immediately, it began to pitch and he heard a man up forward groan with seasickness. There seemed to be small craft everywhere in the lurching sea, rising and falling in the waves. Several times they were blown against the side of the ship, with tremendous metallic crashes as steel clashed against steel, before they unhooked and began to move away.

'Keep in line! Keep in line!' A control officer with a loud-hailer started to shout and the coxswain struggled to get into position, going round in a great ungainly circle to reach his place. On other transports, the boats had been lowered first and men were awkwardly climbing down scrambling nets into the spray. Over the racket of the sea and the roar of the engine the Fox could hear tannoys calling. 'Get your men ashore! That is your primary object! And troops, when ashore, must get up the beach quickly!'

'Remember Dunkirk,' a British voice shouted from the ship. 'Remember the Alamo!'

'Get in there, Yanks! Give 'em hell!'

More and more boats were joining the craft endlessly churning round their mother ships. Already sodden, seasick and miserable, the men in them stared ahead, not seeing, their faces waxy and expressionless, wondering what awaited them at the end of their ordeal.

3

Sixteen converted liners packed with men had anchored in two lines parallel to the beach, eleven miles offshore and beyond the range of the heavy guns believed to be on the Pointe du Hoc. To Iremonger the decision to anchor so far out seemed to be a mistake because the roadstead was wide open to the elements, and the north-west wind had eighty miles of Channel in which to raise the waves that made it difficult for the small craft – and impossible for some – to make the long run to the shore.

The picket boat was already bobbing alongside *Augusta* as they moved to the port side. Looking down the swaying rope ladder, laden with carbine, pistol, pack and Mae West, Iremonger almost began to wish he'd done the same as Pargeter and settled for a simple revolver.

'It'll be all right,' he said out loud, as much to convince himself as anyone else. 'Don't worry.'

Pargeter's head turned. 'Who's worrying?' he asked.

Iremonger gulped. 'Me, for one,' he said.

As he backed away, he saw Pargeter was removing the papers Hardee had given them from the bulky file he carried. Stuffing them into an inside pocket, he threw the file overboard. He seemed quite unruffled.

'I'll be glad when this hoop-la's over,' Iremonger said, envious of his calm. 'And so will you, because a goddam revolver isn't going to be much use against a charging German.' The comment was a bitter one because Iremonger was humble enough to concede that he was more afraid than Pargeter seemed to be. He needed something to bolster his ego and was trying to convince himself that Pargeter simply hadn't the brains to appreciate danger.

Pargeter smiled, his face calm with knowledge. 'It's always been my experience,' he said, 'that there are usually a lot of unwanted weapons lying around in an affair of this sort, just waiting to be picked up. We're not here to do any fighting but, if we have to, we shall find something to fight with all right.'

He patted the revolver holster and, gripping his walking stick, began to climb over the side, the air-raid warden's helmet rakishly over one ear.

Iremonger saw him jump easily into the bobbing boat. Then, helped by Fitzsimmons, he cocked a leg over the rail himself and began to climb after him. Half-way down, a gust of wind coming round the ship's fantail caught him and set him swaying so that he almost lost the carbine, but a moment later he was hanging on to the ladder above the heaving boat which one moment was brushing his feet and the next ten feet below him.

'Jump!' someone shouted and he jumped, fully expecting a long drop. But the boat was coming up to meet him and jarred against his heels in a way that shook his spine and set his teeth rattling.

Away from the shelter of the big cruiser, the little boat lifted and fell in a terrifying fashion. They had left behind an atmosphere of tension, uncertainty and intense readiness. As they had gone over the side, the crew of the ship had been dressed in full combat equipment, and medical stores had been placed at hand in every alleyway, with sick-berth attendants waiting in the wardroom. Tank landing craft were closing up now, and between them and the beach were several control craft. Gunfire and support ships were also moving into position between the transports and the shore, ready to fire if the Germans discovered them.

'*Gussie's* moving up.' The sailor who spoke did so in a tense whisper.

A transport loomed up above them, its grey sides like cliffs, and a rope ladder with wooden rungs clattered down.

'You first,' Iremonger said.

'Better you,' Pargeter replied, staring pointedly at the equipment with which Iremonger had festooned himself. 'Then I can catch you if you fall.'

Iremonger scowled at the jibe but didn't argue. The picket boat was still heaving in an alarming fashion and, as he grabbed the ladder, he felt the deck suddenly fall away beneath his feet and he was left dangling.

'Oh, Jesus!' The cry came involuntarily. Then his scrabbling feet managed to find a rung and he started up the side of the ship, climbing with difficulty. At the top, someone grabbed his jacket and hauled him to the deck with a crash. Pargeter followed.

It was difficult to move among the crowding men. They seemed to be everywhere, already prepared to board their landing craft. The tannoy was crackling and a cheerful American voice was blaring over their heads. 'Now hear this: This is the biggest party you guys are ever going to go to. So let's all get out on the floor and dance.'

An American colonel met them, frowning. He was obviously on edge and desperately anxious that things should go right. 'You've arrived at a goddam fine time!' he snarled.

'Never mind the happy talk,' Iremonger snarled back. 'Let's see this goddam man, Gavin!'

At that moment a bell clattered and an officer shouted from the bridge. 'Lower all landing craft!' Immediately there was a surge forward that almost swept them apart. Davits screeched as the boats dropped to the water.

'For Christ's sake,' Iremonger exploded. 'Tell 'em to hold it!'

'Hold what, for God's sake?' the colonel snapped. 'The invasion? The order's been given! The guys are debarking!'

The cargo nets had been lowered and men were climbing down, laden with equipment. But the slippery decks of the landing craft below were rising and falling wildly, and one of them disappeared between boat and ship. He was only saved from being crushed by a huge fender that was hurriedly thrust over the side, and was dragged to safety dripping wet, white with shock and enraged at the indifference everyone showed.

As Iremonger watched, furious, the colonel started yelling at the men waiting alongside him. 'Get into those boats!'

'Listen!' Iremonger pulled at his arm. 'I want to see this goddam Gavin!'

'What unit?'

'Seventeenth Rangers.'

The colonel pointed to one of the landing craft just beginning to pull away from the side of the transport.

'The Rangers are in that! They're due to land with the DD tanks!'

'Then hold the bastards!'

'Are you crazy?'

Pargeter stepped forward. 'Put us in the next boat,' he suggested. 'One that lands in the same sector.'

The colonel turned towards Iremonger. 'Who the hell is this guy?' he asked, staring at Pargeter's strange helmet.

'This *guy*,' Iremonger yelled, 'is a top British intelligence officer and he's working with me. For your information, I'm the top American. Now get us in that goddam boat!'

The colonel's jaw thrust forward and he pointed. 'That goddam boat, he said, is *full*! And I'm not going to take anybody out of it for General Eisenhower himself. These boats have been planned to the last round of ammunition, and I'm not changing it!'

'There are only two of us,' Pargeter said. 'We can cram in.'

The colonel glared at him but, despite his distrust, he seemed to prefer him to Iremonger. 'Get going,' he said. 'I'm not supposed to do this, but for five minutes I'm not looking.'

Pargeter pushed Iremonger forward. 'It's our only chance,' he said.

Iremonger stared with horror at the net he was expected to climb down. 'For Christ's sake,' he grated, 'we've only just climbed *up*.'

Pargeter seemed unperturbed. 'We can pick up our man on the beach as soon as we land. He'll not be moving forward until the situation's stabilised.'

'Suppose he's *not* our goddam man?'

'Then we nip along to the next beach. And if he's not with the cavalry recce squadron, we move along to Fox Green. *One* of 'em must be our man. The whole landing area's only eight miles long. We ought to be able to cover that before they start moving inland.'

Iremonger scowled, irritated by Pargeter's matter-of-fact manner. 'You *are* allowing for the Krauts shooting at us, aren't you?' he said sarcastically.

The colonel was glaring again. 'This boat leaves in thirty seconds,' he said pointedly.

As they clambered down the net, Iremonger could hear someone below him quoting the Twenty-third Psalm – 'The Lord is my shepherd, I shall not want.' Next to him on the net was a man carrying mortar bombs attached to his neck in a rolled blanket. 'If I go overboard,' he wailed, 'I'll sink like a brick!'

As they squeezed in among the crowded soldiers, the boat was cast off. As it came beam-on to the sea, its plunging movement became a wicked roll and a man near Pargeter groaned as the spray came over in a drenching sheet of water.

A loud-hailer roared – 'Follow me! Follow me! Get into line! Get into line!' – and as the boats swung away from the side of the ship there was a cheer from the British crew of the transport.

As they turned, one of the craft was caught by a heavy wave and capsized at once, throwing its entire complement of men into the water where they struggled for their lives in the half-darkness and the impersonal violence of the sea, fighting to cling to the upturned craft, their sodden equipment a menace as they reached out for friends floating past in their lifejackets.

The men around Iremonger watched silently, their minds filled with thoughts of German secret weapons. They'd heard of them often enough on the radio from 'Invasion Calling', and now they were wondering 'What were they?' There had been hints that there was oil under the sea, which could be ignited at the moment of landing so that they would all be incinerated as they stepped ashore; and they all remembered how the Germans, stymied on the Western front in the last war, had produced the *Flammenwerfer*. Would the sea be a sea of roaring flame? Or would there be gas? Somebody high up had thought there might, because they'd been issued with gas-masks. Goebbels had done a good job on many of them, and most of them knew what had happened to Exercise Tiger off Slapton Sands.

The darkness diluted and three Spitfires went overhead, making a whistling noise. Higher, relays of American fighters formed a second layer of air cover. *Augusta* moved further in towards the shore, blurred in the morning mist. It was daylight now but the sun was hidden in haze, and the land was only a grey panorama. There was still no firing and the landing craft were now moving like water beetles towards the beach, away from the follow-up craft circling near their parent ships. Every time the bow lifted on a wave, the following plunge left Iremonger's stomach in mid-air. He heard a wretched soldier groan. 'The bastard who invented this goddam boat sure has nothing to be proud of,' he wailed.

It seemed almost too quiet ashore to be healthy. Mine-sweepers, which had cleared the entrance channel, were now heading back to sea, their jobs done, and a naval officer in a landing craft began pulling lost assault vessels out of the confusion in the murky daylight and sending them dodging among the bigger craft to their positions. There was still no enemy reaction.

'There ain't no Germans there,' one disgruntled soldier growled.

But even as he stopped speaking, the first enemy gun – what sounded like an 88 from a light battery – opened up. Five minutes later, other batteries started to fire and as the destroyers replied, the big ships followed, until the whole sky was a sustained roar of gunfire. Then the very air about them shook and there was a tremendous flash. Heads jerked up, and they saw ginger smoke surrounding *Augusta* and a perfect smoke ring rolling away as her 8-inch turrets opened up. The concussion seemed to lift the deck beneath their feet. Then they saw a flickering line of exploding shells just behind the dunes on the shoreline, and smoke was added to the mist.

Texas was firing now at the Pointe du Hoc, a spotter plane circling overhead, the shells digging huge craters in the cape and tumbling chunks of cliff into the sea. As they watched, they heard a rushing, whistling roar, like an express train flashing past overhead. There was a crash and a fountain of water was flung skyward two or three hundred yards astern. It looked so clean and so clear it was hard to believe it contained anything lethal, but as it collapsed they heard the ominous sound of automatic weapons over the heavier guns.

'No Germans?' a grizzled sergeant said bitterly. 'You're out of your goddam mind, son.'

4

Flash-masked gunners on the destroyers were firing on machine-gun posts and pill-boxes and the radar station near the Pointe du Hoc, every available gun hammering at the shore in an attempt to pick out strongpoints.

'I don't know which worries me most,' a man near Pargeter observed. 'What Goebbels said about them waiting for us or my goddam stomach.'

'One thing,' Iremonger said, his face grey-green and miserable with sickness, 'if anything's more likely to make troops going into battle care less about living or dying it was that climbing down from the transport into this goddam thing.'

As he spoke, his heart was thumping chokingly in his chest. He could see the land quite clearly now. In front of them lay a high plateau with precipitous cliffs and steep sandy bluffs, here and there eroded by gullies leading inland. It had a gaunt and desolate aspect, and seemed charged with danger.

'That goddam place looks easy to defend, even with rifles,' the grim-faced sergeant said, and there was a growled assent from the men.

'Don't be daunted if chaos reigns,' Pargeter advised. 'Because it undoubtedly will.'

Above them low scuds of cloud whipped past. The men were silent again now, wrapped in cocoons of loneliness. As they crossed the bows of an LCT, a weary voice came through a loud-hailer.

'Keep away from me! I've got seventy tons of explosives on board! It wouldn't do either of us any good if we collided!'

They appeared to be on the wrong heading and the leading landing craft turned slightly. Immediately all the others followed suit.

'When father turns we all turn,' Pargeter observed, and the wretched Iremonger, who was in no mood for jokes, gave him a sour look.

The landing craft was a bad sea boat and seemed to whip in the waves. It was difficult to hold on course in the strong wind, and, like the other vessels, was veering in every direction as the coxswain fought to hold it steady, one minute riding up the stern of the boat in front, the next fighting to avoid the boat behind. Signal flags snapped in the breeze on the naval ships as the columns formed up and headed for the shore where they could see the orange reflections of huge fires started by the bombers. Then a flight of Lightnings passed overhead, the bold black and white stripes on their wings clear in a sudden burst of sunshine.

On shore, dust was rising from the bombs and shells, opaque-looking and ominous, and a man near Iremonger pointed to the line of landing craft in front. 'They say that first line contains all the veterans of North Africa and Sicily,' he said. 'If I'd done it there, they'd have had to hog-tie me to make me do it again here.'

Iremonger became aware of water sloshing about his feet. Not far away, another infantry landing craft was obviously in trouble. It was low in the sea, wallowing badly. Its engine had stopped and it was swinging beam-on to the waves.

'I think we'd better bail,' Pargeter said quietly and, using his helmet, he began to scoop up water and throw it over the side. A lot of it fell back on the men surrounding him but nobody complained. Iremonger took off his own helmet and began to do the same, reckoning that if Pargeter had escaped by boat from Dunkirk and Greece, he ought to know something about what he was doing. One after the other, more men took off their helmets and began to follow suit.

The coxswain bellowed from the stern above the din of the sea and the gunfire. 'Just keep that up, Colonel,' he said. 'It cain't do no harm!'

There was a crash alongside and a man shouted. 'Oh, Jesus God almighty,' he said, and their eyes followed his pointing finger. A shell had landed in the next landing craft, and where men had been massed there was a sudden gap which could only mean heavy casualties. The LCT didn't waver on its course but men were already jumping over the sides and trying to swim away from it, yelling for help. As their own coxswain swung towards the swimming men, the loud-hailer on one of the control craft bellowed metallically.

'You're not a rescue ship! Get ashore!'

'For Christ's sake, those guys are drowning!'

'You know the orders! You don't stop to pick up anybody!'

The coxswain of the foundering landing craft had lowered his ramp, so that the remaining men could fight their way out but he'd forgotten to stop his engines and the ramp was ploughing over the screaming soldiers. Then, abruptly, the bow went down and the vessel slid beneath the grey sea, leaving a scattering of heads dotting the surface and the cries of drowning men coming thinly over the buffeting wind and the slash of the water.

The cries died away and several men bent their heads to avoid looking. The smoke was thickening as British, American and French warships roared in answer to the raking fire of the German guns. Through the din they heard the rumble of aircraft out of sight above the cloud, then the crash of the bombs sent more smoke billowing out of the mist.

'The bastards have dropped them too far inland.' The sergeant's eyes were full of hatred for the airmen. 'All they've done is kill goddam cows and sheep!'

The landing craft were jockeying for position now, trying to arrive in the correct spot at their scheduled time. Iremonger glared at the beach, his head down to avoid the spray lashing into his eyes. As he turned, he saw Pargeter, his head down, studying the soaked papers that Hardee had given them.

He pointed to the right. 'That's where Gavin'll be,' he said. 'The Rangers' job's supposed to be to blast a way through the wire, and if Gavin's Kechinski, he's going to be first through.'

There were so many landing craft now, they were in difficulties from each other's washes. Then the LCT(R)s sent off their rockets in a crackling rasp of sound and, in a billowing sheet of flame, nine thousand rockets hurtled shorewards. Curving upwards and downwards, the rockets exploded in a second great drenching of explosive, again too far inland to be of any use to the men in the landing craft.

By now the packed soldiers had stopped bailing because scattered shots were coming close to them and, jamming their helmets back on their heads, they started checking their life jackets and nervously lifting the safety catches of their loaded weapons. Up ahead the first lines of boats, swarming like sea lice, were crashing through the surf, pitching violently in the waves. They saw the ramps go down, then an escorting patrol craft struck a mine, and at the crash their own boat shook like a piece of sheet tin. The other vessel rolled over and sank, and a few minutes later one of the tank landing craft also struck a mine and went down. As she up-ended, they could see tanks sliding forward towards the ramp and hear the screaming of crushed and trapped men.

'At least, they're not seasick no more,' someone said in a high, strained voice.

Despite the casualties, craft were managing to reach the shore and the soldiers began to pour out into water churned by fire. Men disappeared and rose, struggling to the surface, their loads of bazookas, mortars, bangalore torpedoes, radios and other equipment dropped in their efforts to save their lives.

Immediately behind them, the LCTs were discharging DD tanks with their aprons up. But as the great machines rolled off the ramps, almost immediately half of them were swamped and foundering, their crews struggling to escape through the hatches.

'What a goddam snafu.' The sergeant jumped on to the side of the boat and began to yell. 'Take the goddam things closer in, you bastards. We need the sonsabitches!'

A boy next to Pargeter, his jaw sagging, was staring at the shore with eyes that were glassy with shock. Pargeter nudged him, feeling he needed something to take his mind off what was happening.

'Not as bad as it looks,' he said lightly.

The boy turned, his eyes wide. 'It looks goddam bad to me,' he observed.

'There are a lot of bullets,' Pargeter agreed. 'But there's also a lot of space between them.'

The noise was indescribable. Destroyers were weaving among the big ships now, laying a smoke screen to hide them from the deadly shore batteries, and the head of the boy alongside Pargeter turned slowly, mechanically. 'You done this before?' he asked.

Pargeter smiled stiffly. 'Not going this way. T'other. This time the odds are on our side.'

'I sure wish I felt as certain as you do.' The glassy look had left the boy's eyes as he became interested. 'You an officer, sir?' He was obviously puzzled by the air-raid warden's helmet.

'Yes. Not your outfit, though. Pargeter's the name. Cuthbert Pargeter.'

'I'm Ackerman, sir. Harry Ackerman, of Charleston, South Carolina.'

Ducking from the spray and flinching from the crashes, Iremonger was treated to the spectacle of Pargeter solemnly shaking hands with the boy as if he were at a garden party. Then a shell crashed nearby and Iremonger saw shapes like grey-brown trees rising from the beach through the haze, and it dawned on him that they were explosions.

'Engineers,' the sergeant said. 'Destroying the obstacles and minefields so we can get in.'

The boy looked at Pargeter. 'What are you doing with us, sir?' he asked.

'Sort of a job.' Pargeter indicated Iremonger crouched with his head down. 'With the colonel there.'

The boy's mouth writhed as he forced a smile. 'That hat, sir. It's different.'

Pargeter took off the navy-blue helmet. 'Yes,' he said. 'Borrowed it. Had to have something.'

There was another crash alongside and a shower of spray hit them. Blinking, they spat out the salt water. The boy was still studying Pargeter. He seemed to regard him as if he were a strange animal.

'You in the British army, sir?'

'Middlesex Regiment. They call us the Diehards.'

'That's a goddam funny name.'

'There are funnier ones,' Pargeter said. 'The Poona Pets, for instance, Blayney's Bloodhounds, the Dirty Half Hundred, the Mutton Lancers, the Holy Boys, the Old and Bold, the Emperor's Chambermaids. That's the 14th Hussars. Know how they got it?' He had replaced the steel helmet and seemed to Iremonger almost to be enjoying himself. 'During the wars against Napoleon, they captured the baggage of Napoleon's brother, King Joseph, and among it there was an item of bedroom furniture made of solid silver.'

'A thundermug?' The boy smiled.

Another wave came over as they neared the surf. Pargeter mopped his face with a red handkerchief. 'The very same,' he said. 'They paraded it with whoops of triumph, mounted guard on it and paid it the ceremonial honours due to a "royal throne". When they were first called the Chambermaids by the rest of the army they took it rather amiss and a few fights started, but later they began to consider it rather a good nickname. Mind you, their trophy, unlike some they'd taken, never appeared on their drum cloths.'

The boy was grinning now. Then he glanced ashore again, and his smile vanished. 'That was sure a good story, sir,' he said. 'I appreciate it. But I guess I'm still scared.' He swallowed. 'All the same, I'm glad I'm here. I'd hate to miss what's maybe the biggest thing that'll ever happen to my generation.'

He stopped and glanced ahead. Two amphibious tanks had been abandoned half-way up the beach, and two landing craft, one burning with an extraordinary brightness and throwing out shells and debris, the other smoking like a tar barrel, were stranded at the water's edge, broached to and lopsided. Then a shell hurtled over their bows and struck a landing craft on their port side which heeled over, swung away and burst into flames as it came to a stop, and they realised that the mushrooming explosions on the beach were not engineers' demolitions, after all, but German shells. Iremonger saw Ackerman's adam's apple jerk as he swallowed convulsively.

'One thing, sir,' he said to Pargeter, staring at the shore with eyes that were suddenly bleak. 'I guess you won't find it so goddam hard to die here.'

5

They were closing in on Omaha now. There was a great deal of smoke and the mist seemed thick enough here to cut with a knife, so that it was suddenly difficult to see what lay ahead.

The coxswain was shouting to a man by the ramp, asking which was the disembarkation spot, and the soldier kept pointing at a yellow-brick house behind the beach, with patterns like Xs built into the walls with darker bricks. There were wrecked landing craft everywhere among the obstructions the Germans had erected. The bristling stakes stretched before them in rows, and the mines on them looked as big as mooring buoys. Iremonger could also see graze-nose shells pointing towards them and reflected how ironic it would be to be blown up by something that looked like a bottle of beer.

His steel helmet seemed too big for him. It kept jumping on his head with the concussion of the explosions and coming down over his eyes. Men on the beach were falling, and he thought how surprised they looked as they stopped and how slowly they spun round before they fell. There was another explosion just ahead and he saw men and machines tossed into the air as if they were made of straw.

Almost without being aware of it, he was watching a man loading his seasick friend's rifle because its owner was incapable.

'Soon be off, Chuck,' he was saying. 'Soon be on dry land.'

Ackerman produced a flask from his pocket and passed it to Pargeter. 'Fancy a drink, sir?' he said. 'Just for luck.'

Pargeter gave him a smile. 'Helps to steady the old nerves,' he said.

'You scared too, sir?'

'Scared as hell. Always am.'

Pargeter felt the hot liquor shooting out its tentacles inside him. Ackerman took a gulp himself, and passed the flask to the man alongside him who was too sick to care; it moved along the landing craft until it was empty and was tossed overboard.

'Won't be much use to me if I get shot,' Ackerman said.

Ahead of them, wrecked DUKWs were swinging backwards and forwards in the surf, and along the tide line men were crouching behind the exposed obstacles, flat on their faces, their heads down, firing sporadically towards the bluffs. As they watched, they saw little darts of wet sand leap up as a machine-gun raked the beach; then a small group of men rose to their feet and began to run. Above the crash of the waves, they couldn't hear the weapon which caught them but they saw the spurts of sand and the men staggering, still trying to move forward on legs which had suddenly become like jelly. Those who weren't hit flung themselves down again.

The breakers in front of them looked ominous and were clearly terrifying to the heavily-laden soldiers. A man at the front of the landing craft began to shout. 'Any minute now! Any minute now!'

The vessel pitched violently and a hailstorm of bullets started to drum against the steel plating of the ramp. Private Ackerman looked at Pargeter.

'They said there was nothing but second-rate troops in front of us,' he complained. 'And that they'd throw down their arms and surrender as soon as we appeared. Those sonsabitches are firing like a regiment of veterans.'

Pargeter tapped Iremonger's arm. 'If I were you, old boy,' he said, 'I'd give that front end of the boat a wide berth.' He glanced at Ackerman. 'Do what I do, son.'

The coxswain was standing up now, one hand in the air. 'Stand by to beach,' he yelled, and the lurching bodies crowded against each other, tense with an upsurge of spirit. Any moment now they'd be out of this dreadful craft.

A fountain of water shot up near their port bow and the sergeant glanced at his watch. 'We're early,' he shouted.

'I don't think anybody'll mind today,' the coxswain said.

The forefoot grounded on the sand slightly askew, flinging them all forward and sideways. Pargeter slapped Ackerman and Iremonger on the back, and jumped for the sea-side of the boat. Iremonger followed him and, sitting on the gunwale, they reached down and yanked Ackerman after them just as the ramp slammed outwards. As the men surged forward, a German machine-gunner, who must have had his weapon trained on the landing craft all the way in, let go with a long burst and the pushing men fell in a stumbling, yelling heap. As others tried to fight their way round them, more automatic weapons opened up until the interior of the landing craft was filled with a mush of bloodstained flesh.

Ahead of them was a shallow arc of sand enclosed by bluffs rising in a gentle slope for a hundred and fifty feet in the direction of scattered stone hamlets, and Pargeter knew from experience that it was an excellent defensive position with carefully concealed machine-guns and artillery hidden among the folds of land. Struggling ashore, he trod on men still squirming in the water. One man, freed of his pack, suddenly shot to the surface, gasping, his face purple.

'Oh, God Jesus Christ!' he said. 'I thought I was going to drown!' As he spoke, machine-gun bullets lashed the water, and with a look of surprise on his face he slid out of sight again.

As the battered landing craft swung, the few men who had escaped the slaughter rushed out of the bows, hunched up, heading for a gap that had been blown in the wire. A man was floating on his back in the water alongside, one arm missing and clearly dying, but though his lips moved, he didn't ask anyone to stop and help him. Crouching, chest-deep in the water, at the side of the vessel, Pargeter edged forward. There were three bodies bobbing together nearby, one just a head and shoulders, another without arms or legs. As the machine-guns finished their deadly work and moved on to find fresh victims, he straightened up and ran for the beach.

All round him men were picking their way gingerly through the mined obstacles. No artillery had landed and there were no tanks to support them. It was a terrible distance to the sea wall below the bluffs and wounded men were prone on the wet sand, crawling in with the tide at a yard a minute until, as they grew weaker and the water began to move faster than they did, they finally drowned. Dead men floated face-down, fouled in the wire, until the flooding tide plucked them free and washed them further inshore to catch on the next line of barbs. A destroyed tank just in front was on fire and the ammunition was fountaining skywards as it exploded. Men crouched behind it but a German sniper on the flank was picking them off one by one.

To Iremonger, Pargeter seemed to know exactly where to go. Dashing between the mined obstacles, he ran up the beach in sweeping zigzags, until his feet crunched on the shingle and pebbles, and he flung himself down in the shelter of the sea wall. A moment later Iremonger arrived alongside him, panting, followed a second later by Private Ackerman.

'Made it,' Pargeter said.

For the moment they were safe, though all round them they could hear the cries of wounded and drowning men. The LCMs full of engineers were coming ashore now, loaded with high explosives, and they saw two blow up in quick succession as they touched off the German mines which in turn set off their cargoes. A bulldozer landed but it couldn't do its work properly for the crowd of men sheltering behind it. As it tried to move up the beach, it was hit by a shell and disappeared in a ball of flame and black smoke from which sheltering infantrymen reeled away to flop down, writhing in their burning clothes.

Dozens of men, stripped by the sea of arms and armour, clung to the wall. More men arrived, top-heavy with their loads, and an officer, standing up and yelling at them to go on, suddenly grunted and sank slowly to his knees, then folded up until his helmet fell off and he was kneeling on the sand, head down, quite dead.

Other men were digging in along the wire, unaware that the Germans had its exact range and would shortly start blasting it out of existence and them with it. A sergeant, shouting at them to get up the beach, stopped and sat down abruptly, clutching his knee and weeping over the bloody mess it had become. Men running up the beach set off a mine and, as the smoke cleared, eight of them were lying with their battledresses smoking, the sand around them tinged with red. The only survivor, running for safety, leapt into the air and landed right alongside Iremonger, his eyes already glazing. As Iremonger stared at him, horrified, Ackerman started yelling for the medical orderlies.

Down the beach more ships and landing craft were blazing. Bodies were scattered everywhere and medical orderlies were doing their best to attend to the injured. To Iremonger it seemed as if every gun on the beach was aimed at him personally, and when a bullet glanced off his helmet he dived hastily for shelter. 'Oh, brother,' he said. 'Someone sure did a good job with these hats.'

'You ask me,' Pargeter observed grimly, 'I'd say that the only people who're going to stay here will be dead. They ought to be moved on somehow.'

'That's not our job.' Iremonger flinched as a mortar bomb showered them with grit. 'And I guess it's occurred to other people, too.'

Crawling and scrambling among the crouching men, they made their way along the sea wall, showered constantly by pebbles and sand from the explosions. It was a terribly overcrowded area as more soldiers arrived from the sea, most of them too stunned for coherent thought. There seemed to be little future for them there, because they couldn't go back and the only way they could move – forward to the road that ran behind the sea wall – was barred by coils of concertina wire in the cuttings that carried pathways from the beach. Men with wire cutters who had tried to clear them hung on the coils in grotesque shapes.

'Where the hell are the bangalore torpedoes?' an officer was shouting.

'They were lost in the landing, lieutenant,' his sergeant yelled back above the din. 'Together with our radios and mortars – *and* our goddam tanks and artillery!'

Iremonger crawled up to the lieutenant and, as another mortar bomb landed, they both dived head-first for the shelter of the wall again.

'I'm looking for the Seventeenth Rangers,' Iremonger yelled.

The lieutenant stared at him. His eyes looked wild but he wasn't panicking.

'Why?' he demanded.

'I'm Intelligence. I'm looking for a guy called Gavin.'

'For Christ's sake, Colonel, I got better things to do just now!'

'I've got to find this guy,' Iremonger insisted. 'He might well be a German agent.'

'Here? For Christ's sake, no German agent would be *that* goddam silly!'

'This one might,' Pargeter said.

The lieutenant looked at him. 'Who the hell's this guy?' he snapped. 'He looks like your German agent himself.'

'Major Pargeter,' Iremonger said. 'British Intelligence. We've chased this goddam German all across the South of England and we have reason to believe he's right here on this beach.'

'Well, good luck to you, Colonel. They're over there – what's left of 'em.'

It was difficult to move, and half the time they were scrambling over dead, wounded or frightened men, or men who were simply crouching against the stone wall waiting for someone to emerge as a leader and tell them what to do. The remnants of the Rangers were huddled together in an angle of a low sandy cliff. One or two of them were digging into it with bayonets to make a protecting overhang, and all the time, at every crash, the sand dribbled down on top of them.

Reaching them, Iremonger and Pargeter dived into a shell hole. There were two dead GIs in it, and they scrambled out again and jumped into another which appeared to be a headquarters because there was a man with a radio. The lieutenant in charge looked barely old enough to shave but he was putting on a good show of being a commanding officer.

'Everybody else's dead,' he explained. 'And I sure as hell don't know your Captain Gavin.' He turned to one of his sergeants. 'Do you know Captain Gavin, Sergeant?'

The sergeant had a bandage round his head and another round his hand. He gestured towards a group of men hugging the cliffs twenty or thirty yards away, and Iremonger and Pargeter set off towards them, bent double.

'If it's the new officer,' a haggard-looking soldier told them, 'then he's had it. You ask me, Colonel, I think we've *all* had it.' He jerked a hand towards a body lying face-down at the edge of the shingle. 'That's him, sir. He got us here and went back for the sergeant. That's the sergeant further back.'

Pargeter looked at Iremonger. 'Doesn't sound like *our* chap,' he said. 'Stay here, Linus. I'll go and look.'

'I'll come with you.'

'Don't be damn silly! If they knock us both off, who's going to find Kechinski? You can be the hero next time.'

He pushed Iremonger back among the huddled men and ran bent-double towards the dead man, to fling himself down on the seaward side of the body so that it protected him from the firing. Iremonger saw him roll the body over and lift his head to stare at the dead face, then he scrambled to his knees and began to run for the wall again, the bullets kicking up the sand at his heels.

'It's not Kechinski,' he panted as he crashed into Iremonger. 'Wrong jaw. Wrong nose. Wrong face altogether.'

His back against the wall, he wrenched the list from his pocket and scanned it quickly. 'Lieutenant Loftus, Third Cavalry Recce Squadron; Captain Jones, Ninth Mortar Unit.' He jerked a hand. 'Third Cavalry Recce's on Easy Red and the mortar people are on Fox Green. We've got to get along there.'

Iremonger stared at the beach. 'I sure hope we make it,' he said fervently.

They were just on the point of leaving when one of the soldiers scrambled forward to where they were huddled. His eyes were red-rimmed and there was blood on his hands.

'Colonel, sir,' he said to Iremonger. 'When are we goin' to move off from here? These guys only need someone to kick their butts to get 'em going, sir. They're less scared than mad. They're mad as hornets, sir. For Christ's sake, we'll never win this goddam war if they stay where they are.'

Iremonger glanced at Pargeter. 'Where are your officers, son?'

'They're all down, Colonel. The Krauts got 'em. There's a machine-gun up there just beyond the wire. But there's a sign up there as well. It's for a minefield. There's a gap, sir. I reckon we could get through it and take that goddam gun in the rear.'

Iremonger frowned. 'I'm sorry, son,' he said. 'I've got a job to do.'

The soldier's eyes hardened. 'Where, Colonel?'

Iremonger's hand jerked. 'Right along there, son. I've got to find someone.'

'Getting these guys off their butts is more important than finding someone, Colonel!'

Iremonger's eyes flashed. 'Then get 'em off their goddam butts, soldier!' he snapped. 'You obviously know what to do. Do it!'

'For Christ's sake, Colonel, they won't take any notice of a government issue soldier like me! I got no rank.'

'Then, for Christ's sake, promote yourself!'

'I can't do that, Colonel.'

Pargeter fished in his pocket and, withdrawing a blue pencil, he grabbed the soldier's arm. 'Any NCOs about?' he asked.

'No, there ain't.' The soldier looked at Iremonger, his face grimy and stained. 'Who the hell *is* this, Colonel?' he demanded.

'Never mind who it is,' Iremonger said. 'Just accept that he knows what he's doing.'

The soldier looked at Pargeter, his features white under the dirt. 'There's a sergeant down there,' he said in a stiff prideful manner. 'He's got his head down and he's pretending he's hit, but he ain't. He's shit scared, that's all. Shit scared.'

Pargeter smiled and, licking the blue pencil, began to scrawl three stripes on the soldier's sleeve. 'This makes you a sergeant, old boy,' he said. 'Promoted in the field. Best way to be promoted. Get back up there to your friends and tell them you've just been made up. And get 'em doing what you want 'em to do. By the look of you, I think you can.'

The soldier stared down at the three stripes on his arm, faintly awed. 'They'll take no notice of that,' he said, but he sounded as if he didn't believe it.

–

It was now around eight o'clock and the rhino ferries were heading in to unload. Their arrival had been planned on the assumption that sixteen gaps would have been cleared through the obstacles and wire, and they were in immediate trouble. Only six gaps had been cleared and there was an immediate snarl-up. There were trucks, jeeps, bulldozers, half-tracks and cranes, and, since no paths had been cut through to the road behind the beaches, there was nowhere for them to go, while the beach was narrowing all the time as the tide pushed onwards towards the bluffs.

Shells began to drop among them and a petrol lorry exploded in a vast ball of fire that scattered fragments of metal and wood all over the beach and into the sea. Every time a vehicle was hit and disabled, it jammed up still further what slight movement might have been possible. Offshore, other landing craft and DUKWs, trying to find a place to land and nudging each other in their efforts to force a way in, had to retreat. Scores of dead lay about, and on vast stretches of the beach nothing moved. Groups of men huddled behind broken vehicles or grounded landing craft, waiting for someone to clear a route for them to the bluffs. But the engineers had been decimated and the German gunners turned their weapons on them whenever they gathered to destroy some obstacle.

'This sure is the nearest thing to hell I've seen,' Iremonger growled.

The Germans were cutting the beach in half with their weapons, a blast of fire hurtling down so that it was virtually impossible to move from west to east. Further along, the firing seemed slacker and they made their way back and huddled once more under the sea wall. A sergeant scrambled across the shingle and dropped alongside Iremonger.

'Colonel, sir,' he panted. 'Get on your hind legs, for Christ's sake, and tell these bastards they've gotta move forward!'

Iremonger's eyes narrowed. 'Not me, Sergeant. It's not my job.'

'Colonel, sir, with respect, I guess it's anybody's job.'

'Anybody's but mine, Sergeant. I have an important job to do already.'

The sergeant's face became bitter. 'What's more important than getting these guys forward, Colonel?' he said.

'What we have to do could be a *lot* more important – if not for today, then for tomorrow and the day after and the day after that.' Iremonger gestured towards the sea. 'For your information, we're going back down there to find a landing craft to take us off this beach and put us on again further east.'

'Oh, yeah, sure! I heard that one before, Colonel.'

The sergeant's eyes fell on Pargeter's flat helmet and they narrowed at once. 'Who's this guy, anyway? He sure as hell ain't no American.'

Iremonger looked at Pargeter and then at a group of dead men sprawled in the shingle under the wall, their helmets scattered about them. Abruptly he reached up, snatched off Pargeter's helmet and sent it skimming down the beach. While Pargeter was still protesting, he reached for one of the pudding-shaped American helmets and clapped it on his head in its place.

'This is Major Pargeter, Sergeant,' he said. 'And, due to a misplaced pride in his own uniform, he insists on wearing a half-baked helmet which gives no protection to his neck or ears. Now, for Christ's sake,' he ended with some satisfaction, 'he'll be wearing a decently designed one. Come on, Cuthbert, let's go.'

As they started to move away, the sergeant yelled after them. 'Colonel, sir, we need officers!'

'Then find them, sergeant!'

'Right, *Colonel, sir*!' The sergeant's voice was angry. 'And, by Christ, we'll find *real* officers not chicken-shit pen-pushers. And I hope to Christ you *do* your job, because guys like you ain't no goddam good to us here!'

6

Crouching with his back to the sea wall, the Fox stared at the grey murk above his head. Nearby, an American soldier was moaning over a shattered arm. Around him other men were chattering angrily, blaming their senior officers for the shambles.

He listened with only half his attention on what they were saying, enveloped in his own loneliness and almost unaware of the insane din. There had been a devastating simplicity to the disaster, and no dry landings. Omaha beach was strewn with stove-in craft, drowned vehicles, burned tanks, and scores of bodies sprawled wet and shapeless on the shingle. Only the lightly wounded were being taken away; the more serious cases were still lying under the sea wall and, from one end to the other, the tidal shelf was littered with water-soaked debris washing in the surf. There had been enormous losses of equipment, of supporting artillery, and of the bulldozers that were needed to clear the obstacles for the second tide later in the day.

For a moment he felt physically sick. In all his career he had never experienced anything as awful as this, and even though the Americans were his enemies he felt a tremendous compassion for them in their misery and fear. The less resolute crouched behind the beach obstacles.

Those who had crossed the beach hugged the sea wall, helpless, shocked and leaderless, enfiladed by German guns from the bluffs on the other side. No one could raise his head for the machine-guns behind; and all along the beach, disunited and confused men, without cohesion or artillery support or armour, waited for help to come. Even the gaps that had been blown in the beach obstacles had not been marked before the tide had covered them, and the following landing craft had no idea where they were and wouldn't have until the tide ebbed.

Despite everything, however, despite Hitler's wild promises and the vaunted strength of the Atlantic Wall, the Americans *were* ashore and, staring back at the sea, at the immense weight of shipping, the Fox had a feeling that they were not going to be driven back. Despite the appalling casualties they were suffering, despite the damage, despite the complaints of the men huddled around him. He was an experienced man and he knew that if they had the courage to hang on, they would still be there at nightfall because the naval guns were stopping any counter-attacks from building up.

A mortar bomb exploded nearby. Though the men round him ducked their heads and flinched, he didn't move. He wasn't afraid of dying. Only of dying too soon, because all at once he wanted to survive long enough at least to put right some of the things that, for the first time, here on this awful beach, he had seen were wrong. He had been startled at the hatred there had been in England for the Nazi Party and, regarded from the distance of an opposing country, it did seem to be run by perverted, cruel and stupid men corrupted by too much power. Even Hitler's edicts these days smacked of senility, obsession and madness. Politically, he was already finished because he'd not had the sense to compromise, to stop when he'd achieved everything Germany wanted, and the Fox now desperately needed to be alive to see present policies dropped in favour of subtlety – to align the Americans against the Soviets and make the eastern border secure.

Another cluster of mortar bombs fell and he started, aware that he'd been daydreaming. A young lieutenant appeared, running towards him, and landed alongside in a flat dive.

'The captain's been killed,' he said. 'What should we do? There's a pill-box at the top of the draw.'

The Fox had no doubts at all as to what they should do. There was only one way to go and that was forward. The papers stuffed in the inside pocket of his uniform demanded exactly that. But he knew there were machine-guns covering the pill-boxes, because the Wehrmacht had always been expert at covering fire, and he realised the lieutenant was asking the impossible.

He turned his head. Guns were firing over him towards the sea where men huddled against the beach obstacles and behind wrecked landing craft. They hadn't a chance of moving forward at that moment, and it occurred to him that enough casualties could make the shaken men around him retreat. And if they did, if the beach were evacuated, he could feign death and stay where he was until the advancing Germans arrived.

His body warmed at the thought. 'Who have we got?' he asked.

'Danvers, Kuski, Ryan, you and me. And about thirty-five men, and three sergeants.'

'Get them together. Can Danvers lead?'

'He's an ex-sergeant. He knows what to do.'

'Right. Me, Danvers and Kuski. Then Ryan and you.'

'Shouldn't I be at the front?'

'We can't all be at the front.'

They assembled the men on either side of a gully. None of them was very eager but they seemed willing enough to follow anyone who was prepared to lead.

'You know where the pill-box is?'

Danvers nodded. He was a square-shouldered, tough-looking man, but his face was grey as though he were looking straight at death.

'Bazooka?'

'Right here.'

'Plenty of grenades?'

'Every man has them.'

'Right, let's go!'

He stood up and began to run up the gully. Danvers and Kuski stood up with him, yelling at their men to follow. Immediately, a machine-gun opened up, and as he saw the bullets scattering the sand in front of him, he was caught by an uncharacteristic and wholly unexpected terror. Where it came from he didn't know – perhaps from the wish he'd had to survive, to help put right the things in Germany which had suddenly seemed so wrong – but it was powerful enough for him to fling up his arms and throw himself instinctively into the shelter of the dunes.

When he scrambled to his knees, the panic had gone as fast as it had come and his head was clear again. He saw Danvers stumble to his knees, his head down in an attitude of prayer. Then another burst caught Kuski in the neck, almost tearing his head off his shoulders. A corporal appeared, carrying a bag of explosive charges. As he reached the pill-box, he threw the sack against the base of the concrete wall and began to poke a charge on a long stick into the ventilating hole. The fuse began to splutter and he began to run, but a machine-gun caught him and he went down, rolling end over end like a shot rabbit. As he fell, the explosions came, one on top of another, and chunks of concrete flew into the air and thudded into the sand. The pill-box was split open, smoking and black, and behind it a German soldier was running in circles, burning from head to foot and screaming. A sergeant dropped him with a single shot, then fell himself, and the forward move stopped again as the attack melted away and men dived for shelter. Standing up, feeling he must redeem himself, the Fox grabbed at a man crawling back on hands and knees, and, hoisting him to his shoulders in a bone-cracking heave, stumbled back down the gully.

At the bottom, the lieutenant flung himself to the sand alongside him, his eyes wet with tears. Of the forty men who had started up the gully only twenty had found their way back, their eyes wild, their faces shocked. The Fox dragged the last of them out of sight, still startled that the instinct for survival in him had proved stronger than the ingrained discipline of years. For a moment, he was even faintly ashamed, but he was consoled by the fact that twenty or more casualties added to the total of disaster on Omaha could be directly attributable to him. 'Get down,' the lieutenant yelled. 'Get down!'

The Fox turned to look at him. His fear was gone now and he was eager to prove to himself that he wasn't afraid. He knew the machine-gun firing down the gully couldn't reach him, but, as he turned, a cluster of mortar bombs hit the beach with a series of nerve-shattering crashes, and something struck him at the side of the head, spinning him round. At the same time, something else tore into his thigh just above the knee with the kick of a mule, and he spun round and sprawled in the sand.

The lieutenant dragged him to safety. 'Jesus God,' he was babbling. 'It was my fault! I talked you into it!'

Conscious of the sky whirling about him, his eyes and mouth full of grit, a tremendous feeling of lassitude welling over him, the Fox realised he was muttering in German and forced himself to concentrate.

'How bad is it?' he asked.

'You've been hit in the face but it doesn't look bad. Your leg's different.' The lieutenant had taken out a knife and ripped up his trousers. 'We'll get you to a dressing station.'

'I wish to stay here.'

'Look, you've done all a man could do. Leave it to me.' He tried to protest again but it was no use. Things were fading and little lights were clicking out inside his mind. Doors were shutting one after the other and his thoughts became a jumble as he slipped into unconsciousness.

7

The thin wet line of khaki was still dragging itself ashore. Despite the disaster, fresh waves of men were continually adding to the number sheltering at the head of the beach. There were still a lot of men crouching among the obstacles, but the Germans were turning their machine-guns on them now and only those who could summon the courage to dash up the beach seemed to have any chance of life.

In the congestion offshore, a landing craft was sinking and a control vessel was circling to pick up survivors. The demolition teams trying to blast a way through the obstacles had suffered paralysing casualties but, here and there, crouching in the lee of a scattered bulldozer or a truck, men were still bravely struggling to plant their explosives.

The German artillery continued to harass the circling landing craft, and Pargeter noticed that some of them were turning towards the east. Then, as he crouched under the sea wall, he heard a signaller, trying to snatch some sense out of the tangle of messages in the ether, turn to his next-door neighbour and announce that gaps had been blown in the defences on Easy Red beach and that reinforcements were being directed there.

A small landing craft heading for the shore, caught in the cross current, was swept against one of the tetrahydra obstacles, and there was an immediate explosion. As it swung away, burning, men jumped overboard, only to drown under their heavy equipment, while the German artillery turned their fire on the damaged craft. After four direct hits, it disintegrated and sank.

Every now and then more men arrived with the tide like flotsam, their units mixed, sometimes separated from their commanders by half a mile, and inexperienced leaders were unable to get their bearings. Another landing craft came ashore, but the tide was rising so rapidly its commander kept having to heave his vessel off and rebeach to land his shipload of men. The German gunners over the hill were firing at his barrage balloon, and it suddenly seemed to dawn on him that it was drawing their fire. A sailor ran towards the hawser and swung at it with an axe, and the balloon was swept away by the wind, still fired at by the German gunners.

Three more small landing craft were heading in now and three more sheltering behind the broached-to vessel began to back off. Iremonger jabbed Pargeter. 'Cuthbert, boy,' he shouted above the racket, 'I figure we're in the wrong goddam place! You don't hitch a lift a hundred yards back from the road. We should be down there.'

Pargeter nodded and, jamming his helmet down on his head, he set off after Iremonger. As he ran, a 75-mm gun concealed in the exit from the beach began to fire and was joined immediately by an 88 in a concrete casemate. An explosion just in front of him flung up a shower of wet sand and water and knocked him flying. As he picked himself up, he saw Iremonger still running for the sea. Reaching the water, he flung himself down behind a wrecked bulldozer, and a moment later Pargeter joined him.

There were a dozen men crouched behind the vehicle, poking their heads round the sides to watch the firing. Iremonger nudged Pargeter and, rising to his feet, started running again. As Pargeter set off after him, the men round the bulldozer started shouting.

'You yellow bastards,' they roared.

They splashed down again, soaking wet, near a smashed landing craft.

'One of the hazards of this job,' Pargeter panted, 'is that everybody thinks we're afraid.'

'I'll buy that,' Iremonger yelled back. 'Because they might be goddam right!'

The three landing craft approaching the shore were just grounding. The ramps slammed down and the men poured out. As they emptied, Pargeter and Iremonger leapt to their feet and started to splash through the shallows.

'Hold it,' Iremonger shouted to the coxswain of the nearest vessel. 'For Christ's sake, hold it!'

The ramp was just lifting as he scrambled aboard and pulled Pargeter after him. The coxswain started yelling from the stern.

'Get the hell outa here, you yellow bastards! I'm dumping men, not picking 'em up!'

Iremonger struggled to his feet. He'd long since lost the carbine but he still wore a pistol in its holster at his waist, and he advanced down the length of the craft to the man at the tiller with it in his fist.

'Listen, soldier,' he said, 'if any other bastard calls me yellow, I'll blow his goddam head off! Now shut up! I've got a job to do, and you're going to help me do it!'

The soldier looked scared. 'Look, Colonel,' he said. 'I've gotta get back out there and pick up a bunch of officers!'

'They can wait!'

'They'll sure as hell chew my balls off, Colonel!'

'Take your pick. Either they do or I do.' Iremonger pointed along the beach towards the east. 'Over there,' he went on. 'I've got to contact the Third Cavalry Recce Squadron on Easy Red.'

'When, Colonel?' The man at the wheel was staring horrified at burning landing craft. 'Now?'

'Now,' Iremonger snapped. 'Get going!'

'Colonel, sir—' the soldier clearly didn't wish to go where so much damage was being done '—I gotta get back to the ship for these officers!'

Iremonger whirled. 'For Jesus' sake, man,' he roared, 'you can see what's happening, can't you? It's not a time to go by the book! Unless I get to Easy Red, there'll be a lot more dead men floating in the water here. Perhaps even you! Now back off and get going!'

The ramp slammed into place and, as the engines roared, the vessel went astern into deeper water. All round them the mined obstacles loomed up and Pargeter could see the helmsman's adam's apple jerking as he swallowed nervously. His clothes saturated, his face grimy with smoke and the oil in the water, Iremonger glanced at Pargeter who was just lighting a couple of cigarettes. As Iremonger stared at him, he took one of the cigarettes from his mouth and handed it to him. Then he handed the other to the helmsman who took it in a dazed way.

As they moved in, a gun opened up on them and they could hear the bullets striking the front and sides of the vessel at an angle and whining off over the sea.

'This seems to be a private stretch of sand,' Pargeter said. 'They don't seem to want us.'

The beach obstacles had played havoc with the landing craft ahead and they could see several awash where they had been blown up. Then a DC3, appearing from nowhere and just turning in the sky above them, was caught by the anti-aircraft fire and its port engine fell from the wing, to drop in a curving arc right on to the ack-ack battery that had shot it off.

As they grounded, Iremonger and Pargeter scrambled over the side, and crouched behind a group of corpses. Nearby, as though separated by their rank, were three officers, all captains, all shot through the head, rolling backwards and forwards in the surf.

As the firing died a little, they pounded up the beach to where a crowd of soldiers huddled together under the lee of the cliff, looking like a lot of swarming bees. There were a great many dead about, but the survivors seemed in better shape than the men on Dog Red beach. There were several wounded men with them, their heads or arms bandaged, but they still clutched their weapons and were glaring at the cliff with savage eyes as they wondered what they could do.

'Who's your senior officer, Sergeant?' Iremonger demanded as they dropped among them.

'You are, I guess, sir. Have you come to take over? I sure hope so, because the colonel and the major are down and we left Captain Cruse and Captain Smart right down there.' The sergeant's hand pointed down the beach. 'We're all right. But we're split up a bit, and we need pulling together.'

'I've not come to take over, Sergeant,' Iremonger said. 'I've got another job to do. Haven't you any officers?'

'Lieutenant Cuddy, sir. He's only a kid outa school but so far he's doing okay.'

'Where is he?'

The sergeant pointed to another group of men further along the cliff, and Iremonger slapped Pargeter's shoulder and began to run.

Lieutenant Cuddy looked about seventeen but, as the sergeant had said, he seemed to be well in control of himself and in command of his men. As they dropped down alongside him, he was shouting above the noise into the ear of a husky sergeant old enough to be his father.

He looked up as they appeared. 'Thank God you've come, sir. We seem to need someone here with a bit of experience.'

'I'm sorry, son,' Iremonger said. 'I've got other things to do. I'm looking for the Third Cavalry Recce Squadron and I've sure as hell got to find them. Are they here?'

The lieutenant stared at him. 'You mean you haven't come to take over, sir?'

'No, son, I haven't. I'm afraid you're still on your own.'

'We'll be all right, Lieutenant,' the big sergeant growled. 'We've got these Krauts licked between us. You've only to say the word. The guys'll go.'

The lieutenant nodded. 'Okay,' he said, and Pargeter saw him swallow down his fear.

He pointed. 'Over there,' he said. 'They're supposed to be a mobile signalling station, but I guess their equipment's still down the beach somewhere.'

As he turned, there was a flat thunk behind them and a man who'd been lying stretched out on the sand, squinting along his rifle for the sight of a German head, jerked sideways, a bloody hole in his temple.

'Sniper,' Cuddy said. 'Get these guys further in to the cliffs, Sergeant.'

By this time, the gunfire support ships were pounding the bluffs behind them, showering them with grit and stones and pulverised earth.

'Give those naval guys a chance, sir,' the sergeant said. 'Then I guess we can go. I'll go first, sir.'

'No, Sergeant,' Cuddy said. 'I'll go first. That's my job. You make sure the men follow me.'

He looked at Iremonger and Pargeter and pointed to a narrow gap in the bluffs. 'That's where we're going, Colonel. I hope you find the cavalry boys. Come on, Sergeant.'

He stood up and started running, his young voice thin in the racket. The sergeant rose behind him, shoving and kicking at his men until they were all running too.

Iremonger watched, fascinated and appalled by their courage. Then a machine-gun opened up, and the lieutenant stopped dead. His mouth opened and shut several times but he was unable to speak and all he could do was wave feebly.

'Keep going,' the sergeant roared at the running men. 'Keep running! You're away, so, for Christ's sake, don't stop!'

The lieutenant was still waving, but his arm had dropped and they saw the pistol fall from his hand. He was still standing, shuddering, his tunic red with blood, as the men swept past him. Then the big sergeant snatched him up in his arms and they disappeared out of sight over the bluff.

Iremonger stared after them, his face bleak, then he turned to Pargeter. His mouth opened then snapped shut again.

'Come on, Cuth,' he said. 'I guess we've a job to do too.'

8

Running along the beach in the shelter of the bluffs, they flung themselves down again by a group of men crouching against the cliff. Some of them were wounded and there were several dead sprawled further down the beach. A youngster with glasses was moaning in a loud nasal whine.

'Those goddam Krauts just won't stop fighting and my ma didn't raise me to be shot at! My ma raised me to be a farmer! It was hard too! There wasn't no money and my ma—!'

'For Christ's sake,' another man snarled, 'shut up about your sonofabitchin' ma! *My* ma didn't raise me to be shot at by the goddam Krauts either, but I'm not making no song and dance act out of it!'

'My ma—'

The second speaker leaned over and the complaints came to an abrupt stop as a fist caught the youngster at the side of the head. 'Pass that on to your goddam ma, son, with the compliments of Private First Class Le May!'

As Iremonger pushed among the group, the muttering stopped. Occasionally mortar bombs fell a little further down the beach, scattering them with sand and grit.

'Where's your officer?' Iremonger demanded.

The man called Le May jerked a hand towards a corpse lying a few yards away. 'That's Captain Ward,' he said.

'Lieutenant Trenchard's over there. He's dead too. The bastards caught us just as we reached shelter. I reckon they was waiting for us. They let us get out of the landing craft. Then they blew it up with all our equipment. They let us run up the beach and opened up with machine-guns just as we reached the shingle. They got Captain Ward and Lieutenant Trenchard right off.'

'I'm looking for a Captain Loftus.'

'Ain't no Captain Loftus in this outfit, Colonel.'

'Any new officers?'

'Sure, sir. One. Captain Cornelow.'

'Where is he?'

Le May pointed along the beach. 'We took him over there, Colonel.'

'Took him?'

'Sure, sir. He was hit. That guy sure had guts, sir. We're not supposed to be a fighting outfit, but he sure was set on getting through to the Germans.' He pointed again and they saw several bodies lying in a cutting just above. 'We got him back, Colonel, and took him along to the medics.'

'What was he like, this Cornelow?'

'Big guy, sir. Your age. Sure knew his stuff. No nerves. He wanted to get to them Krauts and he was sure going to try. Lieutenant Gray, sir, went with him.' He indicated one of the bodies on the bluffs. 'That's Lieutenant Gray, sir. He thought that if Captain Cornelow could go, he could go too. The machine-guns got him soon after.'

Pargeter produced the photographs they had of Reinecke. 'That him?' he asked.

Le May looked at Pargeter's unexpected uniform and then at Iremonger. 'Who's this guy, sir?' he demanded suspiciously.

'British officer. We want to see your Captain Cornelow. Is that him?'

Le May looked at the photographs. 'Looks like him, sir, but this guy in the pictures ain't wearing Uncle Sam's uniform. It's – Christ, I don't know what it is!'

'It's a Polish uniform,' Pargeter said.

'He was a Pole?'

'He was a goddam Kraut,' Iremonger growled. 'Thanks, soldier, for your help. If he stopped one, mebbe we can catch up with him. We've been trying long enough.'

–

By this time the beach presented an incredible picture of waste and destruction, the German obstacles swamped by the rising tide in a great wilderness of smashed landing craft and vehicles nudged by the floating bodies of dead soldiers. All around them, men clutched their wounds, their faces pasty with shock, silent, tight-mouthed, trying to reconcile their conduct with the pain of their injuries.

As Iremonger rose to his knees again, brushing off the dirt, a mortar bomb landed a few yards away. His helmet flew off and he was lifted up and flung on to his back. As he sprawled on the sand, a fresh burst of machine-gun bullets cut a swathe around him. Pargeter jumped up and, grabbing him by the ankles, dragged him into cover. After a while, Iremonger's eyes opened and he began to sit up. Pargeter immediately pressed him down and pulled him further under the shelter of the cliff.

His eyes and mouth full of sand, Iremonger struggled to sit up, blinking and spitting out grit. 'Thanks, Cuth,' he said. 'You're better at this sort of thing than you look. I can just see you winning a VC or sump'n for giving me a fireman's carry across a blazing beach. Can you do a fireman's carry?'

A thin smile flashed disconcertingly across the grave face. 'I come from a long line of firemen,' Pargeter said.

Iremonger shook his head. Bells were ringing inside it, and Pargeter looked at him, concerned. 'You all right?'

Iremonger shook his head again. 'They lowered the boom on me, Cuthbert. I can't hear. I'm deaf! I've gone deaf, Cuth!'

Pargeter grinned. 'It'll go,' he shouted in his ear. 'It was a close one. Stay here, I'll go on to the dressing station.'

'Not damn' likely! If you're going, I'm coming too. Just hold your water until I find me a helmet.'

There were several bodies under the cliffs, and a lot of scattered equipment. Iremonger grabbed for the nearest steel helmet and he was just about to put it on when his jaw dropped. He looked up at Pargeter with a sick expression on his face; inside the helmet was part of a man's head and brains.

Pargeter knocked the helmet from his hands and pushed another one at him. Iremonger nodded, his eyes bleak. 'Come on,' he said. 'Let's go.'

But, as he spoke, another clump of mortar bombs dropped just down the beach and they had to dive back for the shelter of the cliff, their heads down, blinking at the crashes which seemed to strip the flesh from their nerves. Then the machine-guns opened up yet again, rippling along the sand in little waves. Iremonger looked up at the sky, as though wondering where the air forces were, then he scrabbled round in the hole they'd made in the shingle with their movements and stared at the cliff. Somewhere above a machine-gun was firing.

'I think we'd better stay where we are,' Pargeter suggested.

'Mebbe you're right. If that goddam Fox *has* been hit, he sure won't be moving far.'

—

They seemed to have been pinned down on the beach for hours and Iremonger glanced at his watch.

'Eleven o'clock,' he said. 'Jesus, is that all? I thought we'd been here weeks.'

His back to the bluffs, he looked across at Pargeter. The Englishman had a gift for remaining motionless for long periods at a time, only his eyes moving. He was as filthy as Iremonger, soaked and covered with oil; a small, strong, grubby figure, self-contained and capable, but still a little remote. His eyes, like Iremonger's, were ringed with tiredness but Iremonger was surprised at the amount of energy his small frame still contained.

'You're a goddam funny guy, Cuthbert,' he said.

Pargeter smiled his secretive smile, as if the day's challenge had lifted his spirits. 'Other people have said that too,' he agreed.

The destroyers were coming in closer now, their guns ranging on the cliffs above them, and as they watched, a landing craft came in at full speed, smashing through the obstacles, and ground to a stop. The men aboard poured out at once and dived for shelter behind stranded vehicles. A second landing craft tried to do the same but, as it crashed up the beach, one of the mines on a tetrahydra exploded against its side. It continued to move ahead, however, and finally ground to a stop alongside the other, and they saw that the coxswains of other landing craft, realising what could be done, were doing the same. Destroyers backing up the movement were so close inshore they seemed in danger of touching the bottom, and at point-blank range they were firing at the German strongpoints all along the bluffs.

The battle, which had produced a lull after the pinning down of the first waves, seemed to have wakened up again. Under the covering barrage, the engineers were completing the demolitions they had begun seven terrible hours earlier. The shore was still a waste of wreckage, burning vehicles and battered craft; and with none of the exits yet open, messages had been sent to the fleet to send no more vehicles, only men. But at last, incredibly, order was beginning to emerge from the chaos, and men were beginning to fight for more than just their lives. Above them the bush fires were still burning on the bluffs, but the morbid fear of mines which had so worried the first men ashore was beginning to recede. For hours, wounded had lain in the minefields, not daring to move, then, seeing the grisly remains of dead men, someone had realised that if they had exploded the mines with their deaths, their friends could at least cross at the points where they'd died.

A few brave men walked erect, cutting wire, taunting others at the water's edge, and an engineer lieutenant was on his face probing the sand with a knife for mines. Slowly, apart from a few units which were beyond rallying, they began to move.

A man with a brigadier-general's star was striding up and down in a hail of fire waving a revolver and shouting to the soldiers to get off the beach. Along the shingle, behind the sea wall and crouched in the coarse marram grass at the base of the bluffs, they stared at him, as though unable to believe that anyone could stand upright and live. Then one of them rose to his feet and ran to an abandoned bulldozer and climbed aboard. The bulldozer's engine exploded into life.

Seeing the general still untouched, other officers began to clamber to their feet and stand upright. A colonel with a wounded hand tied up in a bloody handkerchief was moving through the dead and the dying and the shocked groups of men, talking to them and pointing; gradually, in ones and twos and small groups, they began to rise to their feet and head inland. There was even a trickle of German prisoners, dazed by the gunfire, their hands in the air, anxious to surrender.

The naval guns were knocking chunks off the bluffs by this time. The German fire had slackened, and men who had landed at Sicily and Salerno began to come out of their shock to probe their way forward. A sergeant, lying in the marram grass, used a bazooka to knock out a pill-box at the top of the slope. Another sergeant was running among the groups of huddled men, kicking at them with his boots. 'Get up, you yellow bastards,' he was shouting. 'I'm going. Who's coming with me?'

German fire was still taking its toll, but now the soldiers weren't diving for cover but running, bent double, for shelter higher up the bluffs and off the beach. Suddenly the whole beach was on the move. Men who not long before were cowering in fear of their lives were now standing upright, shouting and cheering, and the groups moving inland clotted together and became a steady stream.

Iremonger swung round to face Pargeter. 'We did it,' he yelled. 'By Christ, Cuth, in spite of everything, we did it! Come on, let's go find that goddam Fox!'

9

The dressing station had been set up in a hole scraped in the beach under the bluffs. The dead lay in rows under blankets, labels attached to their feet for identification. A few bandaged men huddled nearby, their faces blank and expressionless. One of them was a bazookaman who still gripped his weapon with grimy straining fingers. A medical corpsman bent over him, giving him an injection into a bared arm, while nearby a sergeant was busy writing details in a notebook. The beach behind them was clearing now. Exhausted, hungry men were finding time to drink self-heating soup out of tins. Amazingly, above the racket, it was possible to hear birds singing in a way that lifted the spirits, and there were even butterflies fluttering about the bluffs.

Near the sea, amidst the monstrous chaos of charred wreckage and tortured steel, bodies were being laid out in long lines to await collection; and more wounded soldiers, many in severe shock, waited for the medical orderlies. There were so many of them the orderlies didn't seem to know where to start, and there was a terrible politeness among them as they waited. Nearby, oblivious of the machine-gun bullets, a weeping man was throwing stones into the sea as though he had nothing to do with the battle. A group of prisoners was standing knee-deep in the water; gaunt, worn men still dazed by the bombardment.

More men were collecting the waterlogged corpses gruesomely jostling each other in the surf and, as Iremonger and Pargeter arrived, two stretcher-bearers stumbled through the sand with a groaning man. The sergeant with the notebook looked up. 'Right femur,' one of the stretcher-bearers said. 'Hit by a piece of shell. It's sprinkled with sulphanilamide but I guess he's lost a lot of blood.'

The sergeant pointed to the blood transfusion unit. 'Over there,' he said.

A doctor bent over a man who'd been hit by mortar fragments, digging scraps of clothing out of the wounds.

'I'm looking for a guy called Cornelow,' Iremonger began but the doctor gestured without even looking up.

'See the sergeant,' he said. 'I'm too busy.'

Iremonger and Pargeter crossed to the sergeant with the notebook.

'Cornelow,' Iremonger said. 'Captain Cornelow. Third Cavalry Recce Squadron. You got him here?'

The sergeant looked up. He seemed exhausted. 'Colonel, sir,' he said. 'Honest to God, I lost count of the number of casualties we've treated.'

Iremonger's voice was gentle. 'It's important, Sergeant.'

The sergeant seemed almost as shocked as some of the men being treated. 'Colonel, sir,' he said. 'Every one of these guys with me is bone-tired. Out of one guy we picked around two hundred pieces of metal, looking for the one that had done some damage. None of 'em had. He was just punctured like a colander. Then there was a kid with a little hole below his hip that didn't look at all serious. But, underneath, the bone was shattered and the arteries were severed. He's over there.' His hand jerked at the line of blanket-covered bodies. 'There's another guy who was hit in the wrist and the shell fragments went right up his arm to his elbow. It didn't even break the skin but he has a hell of a great blister from the heat of the metal.'

'Sergeant,' Iremonger bent down, speaking slowly. 'It's important that we find this Captain Cornelow.'

'Colonel, sir,' the sergeant raised red-rimmed eyes. 'For all I know, he's been evacuated. A few have. We got 'em down to the water and aboard landing craft.'

'I'd like to know, Sergeant.'

The sergeant looked up. Down the beach, MPs and beachmasters were beginning now to bring some order after the seven hours of chaos. Landing craft still burned, the oily smoke rising in thick clouds to the sky over the pounding surf, and the low tide was exposing the ruin of the earlier hours and the bodies caught under the barbed wire.

'I'll look, sir.' The sergeant turned the pages of the notebook slowly. 'I've been awake now, sir, Colonel, for nearly seventy-two hours.' He began to read out aloud. 'Anderson, Donald; Zimmermann, John; Dube; Cunningham; Janzen; Phillips; Tallerday; Wozenski; Hupfer; Glisson; Jones—' the weary eyes lifted. 'Sir, it'll take all day! There've been so goddam many on this stretch of beach.'

'Sergeant, it's important,' Iremonger urged. 'We have reason to think this Cornelow is a German.'

'Sir, we didn't have no Germans through here. We just looked after our own boys. Any case, there've been goddam few Germans captured round here.'

'He wasn't captured, son. He was in uniform – the same uniform you're wearing.'

The sergeant looked puzzled. He was too tired to take in the implication of what Iremonger was saying.

'We have reason to think he was a German spy, Sergeant,' Pargeter said. 'We have to find him.'

'German spy? I guess you'd better see the lieutenant, sir.'

'Sergeant—' Iremonger's voice grew harsher '—who's got the names of the guys who've been treated here?'

'I have, Colonel.'

'Then look through your list, son, and find him.'

The sergeant shook his head but he went back to his notebook, muttering to himself. 'Tucker, Vandervoort, Sweeney, Schultz, Kirk – Christ, sir, there are hundreds!'

'Keep looking, Sergeant.'

The sergeant struggled through the book, interrupted now and again as one of the medical corpsmen appeared with a question or a wounded man came up or was reported by the men carrying his stretcher. Dazed by weariness, he kept losing his place but, driving him, forcing him against his own inclinations and theirs, they pushed him through to the end of the list of names.

'No Cornelow,' the sergeant said.

Iremonger frowned. 'Could he have died?'

'I got the names here, sir. Ain't many, thank God! We kept most of 'em alive.'

'Go through 'em, Sergeant.'

A group of stretchers arrived and the sergeant had to break off to take down particulars. The men on them were all lightly wounded and talkative, and they had to wait with gritted teeth for them to be cleared.

'Sir, for God's sake,' the sergeant appealed, 'you can see how busy we are!'

An officer joined them. He was a doctor and stood stretching his back, stiff with bending over injured men. He was frowning.

'What the hell's going on here, Sergeant?'

'Mr Willetts, sir, these gentlemen insist on me finding some guy they say is a German.'

The lieutenant turned on Iremonger. 'We have no Germans here,' he snapped. 'We haven't treated any Germans.'

Iremonger drew a deep breath. 'This German was wearing an American uniform, Lieutenant,' he grated.

The doctor looked as weary as the sergeant. 'You can see how busy we are. Now that the beach's clearing, it's only starting.'

Another group of wounded arrived, helping each other. The doctor broke off to direct them to the teams of orderlies, and the sergeant, grateful to be off the hook, followed them to take their names and particulars.

The doctor was just turning away when Iremonger laid a hand on his arm. 'Lieutenant,' he said. 'Doctor. Believe me, I wouldn't be bothering you in the work you're doing if it weren't important.'

'What's more important than saving lives?'

'Lieutenant, that's just what we are doing. This guy, this Captain Cornelow, is a German officer.'

The doctor's eyes narrowed. 'Are you kidding me?'

Iremonger scowled. 'Do I look as if I'm kidding? I've been here since five o'clock this morning. As long as you have. Do you think I'd go through that lot just to be kidding?'

The doctor's expression changed. 'No, I guess not. But, hell, you can see—'

'—how busy you are. Sure I can, Lieutenant. But—' Iremonger's voice rose '—for Christ's sake, just listen to me for a minute, that's all! One minute. If we don't find this guy, it might well be that all those boys going inland now will be driven back into the sea tomorrow. You, too, for that matter. This guy we're looking for knows exactly what the follow-up plans are and he's trying to get them to his buddies over there. We've got to find him. He was with the Third Cavalry Recce Squadron and he was wounded and brought over here. His own men brought him. They told us. We have to find him.'

The doctor stared at Iremonger and then at Pargeter but he made no comment. He stood thinking for a moment. 'Does the sergeant have no record of him?' he asked.

'The sergeant has no record among the wounded. If the guy's died, that's fine. We know where we are. But, Lieutenant, this goddam landing's been jeopardised half a dozen times by the possibility of its secrets leaking out. This is just another. And this is the most important of all because this guy knows what's going to happen tomorrow and the day after and the day after that, all the way to Berlin maybe, for all I know. Now, do you help us find him?'

The doctor said nothing for a moment. Then he called the sergeant to him. 'Give me your notebook, Sergeant,' he said. 'You got another?'

'Yeah, sir, but—'

'Open it. Start a new record. I'll use this for the time being.' As the sergeant went away, grumbling, the lieutenant checked carefully through the list of names. 'No Cornelow among the wounded,' he said. He began to read again, turning the pages over. 'No Cornelow among the dead. You sure he was brought here, Colonel?'

'I'm sure of nothing except that I have to know what happened to him. The guys with him say he was hit and they brought him here.'

The lieutenant frowned, brushing aside a medical corpsman who demanded his attention. His expression distracted, he called the sergeant back.

'Sergeant, did we have any men who were wounded and insisted on returning to their units?'

'One or two, sir. Not many. Most of 'em were glad enough to stay put.'

'Any officers?'

'One or two, sir.'

'Could this guy, Cornelow, be one of them?'

'Christ, sir, I don't know. One of 'em wouldn't even give his name. Nellar told me.'

'Where's Nellar now?' Pargeter asked and the sergeant's hand jerked towards the line of bodies.

'There must have been somebody working with Nellar,' the lieutenant said. 'Find him, Sergeant.'

'Sir, for Christ's sake—!'

'Find him, Sergeant. It's important.'

The sergeant stumbled away, his shoulders bowed.

The doctor followed a medical corpsman who was waiting alongside and bent over a stretcher. Down the beach still more men were trying to land through the line of ruined vehicles that clogged the surf, heading inland in a steady stream now, struggling up the slopes, weighed down by weapons and equipment.

Iremonger sighed, suddenly weary. 'Christ, I didn't enjoy biting that sergeant,' he said. 'The guy was whacked. Come to that, so am I. So are you.'

Pargeter shrugged. '*I'm* hungry.'

'Ain't much here.'

'We could always eat each other.'

Conditions were still improving. German artillery and automatic weapons continued to fire on the beach but with diminished intensity now. The engineers were blowing more gaps through the sea wall, bridging anti-tank ditches and clearing minefields. As the tide had receded, the demolition teams had made a fresh assault on the underwater obstacles in readiness for the next high tide. Ashore, more engineers, not waiting for the last house to be captured, were bulldozing a by-pass through the village of St Laurent to the Bayeux-Isigny highway, and a steady flow of traffic was building up.

The sergeant returned, followed by a medical corpsman wearing spectacles. His hand was bandaged. The doctor looked up from a stretcher case he was examining and joined them.

'This is Corpsman Deery,' he said. 'He was wounded when Nellar was killed. They were down the beach bringing in a wounded officer. Go on, Deery, tell the colonel here what you know about the officer you and Nellar treated. The one who wouldn't give his name.'

Deery shrugged. Like the lieutenant and the sergeant, he seemed to be drugged with tiredness. 'Hell, sir, I got his name.'

'You did,' Iremonger said. 'What was it?'

'I didn't write it down. But I got a look at his dog tags.'

'What was it, son? For God's sake, what was it?'

'Cronelow. Cronlow. Something like that.'

'Cornelow?'

'Might have been. Hard to remember. Hard to remember anything, but I think it was.'

Pargeter produced his photographs. 'Was that him?'

Deery looked at them. He didn't seem to be focusing too well. 'Looks like him, sir. But, Jesus, sir, so much was going on at the time. We were swamped with wounded just then, sir.'

'Go on, son,' Iremonger urged gently. 'You're doing all right. What happened?'

'Well, the guy had been hit in the thigh and the head, sir.'

'Bad?'

'Mortar, I think, sir. The head wound wasn't too bad but the thigh wound was a lulu. No bones broken, but there was a hell of a hole there.'

'Go on, son.'

'He sat up while I was looking at his dog tags and pushed us away. Nellar pushed him down again—'

'And then?'

'And then he got on his feet. I told him, for Christ's sake, sir, you're wounded, but he wouldn't have anything to do with it. Sir, that sure was a brave guy. He just wanted to get back to his unit. Nellar told him he was in no fit state to go back anywhere but he said, for Christ's sake, he was *going* back. Then he said something I didn't understand.'

'Didn't understand?'

'Foreign language, sir. German I thought. My mom was German, sir. I speak a bit of German. It sounded like

"*Ich muss gehen…*" Something like that. I didn't catch it properly.'

Iremonger looked at Pargeter. 'Go on, son,' he encouraged. 'You're doing pretty good.'

'Then he started speaking English. He said, "I've got to go," And Nellar said, "Then for Christ's sake, sir, let me do something about that leg!"'

'What did he do?'

'He seemed to see the sense then. He agreed to let us fix it. We sprinkled it with sulpha powder and put a pad on and bandaged it. That guy sure had guts, sir. I know what I'd have done if I'd had a hole in me like he had.'

'Did he give his name?'

'No, sir. He was kinda impatient. Said he ought to be off. Nellar kept asking. We're supposed to keep records. But he wouldn't give it. "I'm not dead," he kept saying. "I'm not even dying. Forget it. I've never even been here." Sir, that guy oughta had a medal.'

'Go on, son,' Iremonger said gently.

'And then he went off. Limping. His leg bandaged, his face beginning to swell. Me and Nellar watched; then we went down the beach for this officer who'd lost a leg. That's when Nellar was—' the boy gulped. 'The officer was dead when we got to him.'

The lieutenant laid a hand on the boy's shoulder. 'Thank you, Deery,' he said. 'That'll be all.'

'Not quite,' Pargeter said. 'Where did he go, Deery? Back to the Third Cavalry?'

Deery struggled through his tiredness to make his mind work. 'No, sir. He went inland right here.'

His hand moved to indicate the men now filing through the cutting in the bluffs.

'Did he join any particular unit?'

'Jesus, sir, I don't know. He just went. It sure looked like hard work to me, but he went all the same.'

Iremonger nodded. 'Thank you, son.' He turned to the doctor. 'Thank you, Lieutenant. I guess it's up to us now.'

He turned to Pargeter. His shoulders were bowed and he looked as weary as the medical corpsmen. 'I guess the bastard's still one jump in front of us, Cuthbert,' he said. 'We don't know where he's at, who he's with, or any goddam thing. We're right back to square one.'

10

There was a sullen smell of smoke in the air, foul and threatening. The night was full of the grind and groan of moving vehicles. Despite the darkness, the build-up had not stopped and the lorries and men and guns and tanks, directed by the beachmasters from their sandbagged bunkers, were still moving steadily inland. A few German planes had flown over and a few bombs had been dropped, but the worst danger had been from falling splinters from the ack-ack shells which had sliced through tents, torn down branches and clanged on lorries.

Iremonger watched Pargeter. He still preferred to keep things simple, and Iremonger's carbine was all he carried apart from his revolver and the papers in his pocket. Iremonger had now acquired a tommy-gun from among the hundreds of weapons abandoned along the shore. As they'd left the beach, lorries had been rolling down ramps to enter the water, accelerating into the shallows to prevent the sea reaching the ignition. When they failed, and the steam rose in clouds, they were immediately surrounded by men with ropes attached to bulldozers to drag them clear.

The first real sign of France they'd seen had been a ruined cottage on the edge of a village with an advertisement for St Raphaël painted on the wall and, beyond it, a profusion of small fields with clumps of trees and hedges on high banks. Before it had grown dark, the German artillery had wakened up and they'd lain like frightened rats in an orchard, pressed to the ground, their faces in the grass. As they'd moved ahead at last in the lull that had followed, MPs were sticking up notices – 'You are in sight of the enemy', and 'Drive slowly. Dust causes shells'.

The village had been destroyed by the Germans to make a strongpoint and had been captured only a short time before. Several houses were still smoking but, despite the uproar, cattle continued to graze in the fields among the swollen bodies of other animals and, as they watched, a shell had killed a cow, spewing its stomach and intestines all over the grass.

An MP, only his eyes visible under the crust of dust and sweat that covered his face, had given them a warning. 'No straying,' he said. 'Keep off the roads. Don't touch anything. And avoid areas marked by cloth strips. They're still mined.' He jerked a hand at a row of corpses laid out neatly at the side of the road, their faces covered by their helmets. 'And keep your heads down. There are snipers.'

Men pressed around them, crowding the narrow strip of occupied countryside to the point of discomfort. Through the blackness of the night, shouts could be heard over the sound of engines and the clatter of tank tracks, and the darkness was broken here and there by the winking cats' eyes of blacked-out vehicles. Nobody was happy, though news had come through that on Utah Beach substantial gains had been made and the seaborne troops had linked up with the airborne division at Ste Mère-Eglise. The British and Canadians had failed to reach their first-day objective, Caen, but they were firmly established ashore at Gold, Juno and Sword beaches.

There was a jumpiness in the air. There were no rear areas on the Omaha bridgehead and no more than a hundred tons of supplies had been landed; men, thankful to be alive, were writing to relatives to tell them so from the backs of trucks, slit trenches and former enemy strong-points. Field kitchens were moving up and latrines were being dug. A few civilians stood in their doorways, staring at the river of men and machines moving ashore.

Despite the horror of Omaha, it had been easier than had been expected, but the Germans usually had an ace up their sleeve and no one wanted to be where the ace was played. Some men slept the sleep of the exhausted, but there were as many awake, staring nervously into the dark-ness, their ears cocked for the sound of panzers, because no one knew what the Germans were up to. The last of the wounded were being removed, their faces composed and serene as nuns' under their bandages.

Pargeter and Iremonger crouched in a shell-smashed farmhouse in the village. There had been several French civilians there when they'd arrived, mostly women and children, and a knitted tricolour and a bottle of wine had been produced.

'Is it le D-jour?' one of the women had asked.

'Yeah,' Iremonger had said. 'It sure is.'

The civilians were now poking among the wreckage of houses smashed into rubble by shells. They looked like fruit-pickers, taking a dusty item of clothing here, an old chair there, a cooking-pot or an unbroken plate, oblivious of the gunfire behind them and the occasional rattle of a machine-gun in front; indifferent even to the possibility of snipers as they struggled to bring some order to the torrents of stone and timber which had been their homes.

The sky in the west showed red, silhouetting the damaged buildings, and nearby a haystack and a house crackled in flames. The place was full of men, yet somehow in the semi-darkness it seemed deserted, weird and unearthly, like a picture by Hieronymus Bosch. Somewhere a church bell tolled. To Pargeter, who hadn't heard a church bell in England since they'd been reserved for invasion warnings in 1940, it sounded strange. The village was silent but alive, almost as if its breathing could be heard.

He was toying with his K-ration and his smooth round face was calm. Iremonger frowned at him, puzzled as always to have found him a reliable comrade and a useful friend. His views on human beings were changing a lot. Hitherto, he'd always set store by bold, active men willing to take risks, but now he realised he'd been over-conditioned by Hollywood's version of courage. Too many times during the past day he'd seen big men with strong arms and strong jaws cowering with their heads down while smaller, frailer ones, with no pretensions to heroic looks, had done their duty without flinching. Courage didn't come in properly labelled packages. Brave men could be any shape, any size – like the soldier they'd made into a sergeant; like Lieutenant Cuddy; Deery, the medical orderly; Pargeter himself. If anyone failed to fit the established picture of a brave man Pargeter did. Yet he'd never flinched during the whole dreadful day and his experience had more than once saved their lives.

The night was dark, windy, wet and cold. In the next room a man was snoring and another muttered in his sleep. Then Iremonger heard an aeroplane overhead and, the guns of the ships lying offshore and the anti-aircraft weapons, which had been dragged up the beach, started to crash. The battered buildings shook and Pargeter raised his head. As the splinters began to clink and clatter on the tiles, his mouth lifted in a smile.

Occasionally there was a solitary shot in the darkness or the short stutter of a machine-gun as some nervous sentry saw shadows in the night. Because he was hungry and over-tired, Iremonger felt half-frozen and began to wonder if there would ever be a time again when he wouldn't be in danger of his life, cold, damp, worried and sickened by the thought of failure.

With no real knowledge of the Fox's whereabouts or what he was up to, they'd spent the whole of the evening moving among the forward units looking for him. Nobody was interested. Nobody wanted to know. They were all far more concerned with eating, sleeping or making sure they were safe from a snap attack.

'For Christ's sake—' the answer had come a dozen and one times '—you guys think we've nothing better to do than search around for some guy who's got lost?'

It had taken all their patience, sometimes a lot of anger, sometimes even Iremonger's rank and the letter he carried in his pocket signed by Eisenhower himself, before anyone would listen to them. Nobody had willingly believed their story. They were ashore, weren't they? That was all that mattered.

Just before dark they had thought they were close to where the Fox was hiding. He was somewhere just in front of the village where they now waited. Nobody knew who he was but his photograph had been identified several times – not with distaste but with admiration.

'That's the guy,' one sergeant had said. 'Jesus, his face was black with bruising, and he was dragging a game leg, but, hell, that guy was sure determined to get forward!'

'He looked like death,' a young lieutenant, the sole unwounded officer of his regiment, had told them. 'Gaunt, battered and covered with blood, and with his trouser leg slit up to the waist. But he sure as hell refused to give up. If we win this war, it'll be because of guys like him.'

They hadn't bothered to enlighten them. It would have taken too long and they probably wouldn't have believed them, anyway. With the image of a hero in their minds, they just wouldn't have seen things the same way.

Trucks and jeeps loaded with ammunition bumped and skidded into the village and a few tanks clattered up, deploying to stop any sudden counter-attack by the panzers. Further back, in the ruined square, MPs were waving the traffic forward, and engineers were pushing aside the wreckage of houses with bulldozers and filling in the shell-holes. Jeep ambulances, with wounded strapped across the top, jolted back between the taped-off mine-fields towards the beach; and in the fields just off the beach, graves registration troops were burying the dead.

Iremonger stared around him. Like so many French farmhouses, this one looked as though it had been built to withstand a siege. It had thick stone walls, narrow windows, slate roofs that were holed here and there, a pump in the kitchen, and a deep safe cellar that was crammed at the moment with sleeping men. On the wall there was a photograph of three men in uniform, with

French flags in the corners and the dates, 1914–1918, and the words, *Morts pour la patrie*, underneath. A machine-gun burst coming through the window had shattered the glass and riddled the picture, pinning it to the plaster and killing the dead men all over again.

Iremonger shifted uncomfortably. The floor was hard and his backside was sore.

'Cuthbert,' he said, 'are you sure we've done everything we can?'

'I think so,' Pargeter answered in his old-maidish way. 'There isn't a thing we can do now until daylight.'

'Suppose he makes a break for it in the dark?'

'With that leg of his, he'll not make any breaks,' Pargeter said confidently. 'And we've asked everyone to report if they've got him. They'll be sending runners any time now.'

'Yeah, I guess so.' Iremonger tossed a cigarette across. 'He can't move fast. That's one thing.' He paused, frowning. 'It's a goddam funny thing, Cuth,' he went on in puzzled tones. 'When this thing started, I hated this guy's guts. Now I'd like to capture him alive. I'd even speak up for him when he was tried.'

'I don't think he'll give us that pleasure, Linus.'

As they talked, a soldier pushed into the kitchen. 'Colonel Iremonger, sir?' he asked.

Iremonger sat up. 'Sure, that's me. What have you got, son?'

'The captain said to tell you that this guy you're looking for isn't with us, Colonel.'

'He was sure of that?'

'He checked every man, sir. There were a few of the 116th mixed in with us but this guy wasn't one of 'em.'

'Thanks, son. What's your unit?'

As the soldier disappeared, Iremonger sighed and ticked off a name in the written list in the notebook alongside him. Next door a field telephone jangled and a dirty face appeared round the door.

'Colonel, sir. For you.'

Iremonger disappeared to the other room and Pargeter heard him talking. When he came back, he shook his head and placed another tick alongside the list.

'That guy's going to slip through our fingers, Cuthbert,' he said.

During the next hour, the telephone jangled several times and the ticks increased on Iremonger's list. One or two messengers also appeared but there was little joy in the messages they brought.

'For Christ's sake,' Iremonger said. 'Where is the goddam guy? We're going through them with a fine-toothed comb. Every goddam outfit – engineers, signallers, infantry, artillery, mortar men, Rangers, tankmen, cavalry, medical corps; even the outfits setting up signalling stations and dressing stations and refuelling posts. He must be somewhere. He's been seen in this village. He's been identified.'

While he was still talking, a soldier pushed into the candlelight.

'Colonel Iremonger, Intelligence?'

'That's me, son.'

'Lieutenant Doss. Jim Doss, Colonel. 18th Infantry. I think we've got your Colonel Cornelow.'

Iremonger glanced at Pargeter. '*Colonel* Cornelow?' he said.

'That's what he is, sir.'

Iremonger frowned. 'Show him the pictures, Cuthbert,' he said.

Pargeter produced the photographs and Lieutenant Doss stared at them by the light of a pressure lamp on the table.

'That's the guy, sir. Colonel Cornelow.'

'Last time we heard of him, he was *Captain* Cornelow.'

'Well, he sure as hell isn't now, sir.'

Iremonger thought for a moment then his eyes lifted. 'You holding him, Lieutenant?'

Lieutenant Doss shook his head. 'Colonel, sir, my commanding officer, Major Dallas, said *he* wasn't going to arrest him. It would have to be done by you. That guy, sir, arrived up with us, wounded and all – twice, mebbe three times – and all he wanted was to get forward.'

'He sure as hell did,' Iremonger growled. 'So far forward he could join the Germans. Where is he?'

'Right in front of us, sir. We pushed forward an observation post and he offered to go. We'd run out of officers, Colonel, and he said he'd take the job. He'd been with us all evening, sir. And, being wounded and all, the major thought he was a great guy. He didn't want him to go but the guy said, hell, he couldn't run much with his leg but he could sure as hell sit down behind a few sandbags and watch for us; if only to let the rest of the guys get some sleep. We thought he was sure some soldier, sir. That leg of his looks bad. He ought to be evacuated by rights and he probably will be tomorrow. The major didn't believe what you said about him.'

'Nobody does,' Iremonger growled. 'Can you pick this guy up for us?'

'No, sir, we can't.' Doss shrugged, as weary as them all. 'There's a fixed machine-gun playing on the ground between us and where he is. There are three of them: this guy, a sergeant and a private first class. Nobody's getting across that patch of ground. Not even in the dark.'

Iremonger looked at Pargeter who nodded.

'It looks as though it'll have to be us, Linus,' he said.

11

They found Major Dallas sitting at a table in what had once been a farm-worker's cottage. Part of the roof had gone and there was no glass left in the window frames where blankets had been hung to provide a black-out.

He was a gaunt, lean-faced Kentuckian and he looked as exhausted as everybody else. On the floor around him men were sleeping, huddled with their weapons round the walls. His eyes were red-rimmed and he didn't bother to rise as they appeared behind Lieutenant Doss.

Pargeter produced his pictures, rather like a magician producing a rabbit from a hat. 'Colonel Cornelow?' he asked.

Dallas stared at them and nodded. 'Yeah, that's the guy all right.'

'I want him,' Iremonger said.

'What's the guy done? He ought to be recommended for a medal.'

'If we don't get him,' Iremonger said, 'he'll probably get one. But it won't be a Congressional Medal of Honour. It'll be an Iron Cross, with palms, oak leaves, daggers and what the hell else they give them. The guy's a German.'

'He can't be!'

'Major,' Iremonger said, 'you aren't telling me. I'm telling you. His name's Reinecke. Lieutenant-Colonel

Ebert Klaus Reinecke of the Wehrmacht. Also Hans-Heinrich Müller. Also Taddeus Kechinski, 20th Polish Recce Regiment, and Lieutenant Jack Kechinski, 113th Infantry, US Army, and a few others as well. Now, it seems, known also as Colonel Cornelow, of no known outfit, temporarily attached to you.' He looked at Pargeter. 'Show him the one Hardee gave us, Cuthbert.'

Pargeter pushed forward the photograph showing the Fox in German uniform with high-peaked cap, flyaway breeches and polished boots.

'I don't believe it,' Dallas said.

'You heard what happened to Exercise Tiger in Lyme Bay?' Iremonger asked.

'Yeah, sure.'

Pargeter tapped the photograph with his finger.

'You're kidding!'

'Son,' Iremonger said, 'I wish we were. If we were, we sure as hell shouldn't be here, and we shouldn't have been on Omaha yesterday. We'd have been somewhere a goddam sight safer.'

'But this guy went forward,' Dallas said. 'I saw him using an automatic rifle with my own eyes. He's out there now.'

'Sure he is, because the first chance he has, he's going to make a break for the German lines. He's got plenty of reason. In addition to his Iron Cross, they'll probably make him a general for what he's got in his pocket.'

'What the hell *has* he got?'

'Every goddam detail of our moves from here on in. If he could have, he'd have got them to the Krauts long before now and, if he had, *you* wouldn't be here. You'd probably be floating face-down in the sea, together with a lot of other guys. At least we stopped him doing that. Now we have to stop him letting Rommel know what our next move is and where we're heading. That's why he's here and why we're here. There was no other way of doing it. That's why he's out there in front. Because the only way he can get what he's got across will be to let himself be captured or something. It wouldn't matter much if he were killed, so long as he were killed getting into the German lines so they could find the papers we know he's carrying.'

'Which is why he's promoted himself to field rank,' Pargeter said.

Dallas was staring at Iremonger. 'Jesus, Colonel, I sure hope you don't think I didn't check enough on him.'

'Don't worry, son,' Iremonger said. 'He's bluffed plenty of other people. If you'd asked to see his papers, he'd have produced them okay. He's got 'em, I guess.'

'But the guy seemed to have so much guts!'

'That's what everybody says. Even I've got to grant him that. But it's still our job to nail him.'

Dallas stared at Lieutenant Doss. 'I guess I can't leave here,' he said. 'We're too thinly spread and orders are to wait for the armour. But I'll send someone with you to show you the way. He's in front of Max Schneider's section and there's a sniper out there. He'll tell you where to keep your heads down.'

—

Lieutenant Schneider's men were dug in round another cottage a hundred yards further forward. The living room smelled of sweat and gunpowder and there were hundreds of spent cartridges lying on the floor, crushed out of shape by the feet of the men in the room. The furniture was piled against the windows, the wooden chairs splintered and broken by bullets, and the men were sitting on the floor against the walls.

Dawn was breaking, and, all along the fringe of the perimeter, men were waking, cold and stiff and dirty from a night of fitful sleep in shallow scraped holes, pinching themselves to reassure themselves that they were still alive. Behind them they could hear the grind and clatter of tanks and bulldozers trying to drag wreckage aside. They were still desperately in need of supplies and, because they couldn't discharge at sea into smaller ships, the British had started beaching the heavy LSTs. When they didn't break their backs, the Americans had begun to do the same.

As the sky lightened, they could see the shape and curves of the countryside. This would probably be the most important day of the invasion. This would be the day when the counterattacks would come and, at the end of this day, they would either be in the sea again or know they were in France to stay. The men in the cottage looked nervous, and Lieutenant Schneider had the air of a gun dog which had just seen a bird; tense and still, his face against the wall, his eye peering round the corner of the window into the growing daylight.

'There's a tank out there,' he was saying over his shoulder. 'If they bring up tanks, we're French fried, with ketchup.'

'We still got a bazooka and two shells, sir,' a corporal said from the back of the room.

Iremonger glanced at Pargeter. The tension in the cottage was like a coiled cobra.

Schneider withdrew his eye from the window frame and saw Iremonger, Pargeter and the man who had led them forward. 'Hi,' he said. 'You brought reinforcements?'

'No,' Iremonger said. 'We want to get forward.'

Schneider's teeth bared in a grimace. 'That's a laugh, Colonel. Nobody's going forward from here.'

'We have to reach your observation post.'

'Not even there. Those guys'll be lucky if they get back.' The tired eyes clouded. 'I'd be sorry about that. They've got guts, all three of them. But at the moment we can't do a damn' thing because there's an 88 in the far corner of the field and about three goddam heavy machine-guns.' He indicated two or three huddled shapes lying in front of the cottage. 'That was last night. They caught us as we tried to move forward. That's Ufford, Smith and Cohn. Lieutenant Howard's somewhere out there, too. We could hear him crying out for a long time. I guess he'd dead now.'

His face was worn by strain so that he looked like an old man, but he managed another grimace of a smile. 'We've called up the armour for help,' he said. 'But there's nothing we can do until daylight. We know exactly where the Krauts are. Sergeant Duffee pinpointed 'em, just before Colonel Cornelow joined him.'

'Anything else out there?' Pargeter asked.

'Just the tank and some guys behind it. What else do you want? An SS division?'

'Nothing else? Nothing behind?'

'Not that I can see.'

'Where's the observation post?'

269

Schneider pointed. 'See that bank? They're there. Under that bush. Three of 'em. Colonel Cornelow, Sergeant Duffee and Pat O'Neil.'

'And the Germans?'

Schneider's hand moved again. 'Along the line of the hedge. Over to the left. They've moved up. They've been dropping m.g. fire on the field all night. And we know there's a tank, because we've heard it moving.' Schneider indicated the bazooka team waiting near the window. 'The little guy stands in the window and the man who fires rests it on his shoulder,' he said. 'Chiefly it depends on who's got the most nerve, because we've got to let it get within range, and the kid's got to stand in full view until it does.'

The man at the window turned. 'If it comes, Lieutenant, it'll come round by them dead Krauts that Lieutenant Howard knocked over before he was hit last night.'

'Yeah.' Schneider nodded. 'And when it comes, I want nobody firing before the bazooka or the bastards'll know where we are and then *nobody'll* be standing up in *any* window.'

The daylight seemed to come slowly, unwillingly, as if the events of the previous day had unnerved the new one and it was reluctant to appear.

'It's a good job he got that wound in the leg,' Pargeter said, 'or he'd have been away long before now. He's only got to get to the hedge and through it, and we've lost him. There are bound to be Germans on the other side of the bank.'

As the light increased they saw leaves moving briskly and Pargeter's eyes narrowed.

'There's a gun in there.' Pargeter frowned. 'It's going to be hard moving inland.'

'We're getting the tanks ashore now,' Iremonger pointed out.

'Not much good in this kind of country. They have to stick to the lanes and the Germans can lay an ambush at every bend.'

Iremonger scowled; then he gave Pargeter a little shove. 'Come on, Cuth. Let's get moving. You're frightening me to death. Yesterday was bad enough. Don't make it worse by talking about today and tomorrow.'

'Wait! Listen.'

As they cocked their ears, they heard the sound of aircraft, and three Typhoons howled over them, the first of the light catching the underside of their wings. They saw the rockets leave them and heard the explosions as they struck. Banking about a mile away, the aircraft came back along the far hedge. They'd obviously spotted the Germans and they came down with their guns firing. The hedge was torn to shreds and a man fell through it to sprawl in the field in front of them.

'He's got to go now!' Pargeter said excitedly. 'He'll not get another chance! Come on, Linus! We're on!'

Still staring into the increasing light and hardly hearing, Iremonger suddenly became conscious of Pargeter snatching at his sleeve. As he turned, Pargeter pounded on his arm, and Iremonger found himself following the Engishman out of the back of the building.

Conscious of the emptiness of the land in front, his whole being screamed out to him to hug the earth; but

Pargeter, looking slightly mad, was running in front of him, bent double, zig-zagging from right to left and back again, and Iremonger found he could do nothing else but follow.

12

As soon as he saw the men running towards him, the Fox knew he'd been found.

At first he thought they were two more of the lunatic American soldiers rushing to his assistance; but then he recognised the small man in front, and the burly shape of the second man, and he knew they were the Intelligence officers who'd been hounding him for six weeks now.

It had seemed impossible that anyone could have sieved through the vast mass of men in the invasion force to find him. He'd constantly changed positions on the beach, using the desperate hours of the previous day to hide himself, knowing the two men had been on his track in England, but he'd never for a moment believed that they could follow him and find him here in this insignificant corner of France.

Throughout the night, he'd been waiting for an opportunity to cross the field to the German lines. But his leg was numb and dragged behind him now like a rotten pole attached to his body. His face was swollen, and for hours he'd been fighting off the persistent efforts of his two American companions to move him to safety. Then a German machine-gun, spraying the field between him and the German lines, had prevented all movement and finally he had fallen into a fitful sleep just before dawn.

He was almost at the end of his tether now, his jaw aching with gritting his teeth to forget the grinding pain in his thigh. Only his determination kept him going, forcing him to keep his wits about him when all they wanted to do was give, relax, slip away from him; only an obsessive wish to redeem what he saw as a shameful lapse into fear the day before. He'd even wondered several times if he were dying, but then sanity had told him he was suffering only from loss of blood and shock, that he was fit and hard as nails, and that all he needed for recovery was to accomplish his mission.

Why the Americans had been allowed to press this far inland he couldn't understand. He'd not seen any sign of the counterattacks by the panzers that he'd expected, nothing beyond small unco-ordinated nibbles by individual companies. Even the first vicious defence had not been strong enough to withstand the advance of men and machines, which had never stopped landing despite the heavy casualties. Something must surely have gone wrong; and when the three Typhoons had appeared, he knew his chances had diminished even further because the 88 beyond the hedge had been knocked out, its barrel cocked up at the sky. He had to make a move soon.

It was as he raised his head to spy out the land that he saw the German tank and his heart leapt. It had come from the trees where it had been hidden from the aeroplanes and was moving along the hedge, covered with branches and difficult to spot. It could be his salvation.

Staring through the growing daylight, he waited for other tanks to follow, firmly convinced that this was the beginning of the first real drive to throw the Americans back into the sea. Then he realised there weren't any

274

others, that this was one on its own which, for some reason or other, simply happened to be near. But as he saw the German infantrymen behind it, his heart leapt again. Within a matter of minutes his ordeal would be over and he would be among his own countrymen with his loneliness ended.

The two Americans with him were yelling wildly now and firing snapshots at the Germans following the tank. They didn't seem to be hitting anyone but for the first time they'd both got their backs to him. Reluctantly he reached for the automatic rifle he'd brought with him. His stomach heaved at what he had to do but he knew he had to do it. He would have to get out of the foxhole on his own – somehow.

Pargeter had spotted the tank at the same time as the Fox. He squeezed Iremonger's arm, and together they dived for the ditch under the overhanging bushes.

The ditch was less a ditch than a dip in the ground, probably dug years before to help drain the field and now overgrown with grass. As they peered over the lip there was an immediate burst of machine-gun fire that clipped the leaves above their heads, and as they ducked down again they could hear the heavy grinding sound of the tank tracks.

'Here it comes,' Pargeter said.

There was another burst of firing but this time Pargeter looked puzzled.

'That was from the observation post,' he said.

'That bastard isn't giving in without a fight,' Iremonger agreed.

'I don't think he was firing at us. There were two men up there with him.'

'You reckon he's murdered them?'

'He'd have a job running to the Germans without.'

Iremonger's eyes narrowed. 'What do we do now, Cuth?' he asked.

'There's one thing that's pretty obvious,' Pargeter said. 'There'll be no rushing up the field here to grab him. The tank'll stop us.'

'Suppose he makes a dash for it?'

'In that case, we do to him what he's done to those other chaps.' Pargeter indicated the tommy-gun Iremonger had acquired and the carbine in his own hands.

'You any good with that?' Iremonger asked.

'Better than most. And he won't take off in a hurry. He has a wound in the head and he certainly won't be able to run very fast. It's nearly twenty-four hours since he was hit and his leg'll have stiffened. And, now that the drugs have worn off, it'll be hurting like hell. He'll be hoping the tank will rescue him.'

Iremonger nodded. Neither of them felt very much like gloating.

As they started to crawl along the shallow ditch, they were both curiously anxious that the affair should be settled with some honour. The Fox had done his job with skill and the kind of lonely courage that is the hardest of all to muster and sustain. They reached the corner of the field, and found themselves in what must once have been a German strongpoint. It was a hole in the ground with a smashed MG42, torn and scattered sandbags dribbling earth, and half a dozen German bodies, so punctured they looked like colanders. Iremonger's eyes narrowed, but Pargeter continued crawling round the hole, skirting the bodies and the dark-stained earth, and Iremonger was obliged to follow.

They had now moved round to the west of where the Fox was holed out, but there was no sign from Schneider. Like Dallas, his orders seemed to be to stay where he was until vehicles, guns and tanks came up; his job merely to observe and hang on to what he'd got.

They could hear German guns firing over them towards the sea and, occasionally, the heavy concussions of the engineers setting off demolition charges to clear the beach obstacles and make the passage inland easier. Every now and then there was a sound like an express train rushing overhead as the salvoes from the heavy naval guns hurried inland to smash strongpoints, assembly areas and German formations moving up to the front.

It was full daylight now and the Fox still hadn't moved. A machine-gun over on their right was firing across the field ahead and, while they waited, they heard the grind and clatter of fresh tank tracks behind them. Swinging round, they saw three American Shermans appear on the road near the cottage where Schneider's men were hidden.

Immediately, there was a crack as the German tank fired, and the leading Sherman was surrounded by a vast cloud of smoke. As it stopped and started to burn furiously, the crew jumped out and dived for the ditch. The second and third tanks hurriedly backed away into the trees and out of sight.

But now they saw that Schneider's men had begun to work their way from the cottage along the edge of the field towards where the Fox was hiding.

'He'll have to make a break for it soon,' Iremonger growled.

The bazooka team dragged their weapon behind the others, the steel pipe gleaming dully in the daylight.

'Get up there,' the bazookaman said, and his voice came to them quite clearly on the morning air. As his team-mate stood up in the ditch, Iremonger stared at him, certain that now it was really light he could be seen. He seemed to be only in his teens and his cold courage tore at Iremonger's heart.

'We'll know now,' he heard the bazookaman observe, 'whether this goddam thing does what they say it does.'

'Get it over with,' the boy said as the barrel was placed on his shoulder. 'The bastards can probably see me.'

'They're watching the cottage.' The bazookaman was too engrossed with what he was doing to be sympathetic. 'Stand still and hold your breath. Don't put my sights off.'

The boy stood silently, upright, exposed in the ditch. 'There are around twenty or thirty infantrymen with it,' he said in a quiet even voice.

'They'll be in for a surprise,' the bazookaman observed. 'The bastard's turning and I want to do this right.'

The tank's engine faded as it halted again, its machine-gun moving slowly like the antenna of a great steel beetle.

Then they realised that the Fox had emerged from his lair and was standing near the hedge. His clothes were torn and his face was blackened, and as he moved among the foliage, he dragged one leg behind him.

The tank was facing the cottage where Schneider and his men had been, and the tank commander obviously hadn't seen the Americans with the bazooka on his left. Iremonger's heart thumped. How the boy with the bazooka on his shoulder could continue to stand upright without moving, he couldn't imagine.

The tank began to edge forward again, the big gun in the turret pointing towards the cottage. The infantrymen followed it, staring at the empty window.

'For God's sake,' Schneider complained.

'I've got him, Lieutenant,' the bazookaman said.

The tank had moved closer now. It looked like some great creature with an intelligence of its own, sensing danger in the cottage but still unsure. It stopped again and the machine-gun fired, spraying the cottage with bullets, which they could hear clinking and thudding against the plaster. Then the turret gun fired with a harsh whip-like crack. As the shell found its target, the front wall of the cottage collapsed in a cloud of smoke and dust, bringing down part of the roof. As the uproar subsided, Iremonger heard the boy's voice.

'For sweet Jesus' sake—!'

As the bazookaman fired, Iremonger saw the shell moving through the air. It seemed to move slowly and deliberately. Then it crashed against the tank, but for an endless moment nothing else seemed to happen.

'The bastard doesn't work,' the bazookaman said disgustedly.

But suddenly the tank's gun swung and dropped. It was now pointing at the ground and they felt rather than heard the explosion inside, muffled and deep, and saw the wisps of smoke come through the driver's slits and round the hatch. More explosions followed, thick and heavy, and the tank seemed to rock on its springs where it stood. They all stared at the tank. It looked as big and dangerous as ever but it didn't move, and they saw the infantrymen who had been hiding behind it start to run backwards.

'Right,' Schneider yelled. 'Let 'em have it!'

Every rifle and machine-gun in the ditch fired and the air was filled with the smell of cordite. They could hear the ejected cases clinking against each other and the cries of the Germans.

The whole group seemed to have melted away. Most of them were sprawled on the ground, killed, wounded or hugging the shelter of the earth. Only one man was still running and, as Iremonger peered, Schneider's rifle cracked and the running figure vanished into a hedge.

Schneider ran towards the tank, all his men on their feet and yelling excitedly, but Pargeter's mind was on one thing alone.

'That's it,' he snapped. 'He's got to go now!'

They almost fell into the hole where the Fox had been hiding. Sergeant Duffee and Pfc O'Neil lay on their faces, the backs of their smocks torn and covered with blood.

'Shot in the back,' Iremonger growled.

Ducking, they ran towards where the Fox was now concealed. Then they saw him rise and climb the bank to drag himself through the hedge. Pargeter climbed after him, forced a way through the hedge, and fell out at the other side. As Iremonger followed, he saw the Fox moving across the field fifty yards away. There was a desperate look about him, as if he knew he couldn't last much longer.

As Iremonger crashed through the hedge, his helmet was pushed on to his nose with a jolt, bringing tears to his eyes, and as he sat up, he saw the struggling figure forcing its way across the field just ahead, strangely pathetic as it dragged its useless leg. Pargeter scrambled to his feet, and started to walk. The figure in front turned and, from where Iremonger was, he saw the Fox had a machine-pistol in his hands. Desperately he dived at Pargeter and, as they went down, he felt something hit him in the calf like a hammer, spinning him round.

For a moment, he lay winded, staring at the sky, still not quite aware that he'd been wounded. As he struggled to sit up, Pargeter pushed him down again.

'Thank you, Linus,' he said in that maddeningly polite manner of his, as though he were thanking a waiter for bringing him a glass of water. 'You probably just saved my life.'

The Fox was still struggling away from them, and Pargeter rolled over to pick up the carbine he'd dropped. Swinging back to lie on his face, he pulled the weapon towards his cheek and worked the bolt. There was a single shot and the Fox pitched forward, rolling on to his face to lie in a crouched position, as though he were clutching at the earth.

'Got him,' Pargeter said. There was an entire absence of triumph in his voice.

There was an angry shout behind them and they could see Schneider's men approaching at a run. Pargeter had risen to his feet now and was moving slowly towards the huddled figure in front. Scrambling to his knees, Iremonger tried to follow but the wound in his leg made him yelp and fall to the ground again, alongside the tommy-gun he'd been carrying.

Pargeter had moved to his left, walking purposefully forward, to approach the huddled shape from behind and, as Iremonger struggled to a sitting position to see what happened, he saw the figure on the ground turn and the machine-pistol move. Immediately, he swung the tommy-gun forward and pulled the trigger, firing in a long burst that seemed to lift the German from the ground, poised on bent legs for a second before toppling backwards, the machine-pistol flying from his hand, to lay with his arms and legs asprawl, staring at the empty sky.

Pargeter had stopped dead and was standing staring at the body when the Americans came up. One of them took a swing at Iremonger with his fist and he fell sideways. When he sat up, he saw that the soldier had run on and knocked Pargeter flying and was standing over him with the butt of his rifle raised.

A sergeant appeared. 'Quit that, you goddam fool!' he roared.

'That goddam limey killed Colonel Cornelow, Sergeant. I saw him do it!'

'No, he didn't!' Iremonger joined in the argument angrily. 'He wounded him. I killed him.'

Schneider had arrived now and was standing over the Fox's body. Pargeter had risen to his feet, holding his cheek where the soldier's fist had caught him.

'Get me up off this goddam ground,' Iremonger snarled and two of the soldiers lifted him to his feet and helped him towards the dead man.

His burst had hit the Fox in the chest but, apart from the swelling over his eye, his face was undamaged.

'That guy was a German,' Iremonger said. 'We've been on his tail for a couple of months.'

The American soldier who had struck Pargeter was staring down, bewildered, as the Englishman knelt by the corpse and felt in the pockets of its jacket. When he rose, he was holding a thick bundle of papers, torn by the bullets and covered with blood. Without a word, he opened them, studied them for a moment, then handed them to Iremonger.

Balancing on one leg, Iremonger glanced at them. The top sheets were covered with scrawled handwriting in German.

'Thanks,' he said in a flat voice.

There was a curious sense of anti-climax. Overhead another group of fighter bombers howled inland, and they heard the the stuttering of a machine-gun on their right, then the heavy thump of a field gun.

Schneider was talking to the man who had struck Pargeter, pointing to the body as though he were trying to explain the strange phenomenon of an American officer killed by his own side. The soldier turned and stared at the Fox. 'But the guy was so goddam brave,' he said.

'He was still a German,' Schneider said.

The soldier shrugged and hitched his carbine on to his shoulder.

A smell of burning was coming to them on the breeze with the smell of destruction and death. The two surviving American tanks had started to move again and, round them, they could see a whole cloud of men with pot-shaped American helmets edging up along the side of the field.

'I thought those guys had shot a hero,' the soldier muttered, looking at Pargeter. Then he turned and began to move ahead of the others towards the far hedge.

Iremonger stood looking down at the Fox. There was a strange nobility about the dead face, and all at once Iremonger felt overwhelmingly weary. He looked at Pargeter who was still kneeling by the body, going through its pockets, conscious of a strange depression.

'Maybe we did shoot a hero,' he said slowly. 'Maybe we did at that.'